WANDA E. BRUNSTETTER

A Cousin's
PROMISE

INDIANA COUSINS | BOOK 1

BARBOUR
PUBLISHING

DEDICATION/ACKNOWLEDGMENTS

To my dear friends Arlene and Wayne Randolph. Thank you for introducing me to so many wonderful Amish people who live in northern Indiana. To my new friend Dale Burnet. Thank you for your willingness to share the experience of losing a leg with me.

Delight thyself also in the LORD:
and he shall give thee the desires of thine heart.
PSALM 37:4

CHAPTER 1

A*ch*, there's a bee in the van! Somebody, get it out of here before I get stung!"

Loraine Miller looked over her shoulder. Her cousin Katie's face was as pale as goat's milk, and her eyes were wide with fear. Ever since they'd been children and Katie had been trapped in the schoolhouse with a swarm of angry bees, she had panicked whenever a bee got too close. Poor Katie had been pelted with so many stings that day, much of her body had looked swollen. The doctor had said it was a good thing Katie wasn't allergic to bee stings or she would have probably gone into shock.

"Get it! Get it!" Katie screamed. She sucked in a deep breath and ducked her head.

The bee flew past Loraine's shoulder, buzzing noisily.

"Open your window, *schnell*!" Loraine said to her fiancé, Wayne Lambright. "We need to get that bee out before Katie hyperventilates."

Wayne quickly opened the window and shooed the bee with his hand.

"Did. . .did it go out?" Katie's chin trembled as she lifted her head. Her vivid green eyes glistened with unshed tears. Loraine found it hard to believe anyone could be so afraid of a bee, even though she knew the source of her cousin's fear.

"*Jah*, I'm sure it's out. At least, I don't see it anymore," Loraine said, hoping to reassure her cousin.

"It's gone, Katie, so you can relax." Wayne closed the window and nudged Loraine's arm. "You know what I'm thinking?"

"What's that?"

"I'm thinking I can hardly wait to get you on the Side Winder I've heard so much about!"

She grimaced. "It would be just like you to try and talk me into going on the scariest ride at Hershey Park."

Wayne's eyes twinkled. "Do you really think I'd twist your arm and make you do that?"

"She doesn't think it; she knows it," Loraine's cousin Ella spoke up from the back of the van.

Jolene, Loraine's other cousin, giggled behind her hand, while Katie's boyfriend, Timothy, snorted like one of his father's pigs.

"Remember, Loraine, you're the one who suggested we take this trip to Hershey Park," Jolene's brother Andrew said. "So I would think you'd be looking forward to going on all the scary rides."

"That's right," Ella's brother Raymond chimed in. "Getting scared out of your wits is the whole reason for going to an amusement park."

Wayne nudged Loraine's arm again. "Don't you remember how much fun we had when we went to the Fun Spot last Labor Day weekend?"

Loraine nodded. It had been fun to visit their local amusement park, but those rides weren't nearly as frightening as the ones she'd heard about at Hershey Park. Even so, she was excited to take this trip. Ever since she was a little girl, she'd wanted to visit Hershey Park and Hershey's Chocolate World. She loved chocolate and had heard there was a ride inside Chocolate World that showed visitors how the various kinds of Hershey candy were made. Their plans were to travel through the night, arrive in Hershey around 2:00 a.m., and check into the hotel their driver, Paul Crawford, had reserved for them. Then they would sleep a few hours and spend all day Saturday at the park. They planned to rest awhile on Sunday, and then maybe take a drive around the surrounding area. Early Monday morning, they would head for home. Loraine figured this trip could turn out to be more fun than if her parents had taken her when she was a girl.

Even though the Amish didn't celebrate Labor Day, Timothy, Raymond, and Andrew worked at the trailer factory in Middlebury and had Monday off, as did Loraine, who worked at the hardware store in Shipshewana. Since neither Katie nor Ella had full-time jobs, being gone for three days wasn't a problem. The same held true for Wayne, who farmed with his father. Only Jolene, a teacher at the local Amish schoolhouse, was scheduled to work, but she'd been able to get a substitute for Monday.

"I don't know about anyone else, but I'm more anxious to eat some of that *wunderbaar* chocolate than go on any of the rides at Hershey Park." Katie smiled and relaxed against the seat, obviously feeling better now that the bee was gone.

"Listen to you. . .talking about food already, and we're not even to Ashley yet." Timothy bumped Katie's arm. "Can't you at least wait until we leave the state of Indiana to talk about food?"

Katie muffled her snicker.

Loraine smiled. It was good to see everyone in such good spirits. Paul had been laughing and telling jokes since he'd picked them up at Jolene and Andrew's house in Topeka.

"Hey, Paul," Timothy called, "Katie's hungry, so we may have to stop soon and see that she's fed."

"I'll be stopping before we get to Highway 69," Paul said over his shoulder. "Will that be soon enough?"

Timothy needled Katie in the ribs. "What do you say? Can you hold out till then?"

She wrinkled her nose. "If you don't stop teasing, I won't go on any of the rides at Hershey Park with you."

"Is that a threat?"

"It's a promise."

Loraine looked over at Wayne and rolled her eyes. Katie was her youngest cousin, and she'd recently turned nineteen. Sometimes, like now, Katie still acted like an immature adolescent. Timothy, who was twenty, wasn't much better, always goofing around, mimicking others, and making all sorts of weird sounds. But the two of them seemed happy together and planned to be married in the fall of next year. Maybe by then, they'd both have grown up some.

"I wish people would quit cutting me off and tailgating," Paul complained as he merged the van into heavier traffic. "Seems like everyone and his brother is headed somewhere for Labor Day weekend. If it's this bad now, I can only imagine how it will be on the trip home."

"Hershey Park will probably be crowded, too," Andrew put in.

Wayne gave Loraine's fingers a gentle squeeze. "This will be our last chance for an outing with our single friends before we become an old married couple, so we'd better enjoy every moment," he whispered in her ear.

He looked at her so sweetly she wanted to tousle his thick auburn curls, the way she sometimes did when they were alone. In just a little over a month, she and Wayne would get married, and then she could tousle his hair to her heart's content. By this time next year, they might even have a baby, and their lives would take a new direction—one that wouldn't include weekend trips to amusement parks. A baby would mean changing dirty diapers, getting up in the middle of the night for feedings, and so many new, exciting things. Loraine could hardly wait to make a home and raise a family with Wayne. It would be a dream come true.

She leaned her head against Wayne's shoulder and let her eyelids close. She felt safe and secure when she was with Wayne—enjoying his company and happy to know she'd soon be his wife. *I wonder what our* kinner *will look like. Will they have my brown hair and brown eyes, or will they resemble Wayne with his curly auburn hair and hazel eyes? Will they be easygoing and even-tempered like Wayne? Will they have a servant's heart—generous in spirit and sensitive to others in need?*

In her mind's eye, Loraine could see a sweet baby with curly auburn hair, gurgling and reaching chubby hands out to his father.

The van lurched suddenly, and Loraine's eyes snapped open. "Wh–what happened?"

"We're stopping for those snacks I promised you could get," Paul said as he pulled off the road and into a gas station. "If anyone wants anything, you'd better get it now, because I won't be stopping again until I need more gas."

Loraine climbed out of the van ahead of her cousins and turned to smile at Katie. "Since you're the one who said you were hungry, I guess you'd better make sure you stock up on plenty of snacks."

Katie snickered. "I plan to do just that."

～❧ ❧～

With a sack full of snack foods, Loraine crawled back into the van and released a noisy yawn. "Someone wake me when we get there, would you?" She leaned her head on Wayne's broad shoulder again. "I hope you don't mind me using you for a pillow."

He nuzzled the top of her stiff, white head covering with his nose. "I don't mind at all."

Loraine's eyelids fluttered closed once more. She was almost asleep when Katie let out an ear-piercing yelp. "Ach! Another bee's in the van!"

Loraine sat up straight. Sure enough, a bee buzzed irritatingly overhead.

Timothy and Raymond swatted at the troublesome bee with their hats.

"Ella, roll down your window!" Timothy shouted. "Maybe the critter will fly out like the last one did."

Ella quickly did as he requested, but the bee kept buzzing and zipping all around.

Katie screamed when it buzzed past her face. "Get it! Get it! Get it!"

"What's going on back there?" Paul called over his shoulder. "What's all the ruckus about?"

9

"There's a bee on the loose, and—"

"Paul, look out!"

At the sound of Ella's shrill scream, Loraine's gaze darted to the front window. A semi-truck headed straight for them!

Paul jerked the wheel, and the van lurched to the right. As the semi roared past, it slammed into the side of their vehicle. The van skidded off the road and smacked a telephone pole. It flipped onto its side and spun around. Metal crunching! Breaking glass! Screaming voices! Deafening silence. Loraine was sure everyone was dead.

CHAPTER 2

Rivulets of sweat trickled down Loraine's bodice as she stood in front of the window inside one of the waiting rooms at the hospital in Fort Wayne, watching the last orange strand of sky fade into darkness. Her family and the families of those who'd been riding in the van with her should be arriving soon. Oh, how she wished she had better news for the parents of those who had died.

Loraine pressed her forehead against the window and closed her eyes, trying to shut out the memory of the accident.

She took a few short breaths and tried to relax, but it was no use. This terrible nightmare was real and would not go away. If she could only wake up tomorrow morning and find that everything was all right—the way it had been before they'd gotten into the van. If Paul hadn't turned around to see what the commotion was about. If she and her friends had only stayed home today. But all the *if*s wouldn't change a thing. The accident *had* happened, and Loraine, along with the others who survived, would have to deal with it.

Loraine turned away from the window and glanced at her cousin Katie, slouched in a chair across the room. Wearing a blank stare, Katie looked at the floor as though she were in a daze. As far as Loraine knew, she and Katie were the only ones who'd escaped

11

serious injury, although they did have several bumps and bruises.

What can I say to her? How can I offer comfort to her hurting soul? Loraine drew in a deep breath and made her way across the room.

"There's a vending machine in the hall. Can I get you something? Maybe a cup of coffee or a bottle of water?" she asked, taking a seat beside her cousin.

Katie lifted her head but stared straight ahead, knuckles white as she gripped the edge of the chair as though she might fall off if she let go.

Loraine shifted in her seat, unsure of what to say or do. Finally, she went down on her knees in front of Katie. Gently, she pried Katie's fingers loose and held them in her hands. "Please, talk to me, Katie. Tell me what's on your heart."

Katie blinked a couple of times. "T–Timothy's dead." Her chin trembled, and her voice came out in a squeak.

Loraine nodded as tears pricked her eyes. "I'm so sorry for your loss, Katie. I'm sorry for everyone's loss."

Katie pulled her hands away and folded her arms. "I wish we'd never gotten in that van. I wish we'd stayed home where we were safe. I wish Timothy wasn't—" Her voice trailed off, and her mouth snapped shut with an audible click.

"We need each other right now, Katie. We need to talk about our feelings."

No response.

"Katie, please say something. It's all right to cry. Don't hold your feelings in. Don't shut me out."

Katie didn't utter a word. It was as though an invisible wall had been erected between them, and Loraine's cousin had withdrawn to her own little world.

Loraine rose from the floor and began to pace, sending up to heaven a silent prayer. *Dear Lord, please comfort Katie and be with the doctors who are working on the others. Please help me know what to say when their families arrive, and please keep my Wayne alive.*

A middle-aged man with thinning brown hair entered the

room. He smiled and held out his hand to Loraine. "I'm Robert Taylor, the hospital chaplain."

She shook his hand. "I'm Loraine Miller, and that's my cousin Katie Miller." She motioned to Katie, but Katie gave no response—just sat with her lips compressed and her eyes tightly shut.

"I heard about the accident you and your friends were in," he said. "I wanted you to know that I'm here to help in any way I can."

"I—I appreciate that."

"Are you waiting for family members to arrive?"

She nodded.

"I'd like to wait with you and offer my support."

"I'm sure everyone will need it as much as I do." Loraine looked at Katie again. "Katie's boyfriend was killed in the accident, and I think she's in shock. She's only said a few words to me since we left the emergency room and came in here. She seems to have shut me out."

"I'll try talking to her." The chaplain moved away from Loraine and took a seat beside Katie. "I'm the chaplain here, Katie. I'd like to pray with you," he said in a gentle, comforting tone.

No response.

"If you'd like to talk about what happened or how you feel, I'm here to listen."

Several minutes passed, and then Katie's lips started to move. She spoke so quietly Loraine couldn't make out the words. She moved back to the window, praying that the chaplain would be able to get through to Katie—help her deal with the pain.

Someone touched Loraine's shoulder, and she whirled around. Uncle Alvin and Aunt Leah, Jolene and Andrew's parents, stood behind her with worried expressions.

"We came as soon as we heard about the accident," Uncle Alvin said. "They wouldn't give us much information in the emergency room. Just said the doctors are still working on our son and daughter and that we should wait in here." His forehead wrinkled as he shot Loraine a pleading look. "Do you know anything?"

"Not a lot. The last thing I was told was that Andrew had suffered cuts, bruises, and a broken arm."

"And Jolene?" Aunt Leah asked with a catch in her voice.

"One of the nurses said something about possible damage to Jolene's auditory nerves, but that's all I know."

Aunt Leah glanced anxiously at the door. "I wish they'd let me go in. I need to see how my kinner are doing. I'm so worried about them."

"I understand. I'm worried, too." Loraine placed a hand on her aunt's arm, hoping to offer a little reassurance. Reassurance she really needed herself.

"What about the others? Was anyone seriously injured?" Uncle Alvin wanted to know.

Loraine nodded. "Our driver, Paul Crawford, was killed, and so were Katie's boyfriend, Timothy, and Ella's brother, Raymond."

"Ach! That's *baremlich*." Aunt Leah's eyes widened as shock registered on her face. "What about the others?"

"Ella has a concussion, and I was told that Wayne has some serious injuries, but I don't what or how bad they are." Loraine swallowed a couple of times. The not knowing clawed at her heart and made her body feel numb. If Wayne died, she'd probably go into shock the way Katie had.

For lack of anything better to do, Loraine motioned to the chairs across the room. "Should we have a seat while we wait to hear how Jolene, Andrew, and the others are doing?"

Aunt Leah and Uncle Alvin nodded and followed Loraine.

She introduced them to Chaplain Taylor, and they all took seats. Aunt Leah clasped Katie's hand. "I'm sorry about Timothy."

No response.

"Have Timothy's folks been notified?" Aunt Leah's question was directed at Loraine.

"Timothy's parents do know about the accident," Loraine replied, "but they haven't arrived yet and don't know he died soon after we got here."

Uncle Alvin grunted. "I hope we find out about Jolene and Andrew soon. I can't stand the waiting."

"I know it's hard to wait, but I'm sure you'll be told something soon," Chaplain Taylor said.

With a childlike cry, Wayne's mother, Ada, rushed into the room. Her husband, Crist, followed.

Ada clasped Loraine's shoulder so tightly she winced. "Have you heard any news about our son?"

Loraine rose from her chair and gave Ada a hug. "He's still being examined, but I was told earlier that he suffered some serious injuries."

"What kind of injuries?" Crist asked.

"I—I don't know. I'm hoping we'll hear something soon. I've been hoping and praying that he's not—"

"We're waiting to hear how our son and daughter are, too," Aunt Leah spoke up.

Ada's lips compressed into a thin, tight line. "So we don't know how anyone is?"

Loraine swallowed around the lump in her throat. "We do know that three people died in the crash."

"Who?"

"Timothy, Raymond, and our driver, Paul."

Ada groaned as she slowly shook her head. "I knew going to Hershey Park on a holiday weekend was a bad idea. I told Wayne that, too, but, no, he wouldn't listen to my advice. He wanted to please *you*, so he agreed to go." She lifted a shaky hand and pushed a wayward strand of grayish-brown hair under her stiff white head covering. "If Wayne's seriously hurt, then I'm sure you realize there won't be a wedding for the two of you in October."

Loraine cringed. She didn't need that reminder. She wished she could change the subject—say something to lighten the mood. Only she didn't know what to say, especially when she felt so discouraged and frightened.

Crist patted his wife's arm. "Let's not put the buggy before the horse. Our son's injuries might not be as bad as we think. Wayne and Loraine might still be able to get married as planned."

Ada shook her head, saying nothing.

"Would either of you like a cup of coffee or something to eat?" Loraine asked Wayne's folks.

"Nothing for me," Ada mumbled.

"No, I couldn't eat or drink a single thing." Crist shook his head.

A few minutes later, a young man entered the room and announced, "My name is Dr. Mayhew. I'm looking for members of Wayne Lambright's family." He glanced around the room. "Are any of you related to him?"

"I'm his father." Crist motioned to Ada. "This is his mother." He nodded at Loraine. "This is Wayne's fiancée. Do you have information about our son's condition? We need to know—is he going to live?"

Dr. Mayhew took the empty seat on the other side of Crist. When he cleared his throat, his forehead wrinkled into deep furrows, making him look older than he was. "Your son has several broken ribs, cuts, and contusions. His worst injury, however, is to his left leg. I'm afraid it's going to have to be amputated above the knee."

Loraine drew in a sharp breath and grabbed the edge of the chair to keep from toppling over. Wayne was a farmer. He needed two good legs. How would he deal with this tragic news? How would it affect their plans to be married?

"You—you want to cut off my son's leg?" Ada's voice trembled, and her eyes widened like those of a panicked horse. "Wayne's our only child! It would break my heart and his, too, if—"

"I'm sorry, but there's no other way." The doctor shook his head. "We can't save his leg. If we don't amputate, he could die."

Crist offered his wife a weak smile and slipped his arm around her shoulders. "We should be thankful our son's still alive. It could have been worse, you know. He might have died instantly like some of the others who'd been riding in the van. If the doctor can save Wayne's life by taking his leg, then we'll give our permission."

Ada glared at Loraine. "This is all *your* fault! If you hadn't insisted on him going to Hershey Park with you—"

"Now, Ada," Crist said in a calming voice, "don't cast any blame; it won't undo what's been done. Everyone in that van went of their own free will. Loraine didn't force Wayne or anyone else to go."

"That may be true, but you know our son—he'd do anything she asked him to do. He's never been able to say no to her." Ada's voice lowered to a whisper, as her gaze dropped to the floor. "I—I wish he'd chosen to marry Fern Bontrager."

A tremor shot through Loraine's body as hot tears pushed against her eyelids. She hadn't realized until now that Ada Lambright didn't want her as a daughter-in-law.

CHAPTER 3

Whispered voices. Strange smells. A heaviness in his body he couldn't explain. Where was he? What was going on?

Wayne groaned and struggled to open his eyes.

"It's okay, son. We're here."

"Mom, is—is that you?"

"Jah, Wayne." He felt the warmth of his mother's fingers on his hand. He heard the sadness in her voice. Something was terribly wrong.

"I'm here, too, son."

"Pop?"

"Jah."

Wayne's eyes finally opened, and two blurry faces came into view. "Wh—where am I?"

Mom squeezed his fingers. "You're in the hospital."

"Wh—what am I doing here?"

"You were in an accident," Pop said. "The van you were riding in hit a telephone pole, and—"

Pop's voice faded as Wayne's memories took over. There was a bee in the van. Katie was screaming. Paul turned around. A semi-truck came at them. Paul swerved. They hit a pole. Someone screamed. Then everything went black.

"Loraine! Is—is she hurt? Is she—"

"Loraine's all right. She and Katie suffered some bumps and bruises, but neither of them was seriously injured," Mom said.

A sense of relief washed over Wayne. He wouldn't know what to do if anything happened to Loraine. She was the love of his life—soon to be his bride. "Wh–what about the others? Were any of them hurt?"

Mom nodded, and her pinched expression let him know the news wasn't good.

"Who got hurt?"

"Jolene and Ella suffered head injuries, but from what we heard, Ella's was only a mild concussion." Mom pursed her lips. "Jolene suffered damage to her auditory nerves and lost her hearing."

Wayne drew in a sharp breath. "That's *baremlich!*"

Pop nodded. "You're right, it's terrible. Now she'll have to learn to read lips and speak with her hands."

"What about the others? Are they okay?"

"Andrew has a broken arm and a few other minor injuries, but he'll be all right once he heals." Pop slowly shook his head. "The other fellows weren't so lucky, though."

"Wh–what do you mean?"

"They didn't make it, son. Raymond, Timothy, and your driver are dead."

Wayne gulped on the sob rising in his throat. His friends couldn't be dead. There had to be a mistake. "Wh–where's Loraine? I need to see her!"

"She's in the waiting room." Mom glanced over at Pop. "We thought it would be best if we spoke to you first. There's something you need to know."

"What?"

"It–it's about your injuries."

"My brain feels kind of foggy right now, but I—I think I'm okay." Wayne managed a weak smile. "I'm alive, anyway."

"You have lots of bumps, bruises, and a few broken ribs, but the worst injury was to your left leg. It—" Mom covered her mouth with the palm of her hand as her voice broke on a sob.

"What's wrong with my leg?" Wayne struggled to keep his eyes open. He needed some answers. He needed them now.

Pop laid a hand on Wayne's shoulder. "I'm sorry to be tellin' you this, son, but you lost it."

"Wh—what are you talking about, Pop? What'd I lose?"

Mom sniffled. "Your leg was badly injured. It had to be amputated."

Wayne lifted his head off the pillow. "Wh—what'd you say?"

Mom patted his arm as if she were soothing a fussy baby. "The doctor took your leg from just above the knee."

Wayne's head fell back on the pillow as the stark realization of what she'd said settled over him like a dark cloud. He had only one leg. He was a farmer. He needed two good legs. He was getting married soon. His world had been turned upside down!

Sweat trickled from Wayne's forehead and dripped into his eyes. Mom wiped it away with a tissue. "We feel your loss, too," she murmured, "but we'll get through this tragedy together."

Wayne blinked a couple of times. "Does—does Loraine know about my leg?"

Mom nodded. "She was with us when the doctor gave us the news."

"What'd she say? How'd she take it?"

"I think you should ask her those questions." Pop turned to Mom and motioned to the door. "Why don't you go to the waiting room and get Loraine now?"

She hesitated a moment, released a deep sigh, and finally left the room.

Wayne's hand shook as he massaged his throbbing head. After the series of shocks he'd suffered today, he needed something to settle his nerves and block out the pain.

~❧ ❧~

"My son wants to see you."

At the sound of Ada's voice, Loraine jumped out of her seat. "Did—did you tell him about his leg?"

Ada nodded as tears welled in her eyes.

"How'd he take it?"

"Not well. I think he's more upset about losing two of his friends than his leg, though."

"Maybe the reality hasn't set in."

"Jah." Ada glanced around. "I don't see your folks anywhere. Haven't they arrived yet?"

"No, but I'm sure they'll be here soon." Loraine moved toward the doorway. "I'm ready to see Wayne."

As Loraine and Ada walked toward the elevator, the echo of their footsteps resounded in the hall. It reminded Loraine of her horse pulling her buggy up a hill. *Clip. . .clop. . .clip. . .clop.*

"I hope you won't say anything to upset Wayne," Ada said as they stepped up to the elevator.

Loraine bristled. "Of course not. What are you worried I might say?"

Ada pursed her lips. "I don't think you should mention anything about marrying him. At least not right now."

"What are you saying?"

"Wayne's lost a leg. He'll need lots of care, and—"

"We may not be able to get married on the day we planned, but we'll be married as soon as he's sufficiently healed."

A look of shock registered on Ada's face. "Then you're not going to back out on the marriage?"

"Of course not. I love Wayne, and I can't wait to be his wife."

"I—I just thought. . . ." Ada sighed. "I assumed you wouldn't want to marry a man with a handicap such as Wayne's."

Hoping, isn't that what you mean? "Wayne's handicap doesn't affect the way I feel about him," Loraine said without voicing her thoughts.

"You say that now, but you don't know how hard things are going to be for Wayne in the days ahead. He won't be able to farm anymore, and he'll need lots of care."

"I realize things will be difficult. Wayne will have many adjustments to make, but we'll get through it together." The elevator door zipped open, and Loraine stepped in behind Ada. She couldn't believe the woman thought she wouldn't want to marry her son because he'd lost his leg. But then, after Ada's earlier remarks, Loraine was sure Ada wanted Wayne to marry Fern instead of her.

The elevator opened, and as Loraine followed Ada down the hospital corridor, she sent up a silent prayer. *Lord, please give me the right words to say to Wayne. Help me not to break down in tears when I see him, and show me a way to let Ada know how much I care for her son.*

"Here we are." Ada halted in front of a door, drew in a sharp breath, and pushed it open.

Loraine stepped into the room. Her heart pounded against her rib cage, and the scene that greeted her blurred her vision. Wayne looked so pale and helpless lying in his bed. He looked like a sick little boy.

I can give in to my tears some other time, Loraine told herself. *Right now I need to be strong and positive for Wayne.*

"Let's leave these two alone so they can talk," Crist said to Ada. He moved toward the door.

She hesitated but finally followed.

At the door, Crist turned and gave Loraine a reassuring smile. "We'll be in the waiting room."

Loraine waited until Wayne's parents left the room before she moved to the side of his bed. "H–how are you feeling?"

"How do you think I feel? I lost my leg."

She nodded, barely able to speak around the lump in her throat. Wayne had never spoken to her so harshly. But then, he'd never lost a leg before.

He stared at the ceiling. "I guess you know what this means."

She seated herself in the chair beside his bed. "It means there will be some adjustments to make, and—"

"It means there will be no wedding for us at the end of October."

"Maybe not October, but when you're better we can—"

"I'm never going to be any better, Loraine. I'll always be without my leg."

"In time you'll be fitted with a prosthesis, and then—"

"I want my own leg, not an artificial one; it would slow me down. I'm a farmer. Farmers need two good legs." A deep groan escaped his lips. "If I can't farm, I can't support a wife and family. If I can't offer financial support, then I won't get married."

"Maybe you can find a different job—one that doesn't require you to be on your feet so much."

"I don't want another job. I've never wanted to do anything but farm." Wayne shook his head. "We can't be married, Loraine. I won't ask you to make that sacrifice."

"It wouldn't be a sacrifice."

"Jah, it would." His head lolled to one side, and his eyelids fluttered as though it took all his strength to keep them open.

Loraine was tempted to argue about whether they could get married or not but knew it was best not to say too much. Wayne was weak and needed time to heal from his surgery. They could speak of this again when he felt a bit stronger.

"Did—your folks tell you about the others?" she asked hesitantly.

He nodded. "If I'd known we were gonna be in an accident, I wouldn't have agreed to go to Hershey Park. I wish now that I'd said no."

Loraine's spine went rigid. Did Wayne blame her for the accident, too? "I–I'm so sorry. I wish I hadn't suggested the trip. I wish there hadn't been a bee in the van. I wish Paul—" She gulped on a sob, unable to finish her sentence.

"Does Paul's wife know he's dead?"

She nodded. "She took it pretty hard. So did Timothy's and Raymond's parents."

Wayne heaved a labored breath and closed his eyes. "I'm tired."

"Would you like me to leave so you can get some sleep?"

"Jah."

She leaned over and kissed his forehead. "I love you, Wayne."

No reply.

"Wayne?"

No response.

With an ache in her soul such as she'd never felt before, Loraine tiptoed out of the room, wondering what the future held for her and Wayne.

CHAPTER 4

The next few days went by in a blur as Loraine and her family comforted those who'd lost loved ones and those who were dealing with injuries. The day when they would attend Timothy's and Raymond's funerals arrived. Not everyone, however, would be in attendance. Wayne and Jolene were still in the hospital.

"Are you doing all right?" Mom asked when Loraine entered the kitchen that morning. "I see dark circles under your eyes, and your face looks awfully pale."

Loraine pushed a wisp of hair off her forehead and sighed. "I haven't slept well since the night of the accident, but I'm sure there are others in much worse shape than me this morning."

Mom nodded. "I feel terrible for my sister Verna. It's not natural for a parent to lose a child. It doesn't seem possible that Raymond is dead."

The ache in Loraine's heart struck swiftly, and she nearly doubled over from the pain. She felt so guilty for suggesting they make the trip to Pennsylvania. "If I hadn't asked Paul to drive us to Hershey Park, everyone would still be alive and well."

Mom left the stove where she'd been frying bacon and gave Loraine a hug. "I want you to stop blaming yourself. There was no way you could have known when you planned the trip that it would end in a tragic accident."

Loraine sniffed as a film of tears obscured her vision. "In my head I know that, but my heart says something different."

"It's hard not to blame ourselves when things go wrong, but you need to remember that the accident wouldn't have happened if Paul had kept his eyes on the road."

"Are you're saying it was his fault?"

"He made a mistake, but I'm sure he didn't do it on purpose." Mom's shoulders lifted in a brief shrug. "Rather than casting blame, we need to concentrate on helping our family and friends get through the funerals. It's going to be a difficult day."

Loraine nodded. "I've hired a driver to take me to the hospital later this afternoon. I'm sure Wayne and Jolene would like to know how everything goes at the funerals, since they're unable to be with us today. Besides, I need to see how they're both doing."

"Speaking of Wayne," Mom said, "I've been wanting to talk to you about something."

"Something about Wayne?"

"Jah." Mom cleared her throat a couple of times. "I talked with Ada at church yesterday, and she said because of Wayne's injuries, there won't be a wedding for the two of you after all."

Irritation welled in Loraine's soul. "He won't be well enough for us to get married in October as we'd planned, but as soon as he's feeling strong enough, we'll set a new wedding date." She saw no point in mentioning that Wayne had said they couldn't be married at all because of his handicap. She also chose not to mention that she'd overheard Ada say she wished her son had picked Fern Bontrager to marry. It hurt too much to talk about it. Besides, once Wayne felt better, he would change his mind. By then, she hoped to be on better terms with his mother. Things had to work out; she couldn't allow herself to think otherwise.

Mom drummed her fingers along the edge of the table. "I have some concerns about your marrying Wayne."

"What concerns?"

"I'm sure you must realize that his disability will probably keep him from farming."

"He can find another job—something that won't require two good legs. Something he can do from a wheelchair, if necessary."

"Loraine's right," Dad said as he entered the kitchen. "Wayne may have lost a leg, but he's a hard worker with a determined spirit. I'm sure he'll find a job that will allow him to provide adequately for our daughter."

Loraine swiped at the tears dribbling down her cheeks. She knew from what Wayne had said to her at the hospital the other day that he, too, was worried he couldn't provide for her.

The things he said were only the shock of learning he's lost a leg, she told herself. *Once he's had a chance to think more about it, he'll realize we can work through this together. That's what people who love each other do.*

⁓ ❧ ⁓

As Ella Yoder stood in front of her brother's plain wooden coffin, a sense of determination welled in her soul. In a short time, family and friends would arrive for Raymond's funeral. Later this afternoon, they would go to the Lehmans' for Timothy's funeral. Ella would need to remain strong. She'd have to look out for her younger siblings and take care of her mother's needs. Mama had taken the news of Raymond's death hard. She'd barely been able to cope since then.

Ella was glad the injuries she had sustained weren't serious. Her concussion had been mild, and the cuts and bruises on her legs and arms would heal quickly. She wasn't sure how quickly Mama would heal, however. Truth be told, Mama might never get over losing her firstborn son.

Ella heard someone approaching, and she whirled around.

"People are beginning to arrive," Papa said. "Loraine's here with her family. She wants to speak with you."

"Oh, okay." Ella stepped into the living room where Loraine stood with her parents, Amos and Priscilla.

"How's Wayne doing?" Ella asked, giving Loraine a hug.

"As well as can be expected."

"How long will he be in the hospital?"

"I don't know. I've hired a driver to take me to see him later today. I should know more then."

"I'm sure it's hard for Wayne not to be at his friends' funerals today."

"Jah."

"Losing a leg must be hard for him, too."

Tears pooled in Loraine's eyes. "He doesn't want to get married. He thinks he'll be a burden on me." Her voice lowered to a whisper. "Mom doesn't want me to marry Wayne, either. She as much as said so this morning." Her chin trembled. "Wayne's *mamm* is against us getting married, too. I think she's been against it from the very beginning. I just didn't realize it until the night of the accident."

"What are you going to do? I mean, if Wayne wants to call of the wedding, and your mamm and Wayne's mamm think you shouldn't get married—"

"I don't care what they think. I love Wayne, and I promised to marry him." Loraine lifted her chin a notch. "I'm going to keep that promise, no matter what anyone says."

"But if he won't marry you. . ."

"He will. He's just confused and hurting right now." Loraine slipped her arm around Ella's shoulder. "Enough about me. How are you feeling this morning? Does your head still hurt?"

Ella touched her forehead. "It feels better than it did a few days ago. I'm worried about Mama, though. She's having a hard time dealing with Raymond's death."

"I'm sure it's hard for all of you."

"Jah." Ella glanced toward the door. "Oh, there's Katie and her family. I wonder how she's holding up."

Loraine could tell Ella was doing her best to put on a brave front. Worrying about others seemed to be how she'd chosen to deal with her pain. Ella had always been a nurturing person, even when they were young girls. Loraine thought about the time her kitten had drowned in the creek. Ella had been so sympathetic that she'd given up her own kitten so Loraine wouldn't cry.

"Let's go talk to Katie before the service begins." Ella linked arms with Loraine and led her across the room.

❧ ❧

"How are you feeling, Mr. Lambright? Is the pain medicine working for you?"

Wayne grunted as a youthful-looking nurse with short brown hair stuck a thermometer under his tongue. How was he supposed to answer her question with something foreign in his mouth?

When she removed the thermometer, she asked again, "Is the pain medicine working for you?"

"It helps some, but it makes me real sleepy."

"That's to be expected." She slipped the blood pressure cuff around his arm. "Are you in pain right now?"

He shook his head.

When she removed the cuff, she listened to his heart and checked the bandages on the stub of his leg. "The doctor will be in later to examine your leg. Is there anything I can get for you?"

A new leg would be nice. "No, I'm fine."

"Would you like the TV turned on?"

"No, thanks. I have no interest in watching that."

"Oh, that's right. You Amish don't have TVs in your homes, do you?"

"No, and even if we did, I wouldn't be interested in watching it. I have better things to do with my time. At least I used to," he added bitterly.

The nurse quirked an eyebrow and placed the call button close to his hand. "Let us know if you need anything," she said before leaving the room.

Wayne reached for the Bible on the nightstand by his bed. Chaplain Taylor had left it there when he'd dropped by Wayne's room the other day.

Wayne opened it randomly, and his gaze came to rest on John 11:43–44: *"And when he thus had spoken, he cried with a loud voice,*

Lazarus, come forth. And he that was dead came forth, bound hand and foot with graveclothes: and his face was bound about with a napkin. Jesus saith unto them, Loose him, and let him go."

The page blurred, and Wayne blinked several times, hoping to keep the tears he felt pushing against his eyelids from falling onto his face. *Today, two of my good friends will be buried. Tomorrow is Paul's funeral. If Jesus were here, He could bring all three of them back to life. He did it for Lazarus; He could do it for my friends.*

Wayne's stomach twisted as his thoughts raced on. *I wish it had been me who'd been killed in the accident. It would have been better than living with only one leg. I can't marry Loraine. I won't be able to farm anymore, and I wouldn't be happy doing anything else.*

Wayne thought about the excitement he'd felt when he'd climbed into that van with Loraine and the others. The memory of how happy he and Loraine had been that afternoon shot through him like a knife. He was no longer a happy, excited, soon-to-be groom. He was an ugly half-man with a missing limb.

A huge knot formed in his throat as helpless fury swept over him. He grabbed his water glass and hurled it across the room, wincing when it smashed against the wall and broke. Nothing would ever be the same for him. Nothing!

CHAPTER 5

A feeling of heaviness settled on Loraine's chest as she looked out the front window of her father's buggy. A slow parade of black buggies inched their way up the hill toward the cemetery. Two funerals in one day; it was too much to bear. First Raymond's service this morning, and now they were about to bury Timothy.

She swallowed past the lump in her throat. Paul's funeral would be tomorrow, and many of the Amish from her community would attend his contemporary service as well. Paul and his wife, Rachel, had moved to Goshen five years ago, and he'd begun driving for the Amish soon after that. They were a middle-aged, childless couple, with no family living in the area. Loraine figured now that Paul was gone, Rachel would probably move back to Pennsylvania, where two of her sisters lived.

"We're here," Dad said as he guided their horse and buggy into the grassy area outside the cemetery.

When Loraine and her family climbed down from the buggy, her gaze came to rest on the open-bed hearse holding Timothy's coffin. Her heart pounded as the oilcloth cover was lifted and the coffin was carried to the gravesite. The mourners followed solemnly behind.

Once the coffin was set in place, the bishop read a hymn: "Ah, good night to those I love so; Good night to my heart's desire;

Good night to those hearts full of woe; Out of love they weep distressed. Tho' I from you pass away; In the grave you lay my clay; I will rise again securely, Greet you in eternity."

Loraine glanced at Timothy's parents, Calvin and Ruby. Calvin's shoulders shook as he struggled with his emotions, and Ruby, sobbing uncontrollably, had to be held up by her husband and oldest son, William.

A group of men sang a song while the grave was filled in by the pallbearers. Loraine's gaze went to Katie, leaning on her mother's shoulder. The poor girl's face looked drawn, and dark circles under her eyes underscored her exhaustion. She probably hadn't slept much since the day of the accident. Katie's vacant stare sent chills up Loraine's spine. It wasn't a look of acceptance; it was a look of defeat.

When the song ended, the bishop asked the congregation to silently pray the Lord's Prayer. As the others moved away from the gravesite, Katie remained near Timothy's grave, rocking back and forth on her heels. Finally, Katie's father led her away.

As Loraine walked back to her father's buggy, she lifted her tearful gaze to the cloudless sky. *Help Katie and all of us who are hurting today. I thank You, Lord, that Wayne's still alive. I don't know what I'd do if I lost him.*

❧ ❧

When Ella entered the Lehmans' house, where the second meal of the day would soon be served, she spotted Katie in one corner of the living room, standing in front of the window with a vacant stare.

Ella stepped up to her cousin and clasped her hand. "I'm sorry for your loss."

Katie blinked several times, as though waking up from a dream. *"Umkummes waar net not wendich,"* she said, as tears coursed down her cheeks.

Ella nodded. "I know his death was unnecessary, but—"

"It's my fault he's dead. I shouldn't have made such a fuss over that bee. If I'd kept quiet, Timothy would still be alive."

"It wasn't your fault. You were afraid of being stung." Ella slipped her arm around Katie's trembling shoulders. "Blaming won't bring my *bruder* or your *beau* back. We need to somehow move on with our lives and believe that God has taken our loved ones home to be with Him."

Katie's chin quivered. "Do we really know that? I mean, how can we know what was in their hearts the moment they died?"

Ella swallowed around the lump pushing against her throat. She missed Raymond so much. If she had the power to bring him back, she surely would. But heaven was a much better place. "We know that they lived like Christians and had acknowledged Jesus as their Savior when they joined the church." She squeezed Katie's fingers. "We have to believe that they're in heaven."

Katie pursed her lips and resumed staring out the window.

Ella gave Katie a hug and moved away. She'd been putting up a brave front all day and needed some time to be alone.

⤙ ⤚

"Are you all right?" Loraine asked when she stepped onto the porch and found Ella sitting on the porch swing, massaging her forehead.

"I have a headache. I think it's from holding back the tears."

"You shouldn't hold them back. It's okay to show your emotions, you know." Loraine took a seat beside Ella.

"I need to be strong for my mamm. If I give in to my tears, I'm afraid she'll fall apart." Ella rested her hand on Loraine's arm. "Will you be going to see Wayne soon?"

"Jah. Would you like to go along? It might do you some good to get away from here for a while."

"I can't. My family will be going home soon, and I need to stay close to Mama for the rest of the day. It wouldn't be right for me to desert her when she's grieving so hard."

"I understand."

"I spoke with Jolene's parents earlier. They said once Jolene's well enough to leave the hospital, she'll be going to Pennsylvania to stay with her aunt who teaches sign language."

Loraine nodded. "I heard that, too. Not being able to hear will be a challenge for Jolene. She'll be able to cope better if she's given the necessary skills."

"Jah."

"My ride should be here soon, so I'd better say good-bye to Timothy's family."

"When you see Wayne and Jolene, give them my love and let them both know that they're in my thoughts and prayers."

"I will." Loraine gave Ella a hug and went back inside.

She'd just told Timothy's folks good-bye, when Ada stepped up to her.

"I'd rather you not go to the hospital today."

"How come?"

"It upsets Wayne too much when he sees you."

Loraine's fingers curled into the palms of her hands until they dug into her flesh. "Wayne's upset about losing his leg. I don't think seeing me upsets him."

"Jah, it does. One of the nurses told me that he sinks into depression after your visits."

"Maybe that's because he misses my daughter so much," Loraine's father said, stepping between them.

Loraine smiled inwardly. Danki, *Dad. Thanks for sticking up for me.*

Ada's face colored a deep crimson. "My son's in a lot of pain right now—physically and emotionally." She looked at Loraine and squinted. "I think it would be best if you give him some time to deal with things on his own, don't you?"

Loraine shook her head. "I—I can't do that. He needs me!" She rushed out of the house before Ada could reply. She was Wayne's fiancée, and she would see him today no matter what his mother said!

CHAPTER 6

With a multitude of swirling emotions swimming in her head, Loraine entered Jolene's hospital room. She and Jolene had been close since they were little girls, just as they had been with Ella and Katie. Loraine hated to see Jolene leave, yet she knew going to Pennsylvania would probably be a good thing. She just hoped Jolene wouldn't decide to stay there permanently—she would miss her too much.

Jolene offered Loraine a feeble smile, and motioned her over to the bed.

Loraine took a seat and reached for the notebook and pen on the nightstand by the bed. *"How are you feeling?"* she wrote. *"Are you in much pain?"* She handed the notebook to Jolene.

"The pain's lessened some because the swelling's going down. I'm still taking pain medication, though," Jolene said in a voice louder than usual.

Loraine smiled and patted Jolene's hand. She knew her cousin had spoken loudly because she couldn't hear her own voice. Many elderly people who were hard of hearing did the same thing.

"I'm glad the pain isn't so bad anymore," Loraine wrote on the notepad.

"My balance is really off, though," Jolene said. "I have to hang on to things when I get out of bed and walk."

"I'm sure that will get better in time," Loraine wrote.

Jolene's eyes quickly filled with tears. "The hardest part of losing my hearing is knowing I won't be able to teach school anymore. I'll miss my scholars so much. They sent me a card they'd all signed, and I cried the whole time I read it." Her voice broke on a sob, and she swiped at the wetness on her cheeks.

Loraine took the notebook again. *"Maybe after you learn to read lips and talk with your hands, you'll be able to teach deaf students the way your aunt does."*

"I can't think about that right now." Jolene sniffed. "All I'm able to do is take one day at a time."

Loraine handed Jolene a tissue. *"That's all any of us should do,"* she wrote on the tablet.

Jolene nodded and blew her nose. "How's Wayne doing? Did you just come from seeing him?"

"I haven't been there yet," she wrote. *"I'll go to his room after I'm done visiting with you."*

"I'm sorry I couldn't be at Timothy's and Raymond's funerals today. How'd things go?"

Tears clouded Loraine's vision so she could barely see what she wrote. *"Ruby's taking Timothy's death pretty hard, and Katie's dealing with it by shutting everyone out. Ella's trying to be strong for everyone in her family—especially her mamm, who's grieving very hard for Raymond."*

"It must be terrible for all of them. I can't imagine how my family would feel if my bruder had been killed." Jolene yawned, and her eyes fluttered shut. "Forgive my rudeness. I guess the pain medicine's catching up to me."

"That's okay. I'll head over to Wayne's room now and let you sleep," Loraine wrote.

"Come back soon."

Loraine nodded and squeezed Jolene's fingers, and then she rose from the chair and slipped quietly from the room. It grieved her to think that Jolene would never hear again. No more listening to warbling birds, bubbling brooks, buzzing bees, the *clippety-clop* of horses' hooves, or the gentle whispering of tree branches blowing in the wind.

God, grant my deaf cousin a sense of peace, and keep her safe when she travels to Pennsylvania, Loraine prayed.

When she approached Wayne's room, she paused outside the door and whispered another prayer. "Dear Lord, give me the right words today, and help Wayne to be more receptive than the last time I was here."

⤐ ⤏

Wayne had been trying with little success to read a magazine, when he heard someone step into his room. He turned his head toward the door, and the rhythm of his heartbeat picked up speed. It was Loraine.

"How are you doing?" she asked, approaching his bed.

"About the same."

She pulled out the chair by the side of his bed and sat down. "I thought you might like to know how the funerals went today."

He nodded and set the magazine aside.

Tears clung to her lashes as she looked at him. "Timothy's and Raymond's families are deeply grieved, as is Katie. It was a sad time for all."

"Figured it would be." He winced and looked away.

"Are you in great pain?"

He shook his head. "The medicine they give me takes care of that fairly well, but I'm sure I'll have even more struggles once I'm home and the phantom pains begin."

"What's phantom pain?"

"I've been told that it feels as if the missing limb is still there. The doctor said it might feel like someone's twisting my foot up to my knees, even though there's no leg there."

Loraine grimaced. "That sounds baremlich! Isn't there something that can be done about it?"

"Just pain medicine, and that might need to be adjusted. I'll be going home in a few days." He sighed. "I guess that's when the

37

challenges will really begin."

"So soon? I thought they might keep you longer—until you could be fitted for a prosthesis."

"If I decide to wear one, that'll come later. I'll have to use a wheelchair for now." He stared out the window, wishing she would stop asking questions and quit looking at him with such sympathy. It made him feel like even less of a man than he already did.

"Have you been to see Jolene?" Wayne asked, needing a change of subject.

"Jah. I went there before coming here."

"How's she doing?"

"As well as can be expected. She'll be getting out of the hospital soon. Then she'll be going to stay with her aunt in Pennsylvania who teaches the deaf." Loraine's eyebrows pulled together as she frowned. "So many changes for so many of our friends, and all because of one terrible, senseless accident."

He leaned into the pillow and groaned. "What's done is done. We're not God. We can't change the past."

Several minutes ticked by, then she reached for Wayne's hand. "When we get married and start our own family, I hope we can teach them to appreciate each other and make good decisions."

He pulled his hand away as he shook his head. "There will be no family for us because I can't marry you, Loraine."

"Why not?"

"I told you before." He grunted and motioned to his leg. "With only one good leg, how do you expect me to farm?"

"Well, maybe after you get a prosthesis—"

"If I can't farm, I can't earn a living!"

"There are other things you can do, Wayne."

He slowly shook his head. "I've never wanted to do anything but farm, and I won't burden my wife with having to care for an ugly, crippled, half-man."

"You're not ugly or half a man." She shook her head. "And you won't be a burden. Once you adjust to an artificial leg, you'll be able to do many things on your own."

"I won't hold you to your promise to marry me," he mumbled. He folded his arms and stared at the wall. "We're not getting married, so you're free to move on with your life."

"I don't want to move on with my life. Not without you, Wayne." A hint of sweet-smelling soap wafted to meet Wayne's nose as she stood and leaned close to him.

"I've made up my mind; we're not getting married," he said determinedly.

Her eyes filled with tears. "You can't mean that."

"Jah, I do."

"Has your mother been talking to you about us? Has she said something to turn you away from me?"

Wayne shook his head. "Mom has nothing to do with this. I make my own decisions."

She clasped his arm. "Don't shut me out of your life, Wayne. You need me now, even if you don't realize it, and I want us to get through this together."

"Well, I don't." He motioned to the door. "Please don't come back here to see me again. It's over between us."

Loraine sat several seconds, staring at him as though in disbelief. Then, with a childlike cry, she rushed to the door. She stood there a few seconds with her back to him, then turned and said, "I'm not giving up on us. We belong together!"

As the door closed behind Loraine, Wayne squeezed his eyes shut. *Oh, dear Lord, have I done the right thing?* The thought of living without Loraine was unbearable. It wouldn't be any life at all. Yet he couldn't ask her to marry him the way he was now. He had to remain firm in his decision.

CHAPTER 7

As Loraine stumbled down the hospital corridor, her breath burned in her lungs. She needed a place to be alone so she could gain control of her emotions before she went out to her driver's car.

She spotted a women's restroom and slipped inside. Good, no one was there. She leaned against one of the stalls, fighting back tears of confusion and frustration. She couldn't believe Wayne didn't want to marry her anymore. Didn't he realize she still loved him and wanted to be his wife? It didn't matter that he only had one leg. It didn't matter whether he farmed or not. They could work things out if he'd only give them a chance.

As Loraine's fears took hold, she burst into sobs and continued to sob until she could barely breathe. She went to the sink and splashed cold water on her face, and then she patted it dry with a paper towel.

I've got to get a hold of myself before I get into Marge Nelson's van. If I let her see me like this, she'll ask questions I'd rather not answer right now.

Once Loraine had composed herself, she left the restroom and headed outside. When she reached the parking lot and climbed into the front seat of Marge's van, tears welled in her eyes, despite her resolve not to break down.

Marge, who'd been reading a book, buckled her seatbelt and

turned to look at Loraine. "You seem upset. Is Wayne doing all right?"

Loraine shook her head. "He's very depressed and not thinking clearly right now." The tension in her throat rendered her words to a whisper, and a sense of helplessness crept through her body. If only she could make things better for Wayne. If only. . .

"Losing a leg has to be a terrible trauma." Marge turned on the ignition. "All that pain medication he's taking has probably made his brain fuzzy, too."

Loraine nodded. Maybe that was all it was. Once Wayne didn't have to be on so much medication for the pain, he would see things clearly again.

❦

As Priscilla sat at her kitchen table, drinking a cup of tea, her gaze came to rest on the quilting rack she kept in the sunroom next to the kitchen. Several months ago, she'd started making a quilt with the double-wedding-ring pattern to give to Loraine and Wayne when they got married. It wasn't quite finished, but she figured she had plenty of time, since the wedding would have to be postponed until Wayne was feeling better.

Priscilla's forehead creased as worry set in. *How will things be for my daughter after she marries Wayne? Will he be able to support her? Loraine would probably have to keep working at the hardware store, but her salary alone wouldn't provide enough for them to live on.*

She drank the last of her tea and set the cup aside, then turned in her chair and reached for the notepad on the counter. She needed to stop worrying and make out her grocery list before she went shopping in Shipshewana tomorrow morning.

Rice, pickles, potatoes, coffee, tea, laundry soap. . . Her list was quickly growing.

Let's see now. What else do I need?

Bam! The back door slammed shut, and Priscilla set the notepad aside.

"Oh, good, I'm glad you're home," she said when Loraine

41

entered the room. "I was just making out the grocery list and wondered if there was anything you'd like me to include."

"No, not really." Loraine draped her jacket over the back of a chair and sat down with a grunt. Her face looked pale and drawn. Her eyes were red and rimmed with tears. Alarm rose in Priscilla's chest.

"Daughter, what's wrong? Has something happened to make you feel *umgerennt?*"

"Jah, I'm feeling very upset. Wayne called off the wedding." Loraine caught her trembling lips between her teeth. "He—he thinks his life is over because he's lost his leg. He thinks he's only half a man."

"Is it because he won't be able to farm? Is that what's bothering him?"

"Partly."

"Is he afraid he won't be able to support you?"

"Jah, that too."

"Maybe it would be best if you didn't get married."

Loraine's eyes widened. "You can't mean that, Mom."

"I'm just trying to help you see the facts as they are." Priscilla's face grew warm as she fiddled with the edge of the tablecloth. She hoped she could say what was on her heart in a way that wouldn't upset Loraine any further. "If Wayne thinks you shouldn't be married, then maybe you ought to respect his decision. He might know what's best for both of you."

"Wayne's not thinking straight! He's *verhuddelt* about things." Loraine's hand shook as she swiped at the tears running down her cheeks. "He needs time to get used to the idea of having only one leg. I'm certain that after a time of healing, Wayne will change his mind about marrying me."

Priscilla reached over and took Loraine's hand. "I'm sure Wayne is feeling confused right now, but I want you to give serious thought to what I'm about to say."

"What is it?"

"Being married to a man with a handicap such as Wayne's

could put additional strain on your marriage. Do you really want to spend the rest of your life taking care of him and dealing with his melancholy moods?"

"He's only lost a leg, Mom. It's not like he's a helpless invalid, and I'm sure in time his moods will improve."

"I hope so, but there will still be some limitations as to what he can do."

"Some time ago, I read an article in the paper about a man who'd lost both of his legs, but thanks to a pair of artificial legs, he's actually running in races. And then there's a swimmer who—"

"I know there are many who have overcome great odds," Priscilla interrupted. "But even if Wayne does rise above his circumstances, he's got a long road ahead of him—both physically and emotionally."

Loraine's chair scraped across the linoleum as she pushed away from the table. "I know you mean well, but I promised to marry Wayne, and I intend to keep that promise. I don't care what sacrifices I might have to make, either." She moved toward the door. "I'd rather not talk about this anymore."

"I think we should talk about it. It's obvious that you're not thinking straight."

"Jah, I am." Loraine grabbed her jacket and outer bonnet. "I'm going for a ride!"

"But you just got home."

"I need to be alone for a while."

As the door banged shut behind Loraine, Priscilla made a decision. She would do everything in her power to make sure her daughter didn't make the biggest mistake of her life.

❧ ❧

Loraine headed for the barn to get her horse and shivered as a cluster of heavy, dark clouds moved across the sky. It looked like it might rain. "Well, let it pour," she mumbled when she reached Trixie's stall. "It can't dampen my spirits any more than they already are."

Memories of Wayne and all the good times they'd had in the past tugged at her heart. A sense of despair crept in, pushing through the tiny cracks of hope she'd been trying to conjure up. What if she couldn't get Wayne to change his mind about marrying her? How could she go to their biweekly church services and other community gatherings and not burst into tears every time she saw him?

In order to calm herself, Loraine let her mind wander back in time. Back to the night when Wayne asked her to marry him. . .

"Would you mind if we take a little detour before I take you home?" Wayne asked when they left the Essenhaus Restaurant parking lot.

Loraine looked up at him with curiosity. "Where are we going?"

"It's a surprise." He tweaked her nose. "You'll see soon enough."

She smiled. "Okay."

Half an hour later, Wayne pulled his horse and buggy into a grassy spot near the pond on the other side of his folks' property.

"How'd you like to live right here?" he asked, turning to face her.

She tipped her head in question.

"Wouldn't you like our home to be built so it overlooked the pond?"

"Our home?"

A wide smile spread across Wayne's face.

Loraine moistened her lips with the tip of her tongue. "Are—are you asking me to marry you?"

He nodded and slipped his arm across her shoulders. "I love you, Loraine. If you're willing to be my wife, I'd like to build our home right here."

Tears gathered in the corners of her eyes. "I'm more than willing, Wayne."

"Are you sure? I mean, if you still have feelings for—"
She shook her head vigorously. *"It's you I love; no one else."*
"I'm real glad to hear it. Can we be married this fall?"
*"Do you think you'll have the house done by then? Since
you're in the middle of spring planting, there won't be much
time to build a house."*
*"That's true, but I'm sure we can live with my folks until
the house is done. Would you be okay with that idea?"*
"I—I guess so." The idea of living in the same house with
Wayne's mother, who could sometimes be rather picky, didn't
set too well with Loraine, but she was sure it wouldn't be for
long.
Wayne pulled Loraine into his arms, and she melted into
his embrace. She could hardly wait to become Mrs. Wayne
Lambright.

A raw ache settled in the pit of Loraine's stomach, as her
thoughts returned to the present. Would she and Wayne ever get
married? Would they live together in the half-finished home he'd
begun near the pond?

To dampen her spirits even further, the sky let loose. Rain
pelted the front of her buggy. Her hands tingled as she gripped the
reins and reminded herself to calm down. She needed to focus on
the road ahead and make sure the horse obeyed her commands.

*I hope Ella's at home; I really need to talk to her. I'm sure she'll be
more supportive and understanding than Mom.*

❦

Ella had just taken a batch of cinnamon rolls from the oven when
she heard the whinny of a horse and the rumble of buggy wheels.
She glanced out the window and noticed that it was raining
heavily, so she hurried to the door and waited as Loraine climbed
down from her buggy.

"Wie geht's?" Ella asked when Loraine stepped onto the porch
a few minutes later.

"I've been better." Loraine removed her rain-soaked jacket, gave it a good shake, and entered the house. "Are you alone? I really need to talk."

"My mamm's not feeling well today, so I insisted she go to her room and rest." Ella motioned to the kitchen. "I just took some cinnamon rolls from the oven, so I'll fix us a cup of hot tea and we can have a snack while we visit."

"I'll pass on the cinnamon rolls, but a cup of tea sounds good." The chair creaked as Loraine slid it away from the table. She dropped into it with a sigh. "I went to the hospital to see Wayne this morning."

Ella poured tea into a cup and handed it to Loraine. "How's he doing?"

"Not so well. Besides the fact that he's still very depressed and is in a lot of pain, he called off our wedding."

Ella nearly dropped the teapot. "You're kidding!"

"No, I'm not. He also asked me not to visit him at the hospital again."

Ella took a seat beside Loraine. "Wayne's still in shock from losing his leg. I'm sure he'll change his mind once he's come to grips with his loss."

"I've been telling myself that, but it's getting harder and harder to have hope—especially when my own *mudder* isn't supportive."

"What do you mean?"

Loraine picked up a spoon and swirled it around in her tea, as she explained how her mother thought being married to a man with a handicap would be a burden. "Mom thinks Wayne did the right thing by breaking our engagement. How can it be wrong for two people who love each other to be together?" Her chin quivered. "At least, I think Wayne still loves me."

"Of course he does. He's just verhuddelt right now, that's all." Ella patted Loraine's arm in a motherly fashion. "You and Wayne are meant to be together."

"I think so, too." Loraine sniffed. "What would I do without you?"

Ella smiled. "That's what friends and family are for—to offer love and encouragement in the dark times, and to laugh and play together during the good times."

They sat quietly drinking their tea. The only sound in the room was the hiss and crackle of the log Ella had put on the fire a short time ago.

Finally, Loraine pushed her chair away from the table and stood. "I think I'll drive over to Aunt JoAnn and Uncle Jeremy's place and see how Katie's doing."

"I'd like to visit Katie, too," Ella said. "Would you mind if I tag along?"

"Of course not. We can go in my buggy, and I'll bring you back here on my way home."

Ella stood. "I'd better check on Mama first, and let her know where I'm going."

"Better take your umbrella," Loraine said as she peered out the kitchen window. "It's still raining pretty hard."

"Okay." As Ella left the room, she glanced over her shoulder. Loraine remained at the window with her nose pressed up to the glass.

I wish I could make things better for Loraine, Ella thought. *I wish I could think of some way to help ease her pain.*

CHAPTER 8

Wwe need to be careful today not to say anything that might upset Wayne," Crist said to Ada as they walked down the hospital corridor toward Wayne's room.

She halted and smacked one hand against her hip. "Are you insinuating that I upset our son the last time we came to see him?"

"I'm not insinuating anything." Crist shrugged. "As you well know, ever since the accident, Wayne gets easily upset. If either of us says the wrong thing, it might set him off."

"Well, no need to worry; I won't say anything to upset our son." Ada hurried down the hall. She couldn't believe the accusation she'd heard in Crist's voice. Why, he'd talked to her as if *she* were the reason Wayne had become upset on their last visit! Didn't Crist realize the reason for Wayne's sour disposition was because he'd lost his leg?

I've never been anything but supportive and helpful.

With her head held high and a smile on her face, Ada stepped into Wayne's room.

⚜

When the door to Wayne's room swooshed open, he rolled onto his side and opened his eyes.

"How are you feeling today?" Mom asked, stepping up to his bed.

Pop was right behind her.

"About the same," Wayne mumbled.

"Are you in much pain?" Pop asked.

Wayne shook his head. "Only when the pain medicine wears off."

"Then how come you look like you're in pain?" Mom asked.

"Loraine was here awhile ago, and I—"

"Did she say something to upset you? Because if she did—"

"No, Mom. I broke things off with her, but now I'm having second thoughts."

"You called off the wedding?"

Wayne nodded. "But I love Loraine and can't imagine spending my life without her, so it's going to be hard for me to—"

Mom patted his shoulder. "You made the right decision. With your handicap, it would be hard for you to support a wife right now. Besides, Loraine's too demanding. She has high expectations and always wants her way." Deep wrinkles formed in Mom's forehead as she shook her head. "I never thought Loraine was the right woman for you."

Wayne grimaced. "I've never seen Loraine as demanding or having high expectations. She's sweet and even-tempered. She's—"

"I think we should change the subject," Pop said.

Wayne ground his teeth. "What shall we talk about—how lousy I feel, and how disappointed I am because God didn't answer my prayers for a safe trip to Hershey Park?"

Pop placed his hand on Wayne's shoulder. "Sometimes the answer to our prayers isn't what we expected. Sometimes God answers by giving us the strength to make it through trials. Other times, He sends someone to help us." He nodded his head. "Some of our greatest blessings can come because of a prayer that wasn't answered the way we'd hoped."

Wayne grunted and turned his head away. "I don't want any sermons today, and I sure don't feel blessed."

"I have some good news for you," Wayne's doctor announced as he entered the room, bringing their conversation to a halt.

"Barring anything unforeseen, you should be able to go home sometime tomorrow, Wayne."

"Oh, that's wunderbaar." Mom clasped Wayne's hand and squeezed his fingers. "I'm sure you'll be a lot more comfortable at home in your own familiar surroundings."

Wayne nodded mutely. Truth was, he was worried about how things would be for him at home. Would he be able to cope with his disability? Would he be able to farm again? Could he live without Loraine?

~≈ ≈~

Priscilla wrung her hands as she paced from the kitchen table to the window and back again. It gave her no pleasure to upset Loraine, but she felt she'd had the right to say what was on her mind. Loraine wasn't thinking straight and needed some guidance.

She glanced at the clock on the wall above the refrigerator. Where had Loraine gone, and when was she coming home?

"What time's supper?" Amos asked when he stepped into the kitchen a few minutes later.

"Whenever Loraine gets home."

"Where'd she go?"

Priscilla shrugged. "I don't know. She left several hours ago and hasn't returned."

Amos slid one of the chairs away from the table and took a seat. "Loraine's been through a lot lately. She probably needs some time alone."

Priscilla sucked in her lower lip. "We. . .uh. . .had a little disagreement. I think that's why she left."

Amos's eyebrows furrowed. "What was the disagreement about?"

She sat in the chair beside him and quickly related the story of how Loraine had gone to visit Wayne that morning and how he'd broken their engagement.

"I'm sorry to hear that." Amos looked at her with questioning eyes. "What'd *you* say that upset her?"

"I just said that I thought being married to a man with a handicap such as Wayne's could put a strain on their marriage."

"Well, no wonder she took off!" Amos glared at her. "You ought to stop meddling and let our daughter make her own decisions. You didn't interfere in our boys' lives like that when they all still lived at home."

Priscilla stiffened. "I wasn't meddling; I'm just concerned about Loraine and want her to be happy."

"Then you oughta realize that Loraine's happiness is with Wayne. She loves him, and that's why she agreed to marry him."

"I know that, but—"

"You oughta stop giving unwanted advice and just be supportive."

"I am being supportive."

"Whatever." Amos pushed away from the table. "Ring the bell when supper's ready." He rushed out of the house before Priscilla could respond.

⚬⚬⚬

"I hope Katie's doing better than the last time we saw her," Loraine said as she and Ella headed down the road in her buggy.

Ella nodded. "Katie's always been kind of excitable, but I've never seen her so despondent and unresponsive, like she's been since Timothy died. I hope she snaps out of it soon."

"The accident affected everyone, but in different ways. I'm afraid some of us will never be the same."

Ella reached across the seat and touched Loraine's arm. "Are you thinking of Wayne?"

"Jah." Loraine blinked a couple of times, hoping to ward off the tears. Just thinking about the accident made her want to cry. Thinking about Wayne not wanting to marry her made her even more miserable.

"Things will work out between you and Wayne; you'll see."

"I—I hope so." A few tears leaked out and trickled down Loraine's cheeks. "Everything was going so well before the accident. Wayne and I had our wedding date set, my dress has been made, our

51

home was getting close to being done, and we were moving along with our plans. Unless he changes his mind, there'll be no wedding for us at all."

Ella offered a reassuring smile. "We'll just have to pray that he does."

Loraine nodded and clucked to her horse to get her moving faster. At the rate Trixie was plodding along, it would be suppertime before they made it to Katie's, and then they'd have to turn right around and head back home.

They rode in silence the rest of the way, and Loraine forced herself to concentrate on driving her horse and watching out for any cars that might be going too fast or following too close on this rainy day.

When they arrived at the Millers', they found Katie's father in the barn, unloading a bunch of hay from the wagon he had parked there.

"Wie geht's?" he called with a friendly wave. "What brings you by this afternoon?"

"We came to see Katie," Loraine said. "We wanted to see how she's doing."

Uncle Jeremy's eyebrows furrowed. "She and her mamm took a trip to Sarasota, Florida, to visit Katie's grandparents. We decided the change of scenery might help Katie deal with the loss of Timothy."

"This is the first we've heard of it," Ella said. "How come no one told us until now?"

"It was a spur-of-the-moment decision, and I haven't had a chance to tell anyone yet," he said.

"How long will they be gone?" Loraine asked.

"Don't know for sure. Probably a few weeks." Uncle Jeremy glanced at the hay he'd already stacked along one wall. "I hope you don't mind, but I need to get back to stacking this hay so I can get some other chores done."

"Go right ahead. We need to get home and help start supper soon, anyway," Loraine said. "If you talk to Katie on the phone, would you please tell her that Ella and I said hello and that we're praying for her?"

"I sure will." Uncle Jeremy went back to unloading his hay, while Ella and Loraine climbed into the buggy.

"Would you mind stopping by Sara Bontrager's place on the way home?" Ella asked as Loraine guided the horse onto the road. "Since Sara's been recently widowed, I'd like to check on her and see if there's anything she needs."

"Jah, we can do that," Loraine replied. Besides doing a good deed for a neighbor, she figured it might take her mind off her own troubles for a while.

A short time later, they pulled into Sara's place. "If you want to head up to the house, I'll untie the horse and be in as soon as I'm done," Loraine said to Ella.

"That's fine." Ella climbed out of the buggy and sprinted to the house, rain pelting down on her umbrella as she dodged several puddles.

Once Loraine had the horse secured to the hitching rail, she followed. She found Ella and Sara sitting at the kitchen table, sharing a pot of tea.

"Come join us for some tea and banana bread." Sara motioned to the chair next to Ella.

After Loraine had taken a seat, Sara passed her a cup of tea and the plate of bread.

Loraine smiled. "Danki."

Sara smiled in return, revealing a set of crooked teeth.

Well, at least she still has all her own teeth, Loraine mused. *Many people Sara's age wear dentures.*

"How are things going with you?" Loraine asked the elderly woman.

"I'm getting along fairly well. Even though none of my family live close to me now, my good friends and neighbors check in on me regularly and make sure I have all that I need." Sara smiled again, a little wider this time. "Of course, once a month the widows in our community get together of an evening and either go out to supper or make a call on someone who's sick or isn't able to get out much. It makes me feel needed when I do something like that."

Ella reached over and clasped Sara's hand. "We all need to feel needed, and I think it's wunderbaar that you're still able to get around and do helpful things for others."

Sara looked over at Loraine and motioned to the loaf of bread on the table. "Before you came into the house, I was telling Ella that five different people dropped by this week, and each of them gave me some starter for friendship bread. I've made several loaves, but I have more starter than I know what to do with." She grinned at Loraine. "Ella's taking a loaf of bread and some starter home. Would you like some, too?"

"I'd appreciate the bread," Loraine said, "but I don't think I'll have time to tend the starter or make more bread, so I'd better pass on that."

"What about your mamm? Would she be able to tend the starter?"

Loraine shrugged. "I'm not sure, but I think I'll just take the bread if you don't mind. I will let Mom know that you have some starter, and if she wants any, I'm sure she'll be over to see you."

"That's fine." Sara took a sip of tea. "How are you two doing since that horrible accident? Are you fairly well healed of your injuries?"

"I wasn't seriously hurt," Ella said. "Just a mild concussion and some nasty bumps and bruises."

"Bumps and bruises were all I had, too, but I wish we could say the same for the others who were in the van." Loraine sighed. "We just came from our cousin Katie's, and her *daed* said Katie and her mamm went to Sarasota for a while."

"That's right," Ella interjected. "Katie's folks are hoping some time away might help Katie recover from the shock of losing Timothy."

"It's such a shame when someone so young passes on." Sara looked at Ella with sympathy. "I'm sure you and your family must miss your bruder."

A muscle on the side of Ella's cheek quivered. "My mamm's taken it the hardest, but in time, I'm sure she'll come to grips with Raymond's death."

Sara looked at Loraine. "How's your boyfriend doing? It must have been a real shock for him to lose a leg like that."

Loraine nodded. She glanced at Ella, hoping she wouldn't mention that Wayne had called off the wedding.

Sara patted Loraine's hand. "If you and Wayne commit everything to God, and if you'll seek His will in all things, I'm certain that it will work out just as it should."

Loraine dabbed at her damp cheeks with a napkin. She hoped Sara was right about things working out. She had so many doubts swirling around in her head. She'd never admit it to anyone, but Loraine's greatest fear was that she and Wayne might never get married.

CHAPTER 9

"Are you warm enough, son?"

Wayne nodded as his mother draped a small quilt across his lap.

"Are you certain? I can add another log to the fire if you're cold."

"I'm fine, Mom."

"Are you sure you're comfortable enough lying on the sofa, or would you rather go to your room and rest awhile?"

Wayne gritted his teeth. Ever since he'd come home from the hospital this afternoon, Mom had hovered over him like a moth drawn to a flame. It was bad enough that he had to deal with the phantom pain he'd begun experiencing and try to get used to maneuvering around their house with his wheelchair. Did Mom have to smother him to death, as well?

Makes me wish I was back in the hospital, he thought. *At least there, they encouraged me to do some things on my own, and they didn't ask me every few minutes if I needed anything or was comfortable enough.*

Wayne stared at the flames rising from the wood in the fireplace across the room. *I wonder if anything in my life will ever feel normal again. Should I have let Loraine know I was coming home today? What if she goes to the hospital to see me and finds that I've gone?*

He scrubbed a hand down his face. *What am I thinking? I broke up with Loraine yesterday, so she'd have no reason to go to the hospital to see me today.*

❧ ❧

With a sense of urgency, Loraine hurried down the hospital corridor toward Wayne's room. She'd lain awake much of the night, thinking and praying about her situation with Wayne. She loved him and had made a commitment to become his wife. She wanted to rub away any tension Wayne felt today and hoped what she had to say to him might cause him to change his mind about marrying her.

As she approached Wayne's room, she said a quick prayer for guidance. Then, feeling a little more confident, she pushed the door open and stepped inside.

She blinked a couple of times and stared at his bed. It was empty and looked like it had been freshly made. Maybe Wayne was in another part of the hospital having physical therapy.

She left the room and hurried to the nurses' station. "Excuse me," she said to the nurse behind the counter. "I just came from Wayne Lambright's room, and he wasn't there. Do you know if he's having physical therapy right now?"

The nurse shook her head. "Mr. Lambright went home earlier today."

"He did?"

"Yes. His parents came to get him about two hours ago."

"Oh, I see." Loraine turned from the counter, feeling as if she were in a daze. She thought Wayne would have called and left a message on her folks' answering machine in the phone shed they shared with the neighbors. She thought he cared enough about her to let her know that he planned to come home, but apparently she was wrong.

Tears blurred her vision as she stumbled down the hall and out the door. As soon as they got back to Goshen, she'd ask Marge to drop her off at Wayne's. She needed to speak to him today!

57

⁓❧ ❦⁓

Loraine arrived at Wayne's house later that day, and her heart began to pound when his mother answered the door.

"Is—is Wayne here? When I went to the hospital, they said he'd gone home."

Ada nodded, a grim expression on her face. "Wayne's sleeping, and I don't want to disturb him right now. The trip home from the hospital took a lot out of him, and he's in a great deal of pain."

"I thought the pain medication took care of his pain."

"It did, but now he has more than the aftermath of his surgery pain to deal with."

"What do you mean?"

"The phantom pains have set in."

"Oh, I see. Wayne mentioned that those would likely occur."

Ada's pinched expression didn't change. "The doctor said it was likely to happen, but we had no idea it would start this soon or be this bad."

"I'm sorry to hear that. Is it all right if I come inside and wait until Wayne's awake? I really need to talk to him."

Ada shook her head. "That's not a good idea."

"Why not?"

"Do you really have to ask?"

Loraine leaned on the porch railing, feeling the need for some support. She didn't care for the cold reception she was getting from Wayne's mother. She'd been dealing with a lot of Ada's icy treatment since the accident.

Loraine moistened her lips. "You probably know that Wayne broke our engagement."

"Jah, and that means things are over between you and him." Ada folded her arms and glared at Loraine as if daring her to say otherwise.

Loraine grimaced. She didn't understand this sudden hostility. Until the accident, Ada had never acted like this toward her.

"I'm hoping Wayne will change his mind and realize that the

58

loss of his leg doesn't change anything between us." She moved away from the railing, feeling a bit more confident. "I want Wayne to know that I'm still his best friend, and that I love—"

"You can do that best by staying away from here. He needs time to heal without a lot of demands and expectations put upon him."

Loraine's skin prickled. "I wasn't planning to make demands or put expectations on Wayne. I just want him to know how much I love him and want to help in any way I can."

"Are you're hoping to change his mind about marrying you?"

Loraine nodded. She couldn't deny it, even though she knew it wasn't what Wayne's mother wanted to hear. "What have you got against me, Ada?" she dared to ask. "Have I said or done something to offend you?"

Ada's gaze dropped to the porch floor. "I—I just think my son has enough to deal with right now without taking on the responsibility of a wife and family."

"He wouldn't have to do it alone. I'm willing to help in any way I can."

Ada lifted her gaze. "Be that as it may, Wayne has a long road ahead of him. He won't be ready to even think about marriage for a long time to come."

"I realize that, and I'm willing to wait."

Ada rubbed her hands briskly over her arms. "It's getting cold out here, and I need to check on the chicken I have baking in the oven. So if you'll excuse me. . ."

Loraine gave a quick nod, turned, and started down the stairs. "Please tell Wayne I was here," she called over her shoulder. "Oh, and let him know that I'll be back tomorrow morning."

CHAPTER 10

Wayne squinted at the invading light streaming through his bedroom window, letting him know it was morning. He'd had a fitful night, tossing, turning, dreaming, and soaking his sheets with sweat. The pain he felt where his leg had once been was so intense at times he thought he'd go mad. The medicine they'd given him for pain had barely taken the edge off. He wished there was something he could do to alleviate his discomfort. He didn't think he could endure the pain if it went on too long.

Gritting his teeth, he pulled himself to a sitting position, took one step, and fell back on the bed with a groan. It had seemed so normal to be back in his own bed, he'd forgotten he only had one leg. He glanced at his stump and noticed that it had started to shrink. Another thing the doctor had told him would happen.

He reached for the handles of his wheelchair and swung it around. Then, hopping on one foot, he positioned himself in front of the wheelchair and sat down.

"Everything I do takes such effort," he mumbled. "I wonder if it'll ever get any easier for me." At least Mom had moved most of his things to the downstairs bedroom, and he didn't have to navigate the steps on one leg. The wheelchair wouldn't work on steps, either, which was why Pop had built a ramp leading to the back porch.

Mom and Pop have done all they can to make my life easier, Wayne thought as he slipped his arms into a long-sleeved cotton shirt. *I ought to be grateful and quit feeling sorry for myself, but in my circumstances, that's easier said than done.*

Wayne closed his eyes, and an image of Loraine popped into his head. It had only been two days since he'd last seen her, but already he missed her—more than he missed his leg. His arms longed to hold her. His fingers ached to stroke her soft skin. His lips yearned to kiss hers. If only they could be together. If things could just be as they'd once been. If he could only undo the past, he would. . . .

His eyes snapped open, and he shook his head. All the *if onlys* in the world wouldn't change a thing. He'd lost a leg, and he wouldn't be getting it back. He'd made a decision not to marry Loraine, and he wouldn't be changing his mind.

❧ ❧

"I'm heading out now, Mom," Loraine said as she grabbed her jacket from the wall peg where she'd hung it the night before.

Mom's eyebrows raised. "Why are you leaving so early for work? You don't have to be at the hardware store for another couple of hours."

"I want to stop by the Lambrights' on my way to Shipshewana and see how Wayne's getting along. Since he was asleep when I stopped there yesterday, I didn't get the chance to talk to him."

"What are you going to talk about—your broken engagement?"

Loraine nodded. "That, plus a few other things."

Mom opened her mouth like she was going to say something more, but she snapped it shut and turned back to the dishes she'd been drying.

"I'll see you when I get home from work this afternoon." Loraine turned and headed out the door.

As soon as she started across the lawn, she spotted Dad coming out of the barn, leading Trixie.

"Figured you'd be leaving for work soon, so I decided to get your horse hitched to the buggy," he called to Loraine.

She stepped up to him and smiled. "Danki, Dad. That was thoughtful of you. Especially since I'm leaving earlier than usual today."

"Going by to see Wayne on the way to Shipshewana?"

She nodded. "He came home from the hospital yesterday, and I want to see how he's doing."

Dad placed a gentle hand on her arm. "I was sorry to hear Wayne called off the wedding. Sorry to hear you and your mamm had a disagreement about him, too."

"Mom doesn't understand how I feel about things." Tears welled in Loraine's eyes. "She's always had more understanding for James, Harold, Earl, and Ben than she has for me."

Dad shook his head. "I don't believe that. I just think that since your *brieder* are all married, and you're the only one of our kinner still living at home, your mamm worries about you more." He pulled Loraine to his side and gave her a hug. "Your mamm loves you a lot. Surely you know that."

"I do know it, but I wish she'd let me make my own decisions without interference. She doesn't think Wayne can take care of me now that he's lost a leg." Loraine sighed. "Of course, Wayne thinks he can't, either, so I'm really outnumbered."

"It'll all work out in the end; you'll see."

Loraine forced a smile. At least somebody was on her side.

❧ ❧

"Did you get enough to eat?" Mom pointed to Wayne's plate. "You hardly touched your poached eggs."

"I'm not that hungry this morning," he said. "The pain medicine has made my stomach upset."

"That's because you took it without eating first." Mom shook her head. "You need to follow the instructions on the bottle."

"Stop badgering him, Ada," Pop spoke up. "He's a grown man, not a little *buwe*."

She turned in her chair and glared at him. "Don't you think

I know that? I'm just trying to make things easier for him."

"Then stop badgering."

"I'm not."

"Jah, you sure are."

Unable to listen to his parents' squabbling a moment longer, Wayne pushed his wheelchair away from the table and propelled it across the floor. The biggest trouble with being an only child was that Mom had no one to fuss over but him, and sometimes she could be downright overbearing.

Wayne was almost to the hallway when a knock sounded on the door. "I'll get it!" he called before Mom could come running.

When he opened the back door, he was surprised to see Loraine on the porch.

"Wie geht's?" she asked with a smile.

"I'm doin' as well as can be expected."

"Can I come in? I'd like to talk to you."

"Jah, I guess it'll be okay." He opened the door wider. "My folks are about done with breakfast, but I'm sure there's still some coffee left if you'd like some."

"A cup of coffee would be nice."

Wayne pushed the door closed and headed back to the kitchen. He couldn't help but notice the scowl on Mom's face when Loraine entered the room with him. He hoped Loraine hadn't noticed.

"*Guder mariye*," Loraine said, smiling at Mom and then Pop.

"Morning," they said in unison.

"I invited Loraine in for a cup of coffee." Wayne looked at Mom. "Is there still some in the coffeepot?"

She nodded, frowned, and pushed away from the table. When she returned with a cup of coffee for Loraine, she was still frowning.

"Danki." Loraine took a seat at the table and looked over at Wayne. "I came by yesterday, but you were sleeping. So I decided to stop on my way to work this morning and see how you're doing."

"He's got an upset stomach," Mom said before Wayne could respond. "Didn't eat much breakfast because of it."

"I'm sorry to hear that. Do you think you're getting the flu?" Loraine asked Wayne.

He shook his head. "The pain medicine upsets my stomach."

"That's because you took it without eating first." Mom reached for the teapot sitting in the center of the table, poured some into a cup, and handed it to Wayne. "Drink some of this peppermint tea, and I'm sure it'll settle your stomach."

Wayne set the cup down. "I don't care for any tea—especially not peppermint. I never did like the taste of it."

"Well, I'd like you to at least try a little bit," Mom insisted.

Pop poked Mom's arm. "You're doing it again, Ada."

"Doing what?"

"Badgering."

"I'm only trying to make him feel better."

Loraine fiddled with the edge of the tablecloth, obviously un-comfortable. "When I was here yesterday," she said, lifting her gaze to meet Wayne's, "your mamm said you were in a lot of pain."

Wayne was about to speak when Mom butted in.

"Like I told you then, Wayne's been having some terrible phantom pains."

"How come you didn't tell me Loraine was here to see me yesterday?" Wayne asked, leaning close to Mom.

She shrugged. "You were asleep. By the time you woke up, I'd gotten busy and forgot."

Wayne ground his teeth. He had a feeling Mom had deliber-ately not mentioned Loraine's visit. Mom clearly didn't care for Loraine anymore, and he didn't understand why.

They sat in silence for a while; finally, Loraine drank her coffee and pushed away from the table. "I'd better go. I don't want to be late for work." She moved toward the door, but hesitated as though there was something else on her mind.

"I'll see you out," Wayne was quick to say. He sure didn't want Mom walking Loraine to the door.

Once they were on the porch, Loraine turned to him and said, "There was another reason I came by today, only I didn't want to say it with your folks sitting there."

"What's that?"

"I wanted to know if you've reconsidered your decision not to marry me."

Wayne's heart began to pound. Loraine was everything he wanted in a wife. Yet he loved her too much to strap her with a cripple who couldn't even support them by doing what he loved best.

"My answer's still the same," he mumbled. "And if you're gonna keep bringing up the subject, then I think it'd be best if you didn't come over here at all anymore."

"You can't mean that."

"I do mean it. In fact, it might be best for both of us if we didn't see each other except at church."

She stared at him several seconds, tears welling in her eyes. Then she sprinted down the stairs and raced to the hitching rail where her horse and buggy waited.

Exhausted and fighting the phantom pain once again, Wayne turned his wheelchair around and entered the house. With only a glance in Mom's direction, he wheeled down the hall and into his room. He didn't have the energy to deal with anything else.

～❧ ❧～

As Loraine guided her horse and buggy down the road, she replayed some of the things that had been said during her visit with Wayne. Every time she saw Ada, it became more obvious that the woman didn't care for her. And every time she saw Wayne, he seemed to withdraw from her all the more. Even so, Loraine's heart longed to be his wife.

How could he have suggested that I not come over to see him anymore? she fretted. *I was so sure if he had a few days to think things over he'd have changed his mind about his decision not to marry me.*

Tears stung the backs of her eyes, and she blinked multiple times in order to keep them from spilling onto her cheeks. *I still think that at least part of Wayne's rejection has something to do with his mother's dislike of me. If I could only think of something to do that would make Ada accept me, maybe Wayne would change his mind. Oh, I wish I knew what to do.*

More tears came as Loraine passed the one-room schoolhouse where Jolene used to teach. Dorene Lehman, Timothy's thirty-year-old unmarried sister, taught there now, but it was just until the school board could find a permanent teacher. Dorene was planning to move to a small town in Montana soon.

My cousin was well liked at this place, Loraine thought as she slowed her horse and studied the two-story wooden structure where she, too, had gone to school. *The scholars must miss Jolene terribly. Jolene's probably missing them a lot, as well.*

Loraine gripped the reins a little tighter. *I, too, miss Jolene, and also Katie. We four cousins were always so close. In times past, I could go to any of them for comfort when I was upset about something. Now Katie and Jolene are gone, and Ella's so busy trying to comfort her mother and take care of things at their home that I feel guilty for bothering her with my problems. Wayne's pushed me away, and Mom doesn't understand me at all. I feel almost friendless right now.*

Beep! Beep! Loraine startled when she realized that her buggy had drifted into the wrong lane, and she gasped when she saw that a car was coming straight at her!

CHAPTER 11

Loraine jerked on the reins. The horse pulled out of the way just in time to avoid hitting the car coming toward her. "Thank You, Lord," she murmured. "That was too close for my comfort."

She gave Trixie the freedom to trot, and by the time they were halfway to work, the horse had worked up a sweat. Suddenly, a siren blared behind her, and she nearly jumped out of her seat. Thinking that a rescue vehicle must be coming down the road, she guided her horse and buggy to the side of the road. The next thing she knew, a police car had pulled in behind her. She gulped when a uniformed officer got out of the car and headed her way.

"Is there a problem?" Loraine asked when the policeman stepped up to her buggy.

"Someone called in a report about a horse and buggy that had nearly hit them on this stretch of road." He squinted over the top of his metal-framed glasses. "Since your horse and buggy is the only one I've seen on this stretch of road, I figured it had to be you."

Loraine hated to admit that she hadn't been concentrating on the road, but she didn't want to lie to the man, either. "I. . .uh. . . yes, it was me."

"Have you been drinking?"

"No, of course not! I was in deep thought about my fiancé having just lost his leg in an accident he and I were involved in several days ago, and I didn't realize my horse had wandered into oncoming traffic."

His forehead wrinkled. "I should give you a ticket for reckless driving, but since I can see how distraught you seem to be, I'll let you off with a warning. However, I caution you to be more careful from now on."

"Yes. Yes, I will."

The officer glanced at Trixie and squinted. "I see your horse is pretty well lathered up, which tells me you must have been running it too fast. I really should call a vet to come check on the animal." His bushy eyebrows pulled together as he slowly shook his head. "There's too much animal abuse going on these days, and it's got to stop!"

"My horse is lathered up, but I haven't been running her too hard," Loraine said. "She's prone to sweating, so this is perfectly normal for her."

"Are you sure about that?"

She nodded. "If you don't believe me, you can call a vet to check Trixie over."

"Trixie, is it?" The officer chuckled. "Okay, I'm going to trust that everything you've told me is the truth." His smile faded. "Next time, though, you'd better keep a closer eye on your horse. Besides the fact that you should never run a horse too fast, there have been way too many accidents on this stretch of road, and we sure don't need any more."

"Thank you, sir."

His smile was back. "Now run along, and don't forget to rub that horse down good."

"Of course."

The officer returned to his vehicle, and Loraine breathed a sigh of relief. This was not starting out as a good day!

～❦～

Wayne closed his eyes and tried to sleep, but he couldn't stop thinking about Loraine and how dejected she'd looked when he'd said he hadn't changed his mind about marrying her. It almost killed him to give her up, but he saw no other way.

He curled his fingers into his palms as he stared at the stump of his leg. *I don't know if I'll ever be able to accept what's happened to me because I'll never be a whole man again.*

Tap! Tap! Tap!

Wayne turned his head toward the door and called, "Come in."

"I'm glad you're not asleep," Pop said when he poked his head into Wayne's room. "There's something I want to talk to you about."

"What's that?"

Pop stepped into the room and took a seat in the chair next to Wayne's bed. "I've been praying about something for sometime, and I've finally made a decision."

"A decision about what?"

"I'm going to quit farming and turn my hobby of taxidermy into a full-time business."

Wayne's teeth snapped together with a noisy click. "You're kidding!"

Pop shook his head. "This is something I've wanted to do for a long while, and I feel now's the right time."

"What about your land? Who's going to farm it if you open a taxidermy business?"

"I'm going to lease out the land to Harold Fry. I've already talked to him about it, and he's agreed to the arrangement."

Wayne's face contorted. If felt like someone had kicked him in the stomach. He had a hunch Pop's decision to quit farming and open his own taxidermy business was because of him and his missing leg.

Pop tapped Wayne's shoulder a couple of times. "If things go well, like I hope, then I might need a partner in my new business."

"I hope you're not thinking of me."

"I sure was. I think taxidermy would be a good thing for you to try, and it's something you can do from your wheelchair if necessary."

Wayne shook his head vigorously. "No way! Working with a

bunch of dead animal skins isn't for me!"

"How do you know that?"

" 'Cause it isn't, that's all. I'd rather be farming."

"But you can't farm anymore. You said so yourself."

Wayne jerked his head, feeling as if he'd been slapped. "I—I know what I said, but if I should get a prosthesis, and if we were both farming, then maybe—"

Pop held up his hand. "The decision's already been made about the farm, and I think I know what's best. You'll just have to accept things as they are." The floor squeaked as he rose from his chair. "Anytime you feel ready, I'll be happy to teach you what you need to know about taxidermy."

When the door clicked shut behind Pop, Wayne rolled over and punched his pillow. *If he wants to become a taxidermist, that's up to him, but he'll never talk me into messing with it!*

⚜

Priscilla had just taken a seat on the sofa late that afternoon when Loraine entered the room, her face pale and lips trembling. "You look so sad. Is something wrong?" Priscilla asked.

"Es is mir verleed." Loraine sank into the rocking chair with a groan.

"Why are you discouraged?"

"I was so upset after I left Wayne's home that I almost got a ticket for reckless driving."

"I've never known you to drive the horse and buggy recklessly."

"I did today because I wasn't paying attention." Loraine gnawed on her lower lip. "Wayne hasn't changed his mind about marrying me, Mom. To make matters worse, he thinks it would be best if we didn't see each other anywhere except at church."

"Does that mean he doesn't want you to go over to his house anymore?"

"I believe it does." Loraine jumped out of her chair and began pacing. "I don't know how, but I have to get Wayne to change his mind about marrying me. I'll do whatever I have to in order to help us financially, too. I'll even work two jobs if that's what it takes."

Priscilla left her seat and stepped up to Loraine. "If Wayne feels he's made the right decision, then don't you think it's time for you to accept things as they are?"

"No, I can't accept Wayne's decision. I could tell from the tender expression on his face that he still loves me, and unless he says otherwise, I'm not giving up on us because I'm sure we're supposed to be together. I know I've got my work cut out for me, because Wayne keeps pushing me away when he needs me the most, but I can't give up on us."

Priscilla sighed deeply. "I know you care about Wayne, but you really should be taking care of yourself right now. You've been through a great ordeal, and you don't need to be worried about Wayne so much that you're getting yourself all worked up and upset." She patted Loraine gently on the back. "Give yourself a little time to get through all the emotional wounds, and then maybe—"

Loraine shook her head. "I don't care about my own needs right now. I only care about Wayne's needs, and I'll do what it takes to get through to him."

With tears streaming down her face, Loraine fled the room and dashed up the stairs.

Priscilla sank to the sofa and closed her eyes. *I think I ought to pay a call on the Lambrights, and it had better be soon.*

CHAPTER 12

As Priscilla guided her horse and buggy toward the Lambrights' place the next morning, she rehearsed in her mind what she was going to say when she saw Wayne. She had left home after Loraine had gone to work because she didn't want her to know where she was going.

She turned up the Lambrights' driveway, climbed down from the buggy, and tied the horse to a hitching rail near the barn. Then she hurried to the house. A few seconds after she'd rapped on the door, it opened, and Wayne's mother appeared.

"Guder mariye," Priscilla said.

Ada nodded. "Good morning. What brings you by so early in the day?"

"I came to see how Wayne's doing."

"He's having trouble adjusting to only one leg, but he's getting along as well as can be expected."

"Would it be all right if I came in and said hello to him?"

Ada glanced over her shoulder. "He's in the kitchen having a cup of coffee, but he didn't sleep well last night, so I don't know if he's up to any company this morning."

"I promise I won't stay long."

"All right then."

Ada led the way to the kitchen, where Wayne sat at the table in his wheelchair. His slumped shoulders and haggard expression gave indication that he really was tired.

"How are you feeling?" Priscilla asked, taking a seat in the chair beside him.

"I've been better," he mumbled.

"He's in a lot of pain yet." Ada handed Priscilla a cup of coffee.

"Danki." She turned to Wayne. "Doesn't the pain medicine help with that?"

He shrugged. "Sometimes."

"We're going to ask the doctor to try some other medicine for the pain Wayne's been having," Ada said. "There's just no good reason for him having to suffer like this."

Priscilla grimaced. She wished Ada would leave the room so she could speak to Wayne privately, but she didn't think she ought to come right out and make such a request.

"I'd like to talk to you about something," she said to Wayne.

"What's that?"

"It's about you and Loraine."

"What about them?" Ada butted in.

Priscilla gritted her teeth. She'd had just about enough of Ada's constant interrupting. "I understand that you broke things off with Loraine," she said, directing her comment to Wayne again.

"That's right," Ada said before he could respond. "Wayne doesn't feel that he can take on the responsibility of marriage right now."

"That's true," Wayne said. "With only one leg, I won't be able to farm. Besides, my daed's decided to lease out his land so he can become a full-time taxidermist. So even if I could still farm, I have no land to work anymore."

Priscilla couldn't help but notice the bitterness in Wayne's tone. She'd never seen him so negative before. Loraine was right about him being depressed, which was just one more reason Priscilla felt he wouldn't make a good husband.

Ada moved away from the table and turned on the water at the sink. "I don't see how my husband thinks he's going to earn a living making dead animals look like they're alive," she mumbled.

"But if that's what he wants to do, then I'll keep quiet about it."

I'll just bet you will. Priscilla noticed that she was gripping the handle of her cup really hard, and fearing it might break, she set it on the table. *I wish you'd be quiet right now, Ada, and let me speak to your son without your interruptions.* She looked at Wayne to gauge his reaction to his mother's comment, but his gaze remained fixed on his cup of coffee.

"I. . .uh. . .want you to know that I agree with your decision to break off your engagement to my daughter." Priscilla paused to wait for Wayne's response, but he said nothing.

"That's what I told him, too," Ada said over her shoulder. "I'm sure Loraine's upset about it, but she's a nice enough looking young woman. She's bound to catch the attention of some other fellow soon enough."

A muscle on the side of Wayne's neck quivered. "I won't hold Loraine to her promise to marry me, so if she wants to find someone else, she's free to do so." He backed his wheelchair away from the table and swung it around. "I'm tired. I think I'll go back to bed."

As soon as Wayne wheeled out of the room, Ada moved back to the table and leaned close to Priscilla. "I'm relieved to know you agree with me about Wayne breaking up with Loraine. I think it helps that we're thinking alike on this."

Priscilla nodded. "I only hope my daughter learns to accept things as they are and moves on with her life."

❧ ❧

"Guder mariye. How are things going for you?" Esther Lehman asked when Loraine entered the hardware store in Shipshewana.

"Okay." Loraine didn't think her boss needed to hear how she really felt this morning. Work wasn't the place to discuss her personal feelings.

"Are you ready for a busy day of stocking shelves and waiting on customers?"

"Ready as I'll ever be."

"Good, because we just got in a shipment of garden tools. There are also some boxes of weather vanes and birdhouses that need to be set out."

Loraine nodded. "That's fine. I'll do whatever needs to be done."

Esther motioned to the front counter. "You know where everything is, so I'd better get back to waiting on customers and let you get busy."

"Jah, I need to do that." Loraine hurried to the back room. She'd only been working a short time when her hands began to sweat and perspiration broke out on her forehead.

Maybe I shouldn't be working today. I can't seem to keep my mind off the situation with Wayne.

She reached for another birdhouse and was about to set it on the proper shelf, when it slipped from her fingers and crashed to the floor.

"What happened? I heard a clatter," Esther said, rushing up to Loraine.

"I—I dropped a birdhouse." Loraine motioned to the floor. "Thankfully, it doesn't appear to be broken." With a shaky hand, she wiped the perspiration from her forehead.

"Are you all right? Maybe you shouldn't have come to work today." Esther's pinched expression revealed her obvious concern.

Loraine shook her head. "I'll be okay."

Esther glanced over her shoulder. "Oh, there's someone waiting at the front counter, so I'd better go. Feel free to take a break if you need to."

"Danki."

Esther walked away, and Loraine bent to pick up the birdhouse. She was about to place it on the shelf when she heard someone call her name from behind her. She whirled around and was surprised to see Ella.

"I wondered if you'd be working today," Ella said.

"Jah, but I'm not doing a very good job of it." Loraine placed the birdhouse on the shelf and then pointed at it. "I dropped this because my hands are so shaky."

"How come they're shaky? Did something happen on the way to work this morning to get you upset?"

Loraine shook her head. "I didn't sleep well last night."

"Why not?"

"I went to see Wayne again yesterday, hoping he'd change his mind about marrying me." Loraine sighed. "He wouldn't budge and even said we should stop seeing each other socially."

"I'm sorry to hear that. What are you going to do?"

"For now, just try to be his friend. That's the only thing I can do, I guess, because if I keep pestering him about his decision, I'm sure it'll only drive him further away."

"I think you're right about that." Ella moved closer to Loraine. "Speaking of Wayne. . ." Her voice lowered to a whisper. "When I was on my way to town, I saw your mamm's horse and buggy pulling out of the Lambrights' driveway."

Loraine's forehead wrinkled. "Are you sure it was my mamm's rig?"

"Absolutely. She even waved as I went past."

"That seems a bit odd. Mom never mentioned to me that she'd be going over to the Lambrights' this morning." A spot on the side of Loraine's head began to pulsate, and she reached up to massage it. *I hope she didn't say anything to Wayne about him breaking up with me.*

Loraine moved over to a wooden bench that was on clearance and took a seat. "I know Ada doesn't want us to get married," she said after Ella had taken a seat beside her. "Maybe our mamms are in cahoots."

"You think they're working together to keep you and Wayne apart?"

"I wouldn't be surprised. Everything's been so verhuddelt since the accident, and nothing makes any sense. It seems like everyone's at odds with each other, too. It's very discouraging."

Ella took hold of Loraine's hand. "Is there anything I can do to help? Maybe speak to Wayne on your behalf, or have a talk with his mamm or your mamm?"

Loraine shook her head. "You've got enough to deal with in your own home right now. Besides, if anyone should speak to my mamm, it ought to be me." She drew in a deep breath. "In fact, I'm going to do that as soon as I get home. I need to know the reason she paid the Lambrights a visit this morning."

⛧

As Jake Beechy drove through the town of Libby, Montana, he spotted a small store on the left. *Maybe I'll stop and see if they have anything to eat or drink. I need something to tide me over till I get back to the ranch.*

He pulled his truck into the parking lot and turned off the engine. A wave of homesickness washed over him when he entered the store and spotted a middle-aged Amish man behind the counter. He'd heard there were some Amish people living in Montana, but he hadn't seen any until today.

"Are you the owner of this store?" he asked the man behind the front counter.

"Yes. My wife and I are originally from Ohio, but we've been living here for the last ten years. I've been tempted to sell out a few times, yet here we still are."

"Fer was hoscht's net geduh?"

The man stared at Jake like he couldn't believe what he'd said. "Didn't you just ask me why I didn't do it?"

Jake nodded.

"You speak the *Dietch*?"

Jake nodded again. "I'm from Indiana. My family's Amish."

"But you're wearing English clothes. Does that mean you decided to go English?"

Jake raked his fingers through the ends of his short-cropped hair. "I left home almost two years ago and have never returned."

"Mind if I ask why?"

"Why I left or why I haven't gone home?"

"Both."

"I left to work on a horse ranch southeast of here. Figured it was a quick way to make good money, but I still don't have enough to do what I want."

"And that would be?"

"I'd like to raise my own thoroughbred horses. Maybe train and board them, as well."

"Raising horses can be expensive."

"I know, and that's why I'm still working at the ranch here in Montana."

"And the reason you haven't been home?" the man asked as he leaned on the counter.

Jake shrugged. "I've thought about it plenty, and I might go back someday when I'm ready to settle down and my bank account is full of money."

"So what brings you to Libby?" the man asked.

Jake nodded toward the window where his truck and horse trailer were parked. "I'm on my way back from a horse auction, where I bought a couple of horses for my boss."

"I guess your boss must trust you, huh?"

Jake shrugged. "I hope so. As I was on my way out of town, I spotted your little store and decided to stop in and see if you had anything to eat or drink."

The man motioned to the back of the store. "There's water, juice, and soda pop in the cooler. You'll find some cheese and meat packages there, too."

"Sounds like just what I'm looking for." Jake hurried to the back of the store, knowing he needed to quit yakking and get back on the road.

He was about to open the cooler when a young Amish woman walked by. He stared at her a few minutes, then moved on. The woman's brown hair and brown eyes reminded him of Loraine.

Jake's heartbeat picked up speed. He hadn't thought of Loraine in a long while. Not since he'd started dating Roxanne, the boss's daughter. Jake and Roxanne had been dating for six months when she'd decided to go to some Bible college in Missouri. Said she wanted to be a missionary and had asked Jake to join her. He didn't feel called to mission work. For that matter, he wasn't sure his feelings for Roxanne went deep enough for a lasting relationship. In fact, he'd almost felt relief when she'd gone off to college.

Pulling his thoughts aside, Jake grabbed a package of cheese and a bottle of lemonade from the cooler. Then he found a box of crackers on a nearby shelf.

When he headed back to the counter to pay for them, he discovered the Amish man was reading a newspaper Jake recognized as *The Budget*.

"Looks like you found something to eat," the man said, looking up and setting the paper aside.

Jake nodded and chuckled. "This should provide me with enough fuel to get me up the road a few more miles at least."

"What part of Indiana did you say you were from?" the man asked as he put Jake's purchases in a paper sack.

"Northern Indiana. My folks live just outside of Goshen."

The man motioned to the newspaper. "Before you came in, I was reading in here about a vanload of young Amish people who were from Goshen, Middlebury, and Topeka. Guess they were involved in a bad accident a few weeks ago."

"Can I see that?"

The man handed Jake the newspaper.

Jake's lips compressed as he read the article that had been submitted by a scribe living in Middlebury. When he saw the names of those who'd been riding in the van, his heart nearly stopped beating. *Loraine. I've got to go home!*

～❦ ❦～

"I'm glad you're home. I could use some help cutting the potatoes I'll be using in a new casserole dish I want to try for supper," Priscilla said when Loraine came in the back door.

"I'd be glad to help, but first I'd like to ask you a question," Loraine said as she hung up her jacket and outer bonnet.

"We can talk while we do the potatoes."

"Okay. Just let me wash my hands and slip into my choring apron first."

By the time Loraine returned to the kitchen, Priscilla had everything ready.

"Mom, I—"

"Did you hear that—"

They'd both spoken at the same time.

Priscilla snickered. "You go ahead."

"No, you first, Mom."

"I was just going to say that when I went to the shoe and boot place in Topeka today, I overheard someone say that Paul's wife, Rachel, is moving back to Pennsylvania to be near her sisters."

"I guess that makes sense, since she has no family living here now that Paul's gone."

Priscilla nodded and handed Loraine a paring knife. "Now what'd you want to say to me?"

Loraine's mouth puckered. "Ella came into the hardware store this morning."

"That's nice. How's she doing these days?"

"As well as can be expected, under the circumstances." Loraine picked up a potato and started peeling it really fast.

"Slow down some, daughter." Priscilla touched Loraine's arm. "We're not in that big a hurry to get these potatoes done."

"Sorry, I'm just feeling a little frustrated right now."

"What are you frustrated about?"

Loraine started peeling again. "As I was saying, Ella came into the store, and she mentioned seeing you leaving the Lambrights' place this morning. Said you'd even waved at her."

Priscilla's neck grew warm, and the heat quickly spread to her face. "Uh. . .jah, I stopped by there on my way to Topeka."

"But the Lambrights' house isn't on the way to Topeka. You'd have had to go out of your way to drop by there."

"That's true enough, but I hadn't been over there since Wayne came home from the hospital, and I thought it would be good if I dropped by to see how he was doing."

Loraine tipped her head. "Did you talk to Wayne?"

"Jah. You're right about him being depressed."

Loraine flicked a potato peel that had landed on the counter into the sink. "Did he mention me?"

Priscilla shifted from one foot to the other and then leaned her full weight against the sink. "I. . .uh. . .guess your name did come up at some point during the conversation."

"You didn't say anything that would make things worse between me and Wayne, I hope."

"No, no, I'm sure I didn't." Priscilla glanced around, wishing she had some excuse to leave the room. If Loraine kept questioning her like this, she was likely to blurt out everything that had been said between her and Ada after Wayne had left the room.

"Well, I'm glad to know you didn't say anything that might hinder our relationship, because I'm going to try real hard to just be Wayne's friend and not pressure him about changing his mind." Loraine smiled, although it didn't quite seem genuine. "I think it's just a matter of time until Wayne and I are back together."

CHAPTER 13

Jake's heart pounded and his knuckles turned white as he gripped his steering wheel. Ever since he'd read about the accident several of his friends had been in, he hadn't been able to think of anything but how quickly he could get home. After he'd left the store in Libby, he'd gone to the ranch and dropped off the horses he'd bid on at the auction. Then, after explaining things to his boss and saying he wasn't sure when he'd be back, he'd thrown most of his things in his truck and started for Indiana.

As he neared the town of Middlebury, he had a decision to make. Should he stop and see Loraine first or go straight home to his folks?

I have to see Loraine, he decided. *I need to know if she was hurt in that van accident.*

Sweat dripped off Jake's forehead as he turned off the main road and started down the Millers' driveway.

Maybe I should have called first, he thought as he parked the truck near the barn. *No, they might not go out to their phone shed and check their answering machine regularly. Besides, after I've been gone so long, Loraine's probably angry with me and might have told me not to come by.*

Drawing in a quick breath to help steady his nerves, Jake stepped out of his truck and sprinted to the house. He'd just lifted his hand to knock on the door when it swung open.

Jake moistened his lips with the tip of his tongue. "Is. . .uh. . . . Loraine here?"

Priscilla's mouth hung slightly open as she gaped at him. "Jake Beechy. I—I didn't realize you'd come back to Indiana."

"I just got here. Read about the van accident and came right home. Is Loraine all right?"

"She's fine—only a few bumps and bruises." Priscilla's forehead wrinkled. "Some of the others didn't fare so well, though."

"Who all was hurt?"

Priscilla opened the door wider. "Let's go inside. It might be best if I let Loraine tell you about it."

Jake's heart hammered as he followed Priscilla down the hall. Just outside the kitchen door, she turned to him and said, "I'm sure whatever you have to say to my daughter you'd like to say in private, so I'll just leave you two alone."

When she disappeared into the living room, Jake wiped his sweaty hands on the sides of his blue jeans, sucked in a deep breath, and stepped into the kitchen.

⟿ ⟾

Loraine had just begun setting the table for breakfast when a young man with short-cropped, dark brown hair, dressed in blue jeans and a matching jacket, entered the kitchen.

Loraine's hands trembled so badly that the spoon she held clattered to the floor. "Jake."

He took a step toward her. "It's good to see you, Loraine. I came as soon as I found out about the accident."

Afraid she might topple over, Loraine sank into a chair at the table. "Wh–where have you been?"

"I've been working on a ranch in Montana. I had been to a horse auction and was on my way back to the ranch when I read an article in *The Budget* about a van accident in northern Indiana." He flopped into the chair across from her. "Your name was mentioned as one of those who'd been riding in the van, but it didn't say whether you'd been injured or not."

Loraine's head began to pound, and she closed her eyes tightly, hoping to halt the pain. In all the time Jake had been gone, he'd only written her two letters. He had promised he'd come back and would stay in touch, but he hadn't kept his promise. Of course, she'd promised to wait for him, and she'd broken that promise as well.

She could still see the way Jake had looked at her that last night they were together. She could hear his contagious laugh and even smell the licorice on his breath. . . .

"Loraine, there's something I need to tell you."

The urgency in Jake's tone caused Loraine to shiver.

"What is it, Jake? Why are you looking at me so seriously?"

Jake directed his horse and buggy to the side of the road and reached for Loraine's hand. "I. . .I'm planning to go away for a while."

"Go away?"

He nodded. "My cousin Sam, who used to live in Illinois, moved to Montana a few months ago, and. . .uh. . .I thought I'd spend the summer with him."

"Which Amish community in Montana did Sam move to?"

"None of them. Sam's working on a ranch in Montana for an English man who raises horses." Jake swallowed so hard that his Adam's apple bobbed up and down. "I want to try out the English way of life for a while—before I make a decision about joining the church." He paused and swiped his tongue across his lower lip. "The wages the man is offering per week is more than I can make working for my daed in a month, so I really can't pass on this opportunity."

Loraine's mouth hung slightly open. "What?"

"I said—"

"I heard what you said. I just can't believe you said it."

"It's not like I'll be gone forever. Probably just for the

summer, that's all." He squeezed her fingers and gave her one of his winning smiles. "You'll wait for me, won't you?"

Loraine sat, too numb to say a word. If Jake left now, what would it do to their relationship? She'd thought he'd been on the verge of asking her to marry him. She'd thought he would join the church this fall. If Jake went to Montana to work for an Englisher who raised horses, he might never come back.

"Say something, Loraine. Will you wait for me or not?"

Tears welled in her eyes. "For how long, Jake?"

"Until I come back to Indiana." Jake pulled her into his arms and kissed her on the mouth. "Just a few months, that's all," he whispered.

Loraine drew in a shaky breath and nodded slowly. "Jah, Jake. I'll wait for you."

"Loraine, did you hear what I said?"

Her eyes snapped open. "What was that?"

"The article in *The Budget* said that some people in the van had been seriously injured, and that three of them were killed. Who died, Loraine? Was it someone I know?"

Her throat constricted, and she had to swallow a couple of times before she could speak. "Katie's boyfriend, Timothy Lehman; Ella's brother, Raymond; and our driver, Paul Crawford are dead."

Jake groaned as he slowly shook his head. "I'm really sorry to hear that."

"Ella suffered a mild concussion, Andrew broke his arm, Jolene had damage to her auditory nerves, and Wayne lost one of his legs." Loraine paused a few seconds, hoping she wouldn't break down. "The rest of us had bumps and bruises. Oh, and Katie suffered great emotional distress."

"Hearing this news just makes me sick." Jake kept shaking his head. "I wish I'd stayed in better contact with everyone—especially you, Loraine. I should have been here for you."

"What happened, Jake? How come you quit writing and never came back until now?"

He dropped his gaze to the table. "I'm sorry, Loraine. I never meant to hurt you," he said, without really answering her question. "Seeing you now makes me realize what a fool I was. I never stopped caring for you. I was just so wrapped up in—"

"I'm engaged to Wayne."

"What?"

"I said I'm engaged to Wayne."

Jake's eyes widened as he lifted his gaze. "I had no idea you were seeing Wayne, much less planning to marry him. I—I can't believe it."

"When you quit writing, I was brokenhearted." Loraine paused again and drew in a shaky breath. "Wayne was there for me, first as my friend, and later, as the man I fell in love with."

"You're in love with Wayne?"

She nodded. "I wouldn't be planning to marry him if I wasn't."

Jake sat several minutes, staring at her in obvious disbelief. "Guess I don't have anyone to blame but myself for that." He plopped his elbows on the table and rested his chin in the palm of his hands.

"The accident changed everyone involved," Loraine said, unable to meet Jake's gaze. "I think it changed Wayne most of all."

"I imagine it's been hard for him to deal with the loss of his leg, huh?"

She nodded. "Wayne's been very depressed and negative ever since the amputation."

Jake tapped his finger against the little dimple in his chin, the way he'd always done when he was deep in thought. "If I hadn't left home, you and I would probably be married by now and maybe starting a family."

Loraine flinched. At one time, she had wanted a family with Jake; she'd loved him so much back then.

The sadness in Jake's blue-green eyes revealed the depth of his pain. "If I hadn't left home, that horrible accident might not have happened."

"Even if you'd stayed in Indiana, the accident might still have occurred. You could have been riding in the van with us that day."

Jake pulled his fingers through the top of his hair, causing it to stand straight up. Any other time, Loraine might have laughed, but not now.

"Where were you all headed to, anyway?" he asked.

"We were going to Hershey Park in Pennsylvania. It was supposed to be a fun day, but it turned into a nightmare."

"How'd the accident happen?"

Loraine quickly related the story, then said, "Paul ran off the road and hit a telephone pole." The memory of that day threatened to overtake her.

"If I'd known about it sooner, I would have come home right away."

"Are you here for good, or did you just come for a visit?"

He shrugged. "I—I'm not sure. Guess it all depends on how things go when I see my folks."

"You haven't been home yet?"

"Nope. Came here first thing. Guess I was hoping things would be the same between us and that we could start from where we left off."

She folded her arms. "That's not possible."

"I know." Jake rose from his seat. "I'm glad you're okay, Loraine, and I'm real sorry about the others." He moved quickly toward the door as though he couldn't wait to be on his way. "I'd better get going. See you around."

Jake disappeared out the back door, and Loraine moved over to the window and watched as he climbed into his truck. Seeing Jake again had stirred up feelings she thought were dead and buried. But exactly how deep the feelings went, she couldn't be sure.

❧ ❧

Jake's hands shook as he headed down the road toward home. Seeing Loraine again had brought back a flood of memories. Hearing that she planned to marry Wayne had been like a kick in the belly.

It's my own dumb fault, he berated himself. *If I hadn't left home the way I did, she'd still be my girl, not Wayne's.*

He slapped the steering wheel with the palm of his hands. *I can't believe that two of my friends are dead or that Wayne lost one of his legs.* "It's not fair! Bad things shouldn't happen to good people!"

By the time Jake reached his folks' house, he was all worked up. He stopped the truck near the barn, wiped the sweat from his forehead, and headed for the house.

He found the back door open but stood on the porch a few minutes, rehearsing what he was going to say to his folks. Then, drawing in a deep breath, he stepped inside.

"Mom? Dad? Is anyone at home?"

"Jake? Oh Jake, is it really you?" Mom ran down the hall, her arms reaching for him.

"It's me all right." He gave her a hug.

"Ach! We've missed you so much," she said tearfully. "You've been gone such a long time, and we've been so worried. We—we were afraid something had happened to you." Mom's voice broke on a sob.

Jake kept his arms around her and patted her back until the sobs subsided. "I'm sorry, Mom. I didn't mean to make you worry."

"Well, you should be sorry!"

Jake whirled around and saw his father step into the kitchen. His face was red, and deep wrinkles creased his forehead. He obviously wasn't as happy to see Jake as Mom had been.

Jake took a step forward. "It's good to see you, Dad. I've missed you and Mom—and my brothers and sisters, too." He glanced around. "Where is the rest of the family? Are they at home?"

"Vern, Kyle, and Elmer are at school," Mom said. "Marilyn and Jeffrey both have jobs in Middlebury."

Before Jake could respond, Dad shook his finger at Jake and said, "Where have you been all this time?"

"I've been working at a horse ranch, just like I said in the letter I wrote when I first got to Montana."

Dad snorted. "One letter in nearly two years! You didn't even give us an address where we could write to you. What were you thinkin', Jake? Didn't you care enough about your family to keep in touch? How could you be so selfish and immature?"

Jake wiped the sweat from his brow. This was an inquisition—not the kind of homecoming he'd hoped for.

"I asked you a question!" Dad bellowed. "Why didn't you stay in touch with us?"

"I—I was afraid you'd pressure me to come home before I was ready."

"Are you ready now?" Dad stared at Jake through squinted eyelids.

"Maybe. If I can get my business going."

"What business is that?" Mom asked.

"I want to breed and train thoroughbred horses." Jake smiled. "That's what I've always wanted to do."

"Humph!" Dad grunted. "Shoein' horses isn't good enough for you anymore, huh?"

"It's never been about being good enough," Jake said. "I want to do something I enjoy, that's all."

Mom gave Jake a questioning look. "Does that mean you want to build your business here and join the Amish church?"

Jake tapped his chin as he contemplated the best way to answer her question. "I can't make a commitment yet. I need to wait and see how it goes."

"What's wrong?" Dad hollered. "Are you opposed to our plain and simple lifestyle now that you've been out in the modern, English world?"

"It's not that. I just can't make a decision about my future right now."

Mom gave Jake's shoulder a little pat, as if in doing so, he would know that what he'd said had been good enough for her. "Are you hungry, son? Would you like me to fix you something to eat?"

He smiled. "That'd be real nice. Danki."

"At least he hasn't forgotten how to speak the Dietch," Dad muttered.

Refusing to let his father's cool reception rile him, Jake followed his mother to the kitchen. He'd have a little something to eat, then head over to the Lambrights' to see Wayne. He only hoped he'd have a better reception there than he'd had here and at Loraine's.

CHAPTER 14

A knock sounded on the back door, but Wayne chose to ignore it. He'd been sitting in his wheelchair, staring out the living room window ever since breakfast, and he didn't want to be disturbed.

A few minutes later, Mom stepped into the room and touched Wayne's shoulder. "You have a visitor."

"Who is it?"

"Jake Beechy."

Wayne's eyebrows shot up. "Jake's back in Indiana?"

"Apparently so." Mom moved to stand in front of Wayne. "He's waiting on the porch."

Wayne's palms grew sweaty. If Jake had come home, he and Loraine might get back together. After all, she wasn't tied to Wayne any longer, and she had been Jake's girlfriend before he'd gone away. On the other hand, Jake might just be here for a visit and nothing more.

"Did you hear what I said, son?" Mom asked.

He nodded. "I guess you'd better let him in."

"Are you sure you're up to company?"

"Jah."

Mom left the room, and when she returned a few minutes later, Jake was at her side. He looked good—suntanned skin;

thick, shiny hair; and muscles in his arms that pointed to lots of hard work.

"I was sorry to hear about your accident," Jake said, stepping up to Wayne. "I came as soon as I heard the news."

"From what your folks have said, you haven't had much contact with them since you've been gone. How'd you find out about the accident?" Wayne asked.

"I read it in *The Budget*." Jake motioned to the sofa. "Mind if I take a seat?"

"Suit yourself."

Jake glanced at Wayne's missing leg and grimaced. "I'm real sorry that happened to you. Are you in a lot of pain?"

Wayne nodded. "Sometimes it feels like my leg's still there, and then the throbbing pain nearly drives me crazy. It's called phantom pain."

Jake winced as though he were the one in pain. "I've never heard of having pain where there's no limb."

"Guess most amputees experience it to some degree. It's supposed to get better in time, but I'm not holding my breath." Wayne shifted in his wheelchair. "My back's been hurting ever since the accident, too."

"Have you been to see the chiropractor?"

"Nope. Figured it would quit hurting on its own, but if it doesn't get better soon, I'll probably go in."

"That's a good idea." Jake cleared his throat a couple of times. "I. . .uh. . .went over to see Loraine awhile ago. I was surprised when she said you and she had been dating. I. . .uh. . .had no idea you were interested in her."

"Loraine was really hurt when you left the way you did, and if you'd continued writing to her, you would have known." Irritation bubbled in Wayne's soul. " 'Course if you'd continued writing, then she probably never would have turned to me."

"I know what I did was wrong, but I can't undo the past. I just want Loraine to be happy." Jake tapped one finger along the edge of his chin. "She said you and she were engaged to be married."

"That's right, we were."

"What do you mean *were*?"

"After the accident, I broke our engagement."

"How come?"

Wayne motioned to his stump. "Thanks to losing this, I won't be able to farm anymore, which means I can't provide a decent living for us. That's why I called off the wedding."

Jake's eyes widened. "Loraine never said a thing about that. She made it seem like a wedding was being planned."

Wayne shrugged. "Guess she doesn't want to accept the fact that I'm a cripple and that I'm not going to be able to support her."

"But won't you be getting a prosthesis?"

"Maybe. If I decide to go that way."

"I'm sure you'll be able to do lots of things you used to do once you get an artificial limb."

"Maybe so, but it'll slow me down considerably. Besides, my daed's already leased out our land so there's nothing for me to farm."

"What's he going to do if he doesn't farm?"

Wayne glanced up at the wall where a mounted deer head hung over the fireplace. "He's opening his own taxidermy business." He grunted. "Pop wants me to learn the trade and go into business with him."

"Might not be a bad idea. Sounds like an interesting trade if you ask me."

"So, what brings you back to Indiana?" Wayne asked, changing the subject. He didn't want to talk about Pop's new business. "Are you here to stay, or did you come for a visit?"

"I may be staying—I don't know yet. I came back because I found out about the van accident. I was concerned about you and the others, and I wanted to see for myself how everyone was doing."

More than likely it was Loraine you were concerned about, since the two of you used to date, Wayne thought ruefully. "So what were you doing while you were gone so long?" he asked.

"I was working at a horse ranch in Montana."

"I heard something about that but figured you'd be back long before now."

"I would have, but—" Jake's voice trailed off and he stared at the floor.

Several minutes went by before Jake finally stood. "Guess I'd better get going. I still need to visit the Lehmans and Yoders and offer them my condolences. Then I'll probably swing by and see Katie and Jolene."

"You won't find 'em at home."

"How do you know that?"

"Jolene went to Pennsylvania to learn how to speak with her hands and read lips. The accident left her unable to hear."

"That's too bad."

"Jah, and Katie's in Sarasota with her grandparents, trying to come to grips with the loss of Timothy."

Jake slowly shook his head. "Seems like everyone riding in the van was affected in some way or another."

Wayne nodded. "None of our lives will ever be the same."

Jake edged toward the door. "It was good seeing you, Wayne. I'll stop by again soon."

"Before you go, there's something else I'd like to say," Wayne called over his shoulder.

Jake turned around. "What's that?"

"I hope you don't think I stole your girl while you were gone. Loraine and I didn't get together until you'd been gone a year and had stopped writing to her."

Jake's face turned crimson. "Don't worry about it. What's done is done. See you around, Wayne."

"Jah," Wayne mumbled as Jake went out the door, "what's done is done."

~❧ ❧~

As Jake drove away from the Lambrights', his stomach clenched so hard, he nearly doubled over. It was a shock seeing his friend sitting in a wheelchair with only one leg. It was a bigger shock to see the gloomy look on Wayne's face. He'd been so full of life when they were boys, always trying out new things and cracking one joke after another. Today he hadn't even cracked a smile.

Of course, Jake reasoned, *if it was me who'd lost a leg, I probably wouldn't be smiling or cracking jokes, either. I wish there was something I could do to make things better for Wayne. I wish I could undo the past.*

⚬ ❧ ⚬

Ella had just taken a tray of peanut butter cookies from the oven when she heard a vehicle pull into the yard. She peered out the kitchen window. A blue pickup truck stopped near the barn, but she didn't recognize the dark-haired man who got out. When he sprinted toward the house, she wiped her hands on a towel and moved toward the door.

When Ella opened it, her heart felt as if it had jumped right into her throat. The man who stood before had short-cropped hair and tanned, muscular arms. He might not look the same as the young, impetuous teenager who'd left home a few years ago, but the deep dimple in the middle of his chin and his sparkling blue-green eyes gave him away. It was Jake Beechy.

"Hi, Ella," he said. "I came by to say I'm really sorry to hear about Raymond."

Tears sprang to Ella's eyes at the mention of her brother's name, and she blinked a couple of times to keep them from spilling over. "He was too young to die, and so were Timothy and our driver Paul." She swallowed hard. If she wasn't careful, it would be easy to let bitterness take over. "It's been a long time since we've seen you, Jake. Are you home for good?"

"I haven't decided yet."

"I guess you know that Loraine and Wayne got engaged while you were gone."

"Uh-huh. I also know they've recently broken up."

Ella's skin prickled as her face heated up. "I hope you don't have ideas about getting back with Loraine."

"Guess I'll have to see how it goes with her and Wayne first."

Ella clenched her fists so hard that her fingernails dug into her palms. "Things will work out for Wayne and Loraine, so don't even think about trying to get back with her."

"You don't have to get so riled up. I never said I was getting back with her. I just said I'd have to wait and see how it goes."

"So you came back here thinking you could pick up where you left off with Loraine?"

"It's not like that. I came back because I read about the accident. I never even knew Loraine and Wayne had started dating until I spoke with her earlier today."

"Jah, well, you'd be doing us all a favor if you got in that fancy truck of yours and went right on back to your horse ranch in Montana." Ella's hands shook, and her voice cracked on the last word. "You hurt Loraine once, and I won't let you hurt her again!"

Jake's eyes flashed angrily. "You may be Loraine's cousin, but you're not her keeper!"

"I never said I was. I care about Loraine. She's been through a lot lately, and I don't want to see her go through any more."

"I agree with you there. I really think Loraine needs all the support she can get right now." Jake looked Ella right in the eye, as if daring her to say more. "I'm going to give Loraine my support, no matter what you say!"

"You're just saying that because you think it's what I want to hear." Ella shook her finger at him. "I don't trust you as far as I can throw one of my daed's horses. I'll bet you came back home just to stir up trouble."

"You think you know everything, Ella. You were like that even when we were kinner." Jake turned and tromped down the steps.

Ella went back into the house, slamming the door behind her. "Jake Beechy, you're a selfish, immature man!"

CHAPTER 15

Wayne lay stretched out on his bed, watching the shadows of morning lurch off the ceiling and studying the tiny cracks where the ceiling met the walls. He'd had another rough night, tossing, turning, rumpling the sheets, and fighting the phantom pain, as well as a muscle spasm in his back. Around two o'clock, he'd finally quit fighting the pain and had taken a pill. He'd slept fitfully after that, but it was better than lying awake, thinking and brooding about the past. Life had no meaning for him anymore. He felt like he was merely going through the motions of living.

Wayne rolled over and gave his pillow a good whack. He'd been cheated out of a normal life, and it wasn't fair! He'd given up the only woman he'd ever loved, and he'd never love anyone that much again.

He covered his ears in an attempt to stop the agonizing thoughts raging in his head, but it did no good. Jerking the pillow out from under his head, he pitched it across the room. Then he grabbed the damp, wrinkled sheets and pulled himself to a sitting position.

"I need some air," he panted, lowering himself into his wheelchair. He rolled across the floor to the open window and drew in several deep breaths.

Finally, his anger faded to a sense of despair. He could fight this for all he was worth, but it wouldn't change a thing. No matter how much he longed for it, his leg would never grow back.

He rolled his wheelchair back to the small bedside table and picked up the glass of water. Tipping his head back, he allowed the cool liquid to trickle down his parched throat. *Maybe I'll feel better after I've had something to eat.*

He slipped on a clean shirt and struggled with his trousers. Seeing that he'd left the dresser drawer open, and knowing Mom would have something to say about it if he left it that way, he kicked it shut with his one and only foot. The dresser trembled and nearly toppled over. A simple thing like getting dressed, which he'd previously taken for granted, had become a tedious, frustrating chore, and it made him angry.

By the time Wayne wheeled himself out of the bedroom and made his way down the hall toward the aroma of spicy sausage sizzling in the frying pan, he was pretty worked up.

Mom turned from the stove and smiled when he entered the room. "I was wondering if you were up. I was just getting ready to come see if you needed my help getting dressed."

"I'm not a *boppli!*" he snapped. "I don't need anyone's help getting dressed!"

Mom frowned, and her forehead wrinkles ran together. "Of course you're not a baby, but I know how difficult it is for you to manage some things, so I just thought maybe I could—"

"You thought I needed babying. That's what you thought!" Wayne gripped the armrests on his wheelchair until his hands cramped. "Ever since I came home from the hospital, all you've done is hover over me and do everything I should be trying to do on my own!" His voice shook, and he nearly choked on the words.

Mom's eyes narrowed. "How can you say such a thing?"

He pushed his wheelchair up to the table. "Because it's how I feel."

A look of concern flashed in her eyes, and a few seconds ticked by before she spoke. "Maybe the problem isn't me trying to help you. Maybe the problem is you not wanting to rely on anyone for help."

Unable to meet his mother's piercing gaze, Wayne kept his eyes focused on the table. "Maybe. . .maybe. . . It's all just a bunch of *maybe*s," he muttered. "Maybe my pain will get better. Maybe I'll adjust to having only one leg. Maybe it would have been better if I had died in that accident. Then you wouldn't have to put up with my moods!"

She turned his wheelchair around to make him face her, grabbed his shoulders, and gave him a good shake. "Don't you talk that way, Wayne! You ought to thank the good Lord that you're still alive!"

Wayne opened his mouth to spew out more angry words but stopped when he felt a nudge at his heart. His self-pity was taking hold of him—making him say hurtful things, making him turn into a bitter, angry man. He pivoted the wheelchair back around, propped his elbows on the table, and let his forehead fall forward into his hands.

"I know you're hurting, son, but things will get better in time," Mom said in a voice that sounded more forced than cheerful. "You just need to be patient." She placed a glass of grapefruit juice on the table in front of him. "By the time your daed comes in from the barn, I'll have breakfast ready. In the meantime, why don't you have some of this?"

Wayne picked up the glass and flinched when the sharp taste of the tangy juice hit his tongue. "I'm really not hungry. I think I'll go out to the barn and see if Pop needs my help with anything."

"Oh, but you can't—"

"Jah, I can!" Wayne propelled his wheelchair across the room and went out the door. He needed time alone. Needed time to sort out his thoughts.

As he rolled down the ramp and headed across the yard, a brisk wind rustled the cornstalks in the fields and blew leaves from the trees. A wet, earthy smell wafted up to his nose. The falling leaves reminded him of a deer's ear flickering in the distance. It was the first time since the accident that he'd really noticed what was going on outside. It was the first time he'd realized that fall had definitely made an appearance.

Wayne moved on until he came to the barn. When he opened the door, a shaft of sunlight filtered through the beams in the barn, and the smell of freshly placed hay assaulted his senses.

He wheeled across the floor and spotted his father coming out of one of the horse's stalls.

"How are you feeling this morning?" Pop asked with a smile. "Did you sleep any better last night?"

Wayne shook his head. "Besides the phantom pains plaguing me, my back went into spasms. Finally had to give in and take some medicine for the pain. Not that it helped very much."

"Hopefully, the phantom pains will go away soon, and then you won't have to take the medication anymore." Pop moved closer to Wayne and lowered himself to a bale of hay.

"Jah, I'm sure that things will go better for me soon." The words rang false, even to Wayne's own ears. He'd only said them because he thought it was what his dad wanted to hear.

Pop clasped Wayne's shoulder. "Maybe you ought to see the chiropractor and let him work on your back."

Wayne nodded slowly. "I've been thinkin' on that. Might call after breakfast and see if they can get me in sometime today."

"That's a good idea. When you find out what time, let me know, and I'll stop whatever I'm doing and take you in for the appointment."

Wayne cringed. He hated relying on others to take him everywhere. He'd never had to be so dependent before, and it stuck in his craw. "If you could hitch my horse to the buggy, maybe I can manage to drive myself to the chiropractor's office."

"No way!" Pop shook his head. "Your mamm would never go for that, and you know it."

Wayne grunted. "Mom thinks I can't do anything for myself. She treats me like a boppli, and I'm getting real sick of it!"

"I know she does, but I think in this situation, she would be right. If you're going to see the chiropractor, then I'd best take you there."

Wayne shrugged and blew out his breath. "Jah, okay…whatever you say."

Pop smiled and thumped Wayne on the back. "Is breakfast about ready? Is that why you came out to the barn?"

"Mom's still working on it." Wayne's shoulders tensed. "I really came out here to get away from her for a while."

A look of concern flashed across Pop's face. "Did she say something to upset you?"

"She hovers all the time." Wayne grunted. "She thinks I'm handicapped."

"Isn't that how you see yourself?"

Wayne shrugged. "Maybe so, but that doesn't mean I want to be treated like a boppli. I can still do some things on my own."

"I hear bitterness in your tone, son. Don't let it consume you," Pop said, gently shaking Wayne's arm. "Tragedies can either drive people away from God or draw them closer to Him."

"Jah, well, it would be a whole lot easier for me to feel close to God if He'd give me back my leg."

"You need to quit feeling sorry for yourself and ask God to help you be all you can be. He'll give you the grace to deal with your disability if you lean on Him and set your bitterness aside."

Wayne grunted in response.

Pop squeezed Wayne's shoulder. "Someone brought in a nice-looking turkey they'd shot the other day, and it needs to be stuffed. Why don't you join me in my shop later today and help with the procedure?"

"No, thanks."

"Have you got something better to do, or is your refusal to help me because you're hurting too bad?"

Wayne pulled his fingers through the ends of his thick, wavy hair. "After I call the chiropractor, I thought I might take a nap and try to get back some of the sleep I missed out on last night."

Pop gave a nod and rose to his feet. "I'm heading in to see about breakfast. Are you coming?"

"I'm not hungry. Just go on ahead without me."

"Suit yourself." Pop shrugged and headed out the door.

Wayne slouched in his wheelchair and closed his eyes. He wondered how he was going to get through another day.

~※ ※~

As Loraine headed down the driveway to get the mail, the wind rustled the leaves at her feet. The cool breeze carved a scent of damp, musty air to her nostrils. Fall was here; there was no doubt about it.

Until the accident that had changed the course of her life, she'd been looking forward to fall—and to her marriage to Wayne.

I have to keep my mind on other things, she chided herself. *It does me no good to keep dwelling on this.*

Her footsteps quickened. Fallen leaves crackled beneath her feet with each step she took. She opened the mailbox and was pleased to find two letters—one postmarked from Lancaster County, Pennsylvania, and the other one from Sarasota, Florida.

Hurrying up the driveway, she seated herself on the porch steps and tore open Jolene's letter from Pennsylvania:

Dear Loraine:

I wanted you to know that I've decided to stay with my daed's sister indefinitely. She's teaching me sign language and how to read lips, but I have so much to learn, and it's going to take some time. I miss you and everyone in my family, but I know I'm where I should be right now.

How are things going there with you? Is Wayne healing from his surgery? Has he gotten a prosthesis? Have you set another date for your wedding yet?

Loraine swallowed hard as hot tears pushed against her eyelids. She missed Jolene so much—missed not being able to talk with her and share her disappointment over Wayne breaking their engagement.

She finished Jolene's letter and opened the one from Florida. It was from Katie's mother:

Dear Loraine:

I'll be coming home sometime next week, but Katie won't be with me. She wants to stay with her grandparents awhile longer. She's still grieving over Timothy, and her depression and fear of riding in a car seem to have gotten worse. I pray that someday soon Katie will be happy and well-adjusted again, and then she'll return home.

Loraine's eyes glazed over, and she blinked rapidly to keep her tears from falling onto the paper. She placed the letters on the small table near the back door and covered her face with her hands. It wasn't right that Katie and Jolene had been forced to leave their homes and family. It wasn't right, what had happened to them.

Horse hooves clomped against the pavement like distant thunder, causing Loraine to open her eyes. She saw a horse and buggy rumbling down the street, then turning into their driveway.

She quickly dried her eyes and wiped her damp hands on her dress, waiting to see who'd come calling.

A few minutes later, Jake stepped out of the buggy, dressed in Amish clothes.

"I'm surprised to see you driving a horse and buggy," she said when he joined her on the porch. "Where's your truck?"

"I parked it behind my daed's barn." The stiffening breeze ruffled Jake's hair as he gave her a deep-dimpled smile. "I figure as long as I'm home, I oughta do what I can to keep the peace." He touched the brim of his straw hat. "I'll be wearing Amish clothes and driving a horse and buggy as long as I'm here."

A strange sensation prickled the wisps of hair on the back of Loraine's neck, and she shivered. If Jake had decided to stop driving his truck and had put on Amish clothes again, did that mean he was planning to stay permanently?

"If you're cold, maybe we should go inside," he suggested.

"I'm fine. Just felt a little chill from the wind, that's all."

"So you don't want me to go inside with you then?"

"It. . .it's not that. My mamm's busy cleaning, and the floors might still be wet."

"Okay." Jake plunked down on the step beside Loraine. "Looks like you've been out to the mailbox." He motioned to the letters on the table.

She nodded. "One's from Jolene, and the other one's from Katie's mamm. It looks like neither one of my cousins will be coming home anytime soon."

"Guess they're in the place they need to be for now." Jake leaned forward, resting his elbows on his knees. "Sure have been a lot of changes around here since I left home."

"Jah—especially since the accident."

"I should never have left home. If I'd stayed, a lot of things would be different."

Loraine looked away. She couldn't allow herself to think about how things would be if Jake hadn't gone. She couldn't afford to take her eyes off her goal to marry Wayne. She'd promised him her whole heart, and he needed her now, more than ever, even if he didn't seem to realize it.

A sharp wind blew under the eaves of the porch, whisking one of the letters away. Loraine jumped up and reached for it. Jake did the same. They grabbed the letter at the same time.

When their fingers touched, Loraine jumped back, feeling as if she'd been burned. "I've got it," she murmured.

"I can see that." Jake released the letter and jammed his hands into his trouser pockets.

They stood staring at each other until Jake's horse whinnied and stamped his foot.

"Looks like Midnight's getting impatient," he said, glancing over his shoulder. "I guess I'd better get going."

"What'd you come by for?" she asked. "Was it anything important?"

"Not really. I just wanted to see how you were doing."

I'd be doing better if you hadn't come back to Indiana. She forced a smile. "I'm all right; just taking one day at a time."

"That's the best way, I guess." Jake reached his hand out, like he might touch her, but he pulled it quickly away and turned toward his buggy.

She breathed a sigh of relief.

"See you later, Loraine," he mumbled as he walked away.

Loraine gathered up her letters and turned toward the door. *I hope it's awhile before I see you again, Jake,* she thought as she stepped into the house. *Being with you only confuses me.*

❦

"I'm a real idiot," Jake berated himself as he headed for home. "I shouldn't have tried to take Loraine's hand. I probably shouldn't have gone over there this morning."

Jake flicked the reins to get his horse moving faster and continued to fume.

He'd gone over to Loraine's place with the intent of telling her about his conversation with Wayne the day before and to see if he could tell if she might still have an interest in him. He'd changed his mind, though. If there was any chance at all of him rebuilding a relationship with Loraine, he'd have to go slow. For now, the best thing he could do was be her friend, and that's exactly what he planned to do.

❦

"I'm glad you were able to squeeze me in today," Wayne said as Dr. Hopkins helped him onto the table. "My back's so spasmed, I can barely move. Between that and the phantom pains I've been having, I'm about to climb the walls."

"I took a class not long ago and learned about a technique that involves something I think might be helpful in relieving not only your back pain, but the phantom pains you're experiencing, as well."

"Something besides chiropractic adjustments?" Wayne asked.

The doctor nodded. "Are you familiar with acupuncture?"

Wayne nodded. "I've never had it done to me, though."

"Well, there's a fairly new technique that involves tapping one's finger along certain acupuncture points, while stating an affirmation. If you're willing to give it a try, I'd like to show you how it's done."

"With the kind of pain I've been having, I'm willing to try most anything."

The doctor gave Wayne's arm a gentle squeeze. "All right then. I'll do some adjustments on your back, and then I'll teach you how and where to tap, and what you'll need to say while you're doing it."

Wayne rolled onto his side and closed his eyes. He didn't know what kind of weird thing he'd agreed to try, but if there was even a remote possibility that it might help relieve his phantom pains, he'd stand on his head and wiggle his ears.

CHAPTER 16

Looks like we're gonna have ourselves one less sheep," Pop said when he entered the house after breakfast on Friday morning.

"What happened?" Mom asked. "Did some critter kill one of our sheep?"

"One of the young lambs got into the horses' pasture and got her left front leg stepped on pretty bad."

"Is she dead?" Mom asked.

Pop shook his head. "Nope, but her leg's badly mangled. I'm afraid she's gonna have to be put down."

"Did you call the vet to see if he can amputate the leg?" Wayne asked from where he sat in his wheelchair near the stove.

"Nope." Pop gave his beard a quick tug. "Even if the vet takes the ewe's leg, she won't be good for much."

The hair on the back of Wayne's neck bristled. "Did you put me down because I lost a leg? Do you think I'm good for nothing?"

Pop's face reddened, and a muscle on the side of his neck quivered.

"Of course you're good for something," Mom said before Pop could respond. "You're our only son, and we love you just as much now as we did before the accident."

Pop nodded vigorously. "You're mamm's right, and I didn't mean you were good for nothing, Wayne."

"What did you mean?" Wayne asked.

"I meant that you can't compare the lamb's situation to your having lost a leg or how it's dealt with."

"Well, I think that ewe has as much right to live as anyone." Wayne pointed to the stump of his leg. "I'm gonna have to adjust to only one leg, and so can the lamb."

Pop gave his earlobe a tug. "The lamb would need a lot of care, and with all the chores I have to do, I don't need another one right now."

"I'll look after it myself."

"Oh, Wayne, do you think you're up to that?" Mom asked.

Irritation flared in Wayne's chest. "I'm not a complete invalid!"

"I know that, but—"

"If he thinks he can do it, then maybe we should give him the chance." Pop squeezed Wayne's shoulder. "I'll go down to the phone shed and call the vet right now. If he thinks it's a good idea to take the ewe's leg rather than putting her down, then she's all yours."

Wayne smiled. It was the first genuine smile he'd been able to muster since the accident. He'd make sure that lamb survived, no matter what anyone said!

❦ ❦

Loraine had just left the hardware store to take her lunch break when she spotted Jake in the parking lot, getting out of his buggy.

Her mouth went dry, and her palms grew sweaty. So much for trying to avoid her ex-boyfriend. She wished she had gone out the back door, but the Wana Cup Restaurant was across the street, closer to the front of the shopping center where the hardware store was located. *Maybe Jake won't see me,* she thought as she hurried her steps. But it was too late. Jake was heading her way.

"Heard you were working here," he said, stepping up to Loraine. "I didn't think you'd be getting off work so early in the day, though."

She wiped her damp hands on the sides of her dress and forced a smile. "I work until four. I'm on way over to Wana Cup for some lunch."

Jake reached under his straw hat and scratched the side of his head. "I haven't had lunch yet, either. Mind if I join you?"

Truthfully, she did mind. Being with Jake after all this time made her feel uncomfortable and jittery. It hadn't always been so. Loraine used to long to be with Jake. She had felt happy and carefree back when they were together. Things were different now. She was in love with Wayne. It was too late for her and Jake.

Jake nudged her arm. "Your silence makes me wonder if you'd rather not have lunch with me."

"It's not that." She didn't want to appear rude. "I. . .uh. . .guess it would be okay."

A wide smile spread across Jake's handsome face. "Great! I'll even treat you to an ice cream cone for dessert."

She smiled, despite her reservations. "That does sound good."

He nudged her again. "We'd better get going before the restaurant gets too busy with the lunch crowd, and then there'll be no seats left for us."

❧ ❧

As Jake and Loraine sat at a small table near the back of the restaurant, eating burgers and fries, he studied the curves of her slender face, her ebony-colored eyes—even the smattering of freckles on her nose. Being with her again made him keenly aware that he'd missed her more than he'd realized. He knew he would have to work hard at rebuilding the walls of trust between them. Loraine had trusted him to come home, and he'd trusted her to wait for him. They'd both let each other down.

"This burger is sure good. I didn't realize how hungry I was until I started to eat." Loraine dabbed at the corners of her mouth with a napkin.

"You've got a spot of mustard on your chin." Jake reached across the table and blotted her chin with his napkin. He was pleased when she didn't pull away.

109

They ate in companionable silence for a while, and then Jake decided to bring up the subject of Wayne.

"I went to see Wayne the other day."

"Was he surprised to see you?"

He nodded. "You were right about him being depressed. He didn't seem like himself at all."

She reached for her soda and took a drink. "He's not the same. Because of the accident, none of us will ever be the same."

"I was surprised when he told me that you two had broken up. When you and I spoke, you never mentioned that."

"We...uh...didn't really break up. Wayne called off the wedding, but I'm sure when he feels better he'll change his mind."

"What if he doesn't?"

"He will."

"How do you know?"

"Because he loves me. Eventually, he'll realize that losing his leg doesn't mean we can't get married."

"What about you, Loraine? Do you love Wayne?"

"Of course I do. I wouldn't have agreed to marry him if I didn't."

"Do you love him as much as you did me?"

Loraine's face flamed. "That's not a fair question, Jake."

"I think it is."

She toyed with her knife and stared at the table.

He reached over and covered her hand with his. "I didn't mean to upset you. I just need to know if the love you feel for Wayne is stronger than what you felt for me."

Deep wrinkles formed in her forehead, and she pulled her hand away. "We shouldn't even be having this conversation."

"Why not?"

"Because you gave up your right to ask anything of me when you left home and didn't come back."

"I made a mistake; I realize that now."

"What's done is done. It's in the past."

"There's still the future." He laced his hands behind his head and stared at her.

"My future's with Wayne."

Jake was tempted to argue but decided it was best not to push. Even though Wayne had made it pretty clear the other day that he wasn't going to marry Loraine, she seemed convinced—almost determined—that he would change his mind.

The best thing I can do, Jake told himself, *is be patient and let Loraine know that I want to be her friend. Maybe after we spend a little more time together, she'll realize that she loves me more than she does Wayne.*

※ ※

When Ada stepped into the Wana Cup Restaurant, the tangy odor of cooked onions and grilling burgers wafted up to her nose. Her stomach rumbled. She'd been running errands all morning and had worked up quite an appetite. She was also desperately in need of a cup of coffee.

She headed for the back of the restaurant, thinking she'd use the restroom before finding a table, and screeched to a halt. Loraine sat at a table on the other side of the room, and Jake Beechy sat across from her!

That sneaky fellow wasted no time in trying to get her back, Ada fumed. *From the way she's looking at him, I'd guess she wants that, too. I knew Loraine wasn't right for my son. I've known it all along!*

Ada compressed her lips as she contemplated what to do. Should she go over to their table and say something—ask what they were doing together? Or would it be better to leave the restaurant and say nothing to Jake and Loraine?

Her hands trembled as she held them tightly at her sides. *I think it would be best if I don't make a scene here in the restaurant. I need to go home and tell Wayne what I've seen. He needs to know that the woman he loves was seen having lunch with another man—the man she used to date, no less.*

Ada whirled around and marched out the door.

CHAPTER 17

W here's Wayne?" Ada called to Crist as she guided her horse and buggy up to the hitching rail near their barn.

Crist motioned to the barn. "He's in there with that crippled sheep he's taken on as a project."

"I need to speak to him." Ada stepped out of the buggy. "Would you mind taking care of my horse for me?"

"Sure, I can do that." Crist took the horse's reins, and Ada scurried into the barn. She found Wayne sitting in his wheelchair, holding the crippled lamb in his lap.

He turned his head and smiled at her. "Tripod's doing pretty good. I think she's gonna make it, Mom."

Ada tipped her head. "Tripod?"

"Jah. Just like a camera tripod that has three legs."

She lifted her gaze to the beams overhead and rolled her eyes. "If you ask me, Tripod's a silly name for a lamb."

He rubbed the lamb's ears, then patted its head. "I think it fits her just fine."

Ada shrugged, then lowered herself to a bale of straw, smoothing the skirt of her dress as she did so. "There's something I need to tell you."

"There's something I want to tell you, too."

"What's that?"

112

"When I was at the chiropractor's having him work on my back, he showed me a new technique to try for my phantom pain."

"Oh, what's that?"

"It involves tapping your fingers on different acupuncture parts of the body while you make an affirmation."

Ada's eyebrows lifted high on her forehead. "What kind of *narrisch* treatment is that?"

"It's not foolish. It's proven to work on a lot of different things, and Dr. Hopkins thought I should at least give it a try."

"And have you?"

He nodded. "It did bring some relief, so I'm going to keep doing it every day and see how it goes."

Ada clicked her tongue against the roof of her mouth. "I can't believe you'd actually try something like that! Sounds like a bunch of hooey to me, and it might even border on superstition."

"It's not superstition! I thought you'd be glad to know that I've had less pain."

"I am glad about that, but—"

"What was it you wanted to talk to me about?" Wayne asked, feeling the need for a change of subject.

Ada's eyes narrowed into tiny slits. "Before I left Shipshewana around noon, I decided to get some lunch at the Wana Cup Restaurant. You'll never guess who I saw there."

"Who was it?"

"Loraine and Jake Beechy—sitting at the same table together!"

"Why would I care about that? Loraine has a right to have lunch with anyone she pleases." Wayne's face reddened. "I broke up with her, remember?"

She nodded. "I just thought you'd like to know how fickle she is. Couldn't even wait a week before she took up with her old boyfriend."

"Like I said, she has the right to see Jake if she wants to. In fact, it's probably for the best. Since Loraine and I won't be getting married, she needs to move on with her life."

"Do you truly mean that?"

He gave a slow nod.

"I'm real glad to hear it." Ada smiled and touched his shoulder. "Since I didn't eat lunch in Shipshewana after all, I'm going into the house to fix myself something to eat. If you haven't eaten already, I'd be happy to fix something for you, too."

"No thanks. Pop and I had a ham sandwich about an hour ago."

"Wouldn't you at least like to come inside and keep me company?"

He shook his head. "You go ahead. I'm gonna stay out here with Tripod awhile longer."

"All right then." Ada patted the top of Wayne's head and left the barn, wearing a satisfied smile. It looked like she wouldn't have to do a thing to see that Wayne didn't marry Loraine. He'd taken care of that himself, and she was pleased that he seemed to have accepted the fact that he was better off without Loraine. She just wished there was some way to get him back with his old girlfriend again. Too bad Fern and her family had moved to Ohio.

❧ ❧

As Loraine pedaled her bicycle home from work that afternoon, she allowed her thoughts to wander. She had enjoyed being with Jake today. Sitting in Wana Cup, eating a juicy burger, had brought back memories of the days they'd been dating. Jake was fun to be with, and his lighthearted attitude made him easy to talk to.

Of course, she reasoned, *Wayne was easy to talk to before the accident. Now I feel like I'm talking to the barn wall whenever I visit with him. If he'd only take down the barrier he's erected and let me get close to him again.*

She blinked against stinging tears, remembering how peaceful and content she used to feel when she and Wayne were together. Now she felt as if she was skating on thin ice. Every time she opened her mouth, she was afraid she'd say the wrong thing. She thought about the verse of scripture that Ella had attached to the loaf of friendship bread she'd given her a few weeks ago. She wondered if she would ever really have the desires of her heart

114

that Psalm 37:4 spoke of.

Of course, she thought, *I'm not sure what my desires are anymore.* A few months ago, Loraine had known exactly what she wanted and had looked forward to the future with gladness. Now she just felt confused and frustrated.

Wayne and I will never get back together if we don't see each other. I've got to go over to his place and check on him from time to time, even though he asked me not to. I'll just have to be careful what I say when I'm near him and make sure I don't bring up the subject of marriage.

Loraine turned her bike up the road leading to the Lambrights' place. She would stop there right now and say hello to Wayne before she went home.

She left the bike around the back of the house, stepped onto the porch, and knocked on the door. A few seconds later, Ada answered her knock.

"I came by to see how Wayne's doing," Loraine said. "Is he at home?"

"He is, but he doesn't want to see you." Ada's tone was about as cold as a block of ice. There wasn't even a hint of a smile on her face.

Loraine's jaw clenched. "I know what he said, but I thought—"

"I saw you with Jake Beechy at the Wana Cup Restaurant today." Ada's lips compressed tightly together. "Are you two dating again?"

"No, of course not. I was taking my lunch break when I ran into Jake. He asked if he could join me."

Ada folded her arms and leaned against the doorjamb. "Humph! You could have said no."

Irritation bubbled in Loraine's soul. "I didn't want to be rude. I thought—"

"What's going on?" Wayne asked as he wheeled up to the door.

Loraine smiled, feeling a sense of relief. "I'm glad to see you, Wayne. I came by to see how you're doing and ask if there's anything I can to do to help."

"We're getting along just fine," Ada said in a none-too-friendly tone.

Wayne looked up at his mother. "If you don't mind, I'd like to talk to Loraine for a few minutes alone."

Ada's face blanched. "But you said you didn't want her coming over here again."

"I know what I said, but I want to talk to Loraine alone."

Loraine held her breath and waited for Ada's response.

After several seconds ticked by, Ada gave a muffled grunt, spun around on her heel, and marched into the house.

Wayne motioned to the wicker chair on one end of the porch. "Would you like to take a seat?"

"Okay." Loraine lowered herself into the chair, and Wayne maneuvered his wheelchair next to her.

"I'm surprised to see you here," Wayne said. "After what I told you last week, I didn't think you'd come over again."

She shook her head. "I can't stop coming to see you, Wayne. I care for you too much."

"Guess I can't stop you from coming over, but you need to know that we can never be more than friends."

"I wish you wouldn't say that. I wish—"

"I heard you had lunch with Jake today."

She nodded slowly, as a rush of heat cascaded up her neck and onto her cheeks. "I guess your mamm couldn't wait to tell you that she saw us at the restaurant, huh?"

"She did mention it."

"I hope you know there's nothing going on between me and Jake."

He shrugged. "Since we're no longer engaged, I have nothing to say about it. You have the right to see anyone you choose."

Loraine fought the temptation to say more on the subject but remembered her decision not to push Wayne or bring up marriage. "How are you feeling?" she asked. "Are you still having that phantom pain?"

He shook his head. "Not so much this week as I did before."

"That's good to hear. I guess the pain medicine must be helping."

He shrugged. "It's helped some, but I've had even less pain since I started using a new technique."

"What technique is that?"

"It involves tapping on various acupuncture points in the body."

Loraine listened with rapt attention as Wayne explained the principles of the tapping method he'd been shown and said his chiropractor had suggested that he give it a try.

"Then, too," he added, "I've been keeping busy taking care of Tripod, so that has helped to take my mind off my own problems for a while."

"Tripod?"

"She's one of our young ewes. Got her left front leg stepped on by one of our horses, and the vet had to take it off." He glanced at the place where his own leg had been. "My daed wanted to put her down, but I talked him out of it." He paused and stared off into space. Then he turned to look at her again. "Tripod and I have one thing in common."

"What's that?"

"We've both lost a leg and will have to learn how to walk all over again."

"Does that mean you've decided to get a prosthesis?"

"Haven't made up my mind yet. Those things are expensive. I was told they can run anywhere from three thousand dollars all the way up to fifteen thousand for the really fancy ones."

"I'm sure our community will help with your expenses. In fact, my daed mentioned the other night that some folks are making plans to hold a benefit auction to help with the medical bills for everyone who was involved in the accident." She smiled. "If you had a prosthesis, you might be able to farm again."

Deep creases formed across Wayne's forehead. "A lot of good that would do me, since Pop's already leased out our land."

"I'm sure you can find something else to do—something that's not as physical as farming. Or maybe you can farm for someone else."

"I don't know about that. Pop wants me to learn taxidermy, but I'm not so sure that kind of work's for me, either." He rubbed the bridge of his nose and grimaced. "I'll have to find something to do, though. Sure can't expect my folks to support me for the rest of my life. They won't be around forever."

The dejected look on Wayne's face was almost Loraine's undoing. She wanted to reach out to him—wrap her arms around him and assure him that everything would work out okay. She wanted to tell him that she thought he should take his father up on his offer to become a taxidermist and then they could be married as planned. She knew that would be a mistake, though, so she kept those thoughts to herself.

Finally, Loraine rose from her chair. "I'd better get going. Mom will be starting supper soon, and I should be there to help."

"I appreciate you coming by," he said. "Next time you come over, maybe I can introduce you to Tripod."

"I'd like that," she said, smiling down at him. "Good-bye, Wayne."

As Loraine hurried toward her bike, a renewed sense of determination welled in her soul. She could not allow her feelings for Jake to surface. She needed to concentrate on Wayne. With a little time and some patience, she was sure he would realize they were meant to be together. She hoped, however, that she wouldn't have to wait too long, because the more time she spent with Jake, the more confused she became.

CHAPTER 18

The following day, Loraine decided to stop and see Ella on her way home from work. It had been awhile since they'd had a good chat, and she was certainly in need of one.

She found Ella in the kitchen, stirring a batter of yeasty-smelling dough.

"It's good to see you." Ella smiled. "Are you ready for some more friendship bread?"

"If you have some made, I could take a loaf, but I'd prefer not to take home any starter."

Ella motioned to the stove. "There are a couple of loaves in the oven, and they should be done shortly, so I'd be glad to give you a loaf." She glanced at the table. "If you'd like to have a seat, I'll fix us some tea."

"That sounds nice. I'm in need of a good visit." Loraine pulled out a chair at the table and took a seat.

A few minutes later Ella placed a pot of tea on the table, along with two cups and a plate of ginger cookies. "Is there something specific you wanted to talk about?" she asked, seating herself in the chair beside Loraine.

Loraine nodded as she poured herself a cup of tea. "I'm really verhuddelt."

"What are you confused about?"

"I had lunch with Jake the other day, and being with him conjured up some feelings I thought I'd forgotten."

Ella gasped. "You're not in love with him, I hope."

"No, I'm not. It's just that being with Jake makes me think about the past and how happy we used to be when we were dating." Loraine took a sip of tea. "He's easy to talk to and so full of life. Being with him takes my mind off my troubles, and he makes me laugh, which is something I really need right now."

"Have you forgotten that he walked out on you so he could try out the English world and make lots of money?" Ella's face contorted. "Have you forgotten that he quit writing after only a few letters and didn't return home until he heard about the accident?"

"I haven't forgotten any of that, but it's not right to harbor resentment, and he did say he was sorry." Loraine sighed deeply. "I think Jake and I can still be good friends, and we are moving on from the past."

"I'm not saying you should harbor resentment. I'm reminding you not to get involved with Jake because he'll only hurt you again." Ella touched Loraine's arm. "And what about Wayne? Are you just going to walk away from him now that Jake is back?"

"No, of course not." Loraine frowned. "I went by to see Wayne after work yesterday. Would I do that if I planned to walk away?"

"I guess not." Ella drank some tea, set the cup down, and fiddled with the handle of her spoon. It seemed like she always had to be doing something to keep her hands busy. "How's Wayne doing? Is he still in a lot of pain?"

"He's said his pain's some better because of some new thing the chiropractor asked him to try, but I could tell that he's still struggling with depression. He's really upset because his daed leased out their land. That leaves Wayne no chance to farm even if he does get a prosthesis and learns to walk well with it."

"Does he plan to get one?"

"I don't know. He's concerned about the cost, but I know it'll be easier for him to adjust if he gets one soon."

"Maybe after the benefit auction, he'll have the money he needs."

"I hope so, but remember, whatever money's brought in will be divided among everyone who has hospital and doctor expenses due to the accident."

Ella nodded. "We'll need to pray that a lot of things will be auctioned off and that there will be plenty of money in the fund."

~⚘ ⚘~

When the back door swung open, Priscilla turned from peeling carrots to see who had entered her kitchen. "Oh, it's you, Amos. I thought it might be Loraine."

"She's not home from work yet?" he asked, removing his stocking cap and hanging it on a wall peg near the door.

Priscilla shook her head. "Maybe she stopped off to see Wayne on her way home from work. She went by there yesterday, you know."

He pulled out a chair at the table and took a seat. "Speaking of Wayne, I ran into his daed when I was Topeka earlier today."

"What'd you go to Topeka for?"

"Went to the shoe and boot store. I told you I was going there, remember?"

"Guess I must have forgotten." She reached for another carrot to peel. "Did you take time out to visit with Crist?"

"We talked for a few minutes." Deep wrinkles formed across Amos's forehead. "He said something kind of disturbing to me."

"What was that?"

"Said his wife saw Loraine having lunch with Jake Beechy yesterday." He grunted and slapped at the dirt on the sides of his trousers. "If she's in love with Wayne and hopin' to marry him someday, you wouldn't think she'd be having lunch with another man."

Priscilla leaned against the sink as she stared out the window. "Hmm. . ."

"Hmm, what?"

"Maybe Loraine and Jake will get back together. She was

pretty smitten with him when she was a teenager, you know."

"Maybe so, but she promised to marry Wayne."

"True, but he doesn't want to marry her now, and I think it might be for the best."

His eyebrows shot up. "How can you say that, Priscilla? I thought you liked Wayne as much as I do."

She pursed her lips. "He's a nice enough fellow, but he's become awful moody since the accident. Besides, I think dealing with his handicap would be hard on Loraine."

"Loraine's a strong woman. I'm sure she could deal with most anything if she wanted to badly enough."

She shrugged. "Jah, well, between you and me, I felt a sense of relief when Wayne broke things off with her."

"I think you're wrong, and it would be best if you kept quiet about this and let our daughter make her own decisions." Amos pushed away from the table. "I'll be out in the barn. Ring the dinner bell when supper's ready."

"Despite what you think, I do know what's best for our daughter," Priscilla mumbled as he rushed out of the room.

❧ ❧

"This is sure not my favorite thing to do," Jake grumbled as he laid out some horse shoeing supplies. "I'd rather be breaking horses than shoeing 'em."

Jake knew he shouldn't complain. For as long as he chose to live at home, he'd need to work and contribute to the family's income. He just hadn't expected Dad to come down with the flu this morning, leaving him stuck shoeing all the horses lined up for the day. Charlie Albright, Dad's hired driver, would be here in a few hours to take him to several farms out of the area where horses needed to be shod. In the meantime, he had to shoe a couple of buggy horses that had been brought here to his dad's place. Their closest neighbor, Melvin Smucker, had dropped off his son's horse, as well as one of his own, while he ran some errands in Goshen. If Charlie arrived before Melvin got back,

Jake would leave Melvin's horses in the corral.

As Jake removed the old shoes from the first horse, he allowed his thoughts to wander. He'd enjoyed his lunch with Loraine the other day and looked forward to seeing her at church on Sunday. He'd like to have another lunch date with her or maybe take her for a ride in his buggy.

When I think the time is right and I've worked up my nerve, he decided, *I am going to ask her out for a real date.*

Years of regret tugged at Jake's heart. He'd been a fool to leave her the way he had. Jake gritted his teeth. *By staying away so long, and not keeping in touch, I opened the door for my best friend to swoop in and take my girlfriend away. Loraine's even prettier now than she was two years ago.* Jake frowned. *I wonder if it's really over between her and Wayne.*

He slapped the side of his head. *I've gotta quit thinking about this or I won't be able to concentrate on the job at hand.*

He set right to work on cleaning the horse's hoof and had just picked up the nippers to trim it, when the horse backed up and stepped right on his foot. Despite the fact that Jake wore boots, it hurt like crazy.

"Yeow!" Jake dropped the nippers and crumpled to the ground as searing pain shot from the top of his foot all the way up his leg.

He tried to stand, but the pain was so intense he just couldn't. Since his folks were in the house, and he was clear on the other side of the barn, he figured there'd be no point in hollering for help. Besides, Dad was sick in bed, and Mom sure couldn't carry him up to the house by herself.

There's only one thing I can do, he decided. *I'll have to stay on the grass and roll my way back to the house. I just hope I can get there before I pass out from the pain.*

By the time Jake made it up to the house, he was so exhausted he had to drag himself onto the porch.

Bam! Bam! Bam! Unable to stand, he reached up and pounded on the door with his fists.

Finally, the door swung open. "Jake! Why are you lying on the porch like that?" Mom asked.

"Stupid horse stepped on me when I was trying to clean his hooves." Jake moaned. "My foot hurts so bad I had to roll my way up to the house."

"Ach! Let's get you inside so I can take a look at your foot. It might be broken."

Jake shook his head as he gritted his teeth. "I think it's just a bad bruise."

"You're gonna have to help me now," Mom said, bending down and slipping her hands under Jake's arms.

Using every ounce of strength he could muster, Jake grabbed the edge of the chair near the door and pulled himself up. Then, using Mom as a support, he hopped into the house on one foot.

"Take a seat at the table," Mom instructed. "I'll get your boot off and see what I think."

Jake did as she asked and groaned when she tugged on the boot. "Not so hard, Mom! It hurts so bad I feel like I might pass out."

"Put your head between your knees," she instructed. "And take in a couple of deep breaths."

Jake complied, then winced when she pulled off the boot.

"It's already swollen," Mom said after she'd removed Jake's sock. "I think you need to go the hospital and have it x-rayed."

"It'll be fine," Jake argued. "I just need to put some ice on it and rest awhile."

Mom shook her head. "Resting it isn't good enough, son. You need to have it looked at."

Jake leaned over and stared at his purple, swollen foot. "I'm lookin' at it now, and I say it's not broken."

Mom gave him a light tap on the arm. "No funning around. If it's broken, it will need to be set and put in a cast."

Jake sighed. "Okay, okay. If it's not feeling better by the time Charlie gets here, I'll ask him to give me a ride to the hospital in Goshen."

CHAPTER 19

Loraine smiled when she saw Crist Lambright pushing Wayne's wheelchair across the grass. It was good to see Wayne attending church again. He needed to be in fellowship with his friends.

She was tempted to rush over but held herself in check, not wishing to appear overanxious or pushy. When Wayne looked her way and made eye contact, she offered him a smile and a friendly wave.

He lifted one hand and gave a quick nod. Then, grasping the wheels on his chair, he pushed himself up the path leading to the Lehmans' barn where several other men had gone.

Loraine headed for a group of women standing near the front porch but had only taken a few steps when she spotted Jake hobbling across the lawn.

"What happened to you?" she asked.

"I was getting ready to shoe a horse the other day, and the stupid critter stepped on my foot."

"That must have hurt."

"It sure did. It hurt so bad I couldn't even stand up or put any weight on my foot. I ended up having to roll my way to the house." He chuckled and gave his chin dimple a couple of taps. "Had to stop every few rolls in order to rest up for the rest of the trip."

Loraine could almost picture Jake lying on the ground, rolling

125

across the grass. It brought a smile to her lips, even though she knew he must have been in a lot of pain.

"The whole episode is kind of funny now," Jake said, "but at the time, it sure wasn't. Thought for a while it was broken, but it turned out to only be a bad bruise."

"How do you know? Did you have it looked at right away?"

"Sure did. I looked at it every chance I got," Jake said with a wink.

She poked his arm. "You're such a tease. Seriously, did you have it x-rayed?"

"Jah, Charlie, my driver, was scheduled to give me a ride to shoe several horses. When he got to our house and took one look at my big foot, he said, 'Jake Beechy, you're going to the hospital to get that x-rayed, whether you like it or not!'"

Jake thumped his chin a couple of times. "I had it x-rayed and checked over real good, but the doctor said it was just a bad bruise and that a couple of blood vessels had busted." He tipped his head and gave Loraine a crooked grin. "Don't think I would have liked being laid up in a cast. It would've slowed me down too much."

Loraine's thoughts went to Wayne. *I can only imagine how he must feel being confined to a wheelchair. I'm sure he'd give just about anything to be in Jake's place right now.*

Jake nudged Loraine's arm and pointed to the Lehmans' house. "Guess you'd better go; your cousin's calling you."

Loraine turned her gaze in that direction and saw Ella on the porch, motioning for her to come.

"You're right; Ella does seem to want me. See you later, Jake."

⌘ ❧

As Jake limped into the barn, he thought about Loraine and how pleasant she'd been to him. It seemed like each time they were together the barrier came down a little more. Maybe she was beginning to trust him again. Maybe he had reason to hope that they might get back together. He thought about asking her out right now but knew it wouldn't be the proper time. Oh, how pretty she looked this morning. It was enough to take a man's breath away.

"How come you're limping?" Wayne asked when Jake entered the barn and found him sitting off by himself.

Jake quickly related the story of how the horse had stepped on his foot and ended it by saying, "I'm just glad there was nothing broken. I can't afford to be laid up right now."

Wayne winced as though in pain, and Jake could have kicked himself. He didn't know what he'd do if he were in Wayne's place.

"So how are you doing?" Jake asked. "Are things going any better for you?"

Wayne shrugged. "My doctor talked me into getting a prosthesis, but now I'm having second thoughts."

"How come?" Jake asked as he lowered himself to a bale of hay.

"I've already gone through so much physical therapy and pain, and I'm not sure I want to go through any more."

"Guess I can understand that," Jake said. "As much as my foot hurts, I can't even imagine what all you've been through."

Wayne motioned to the men who'd begun heading into the buggy shed where their church service would be held. "Looks like church is about to begin, so I guess we'd better get in there."

Jake nodded and followed Wayne out of the barn.

❦ ❧

Ella grabbed Loraine's arm and pulled her close to her side. "What were you doing with Jake over there?"

"Don't look so worried; we were just talking."

"Humph!" Ella crossed her arms. "I thought you had better sense than to get involved with him again."

"We're not involved. I was just asking why he was limping."

"And why is that?"

"He got stepped on by a horse, but lucky for him, he only suffered a bad bruise." Loraine's eyebrows drew together. "It could have been much worse. It could have been broken or mangled like Wayne's sheep."

127

"What sheep is that?" Ella asked.

Loraine was about to reply when Ella's sister stepped between them and said, "Church is about to start. The men are heading for the buggy shed."

"Guess we'd better get in there, then." Ella led the way and quickly found a seat on one of the backless wooden benches on the women's side of the room.

During the service, Ella had a hard time concentrating. It was hard not to watch Jake as he kept looking over at Loraine.

Looks like I'd better have another talk with that fellow, she fumed. *He seems determined to get Loraine back.*

Ella's thoughts shifted gears when she noticed a little girl sitting on her mother's lap, holding a blanket while sucking her thumb.

A fly buzzed around the room, and some of the babies were getting fussy. A couple of the younger boys were bent over at the waist; it looked as though they might have fallen asleep.

Then Ella noticed her mother lift a shaky hand as she wiped her forehead with a handkerchief. Had the words from the song they were singing struck a nerve?

Ella glanced down at the *Ausbund* hymn book in her lap and figured the words from Song 76 had probably touched Mama's heart. *"Where shall I turn to, I the least of the brethren? Alone to God my Lord, Who will be my helper. In all my needs, I trust in you, O God! You will not forsake me; And will stand by me until death."*

Ella hoped her mother had decided to give God all of her needs and to trust only in Him. Mama would always miss Raymond, but with God's help, she could carry on.

❧ ❧

When church was over and everyone had eaten their common meal, Wayne decided to maneuver his wheelchair across the grass and find a spot near the pasture to look at the horses. It was nice to attend church service again, but ever since the accident, he'd had a difficult time socializing, so he preferred to be off by himself for a while.

He closed his eyes and lifted his face to the sky. It might be a bit chilly, but at least the sun was out.

"Are you sleeping?"

Wayne's eyes snapped open, and he turned at the sound of Loraine's voice.

"Uh. . .no. . .I was just sitting here, thinking."

She smiled. "I'm glad you felt up to coming to church today. You've been missed." Her expression was so intense it made his stomach lurch with nervous anticipation. Every nerve in his body tingled.

As Wayne turned back around, tension knotted his shoulders. He could almost feel her staring at him.

"You seem so tense." Loraine placed her hands on his taut shoulders. Fire flared up his arms as she made little circles along his shoulder blades. He feared if he didn't move away soon he might die from longing to hold her. Loraine's presence made Wayne feel like one of the old martyrs of Germany who had led the Amish to flee to America so many years ago.

"I. . .uh. . .have decided to go ahead and get a prosthesis," he mumbled, needing to get his mind on something else.

"Oh, that's good to hear." She continued to lightly massage his shoulders.

"I've got another doctor's appointment later this week, but I'm not looking forward to going."

"Would you like me to go with you?" she asked.

"That's not a good idea! Besides, my folks will be going with me."

"Oh." She stopped rubbing his shoulders and moved to stand near the fence. As she did so, an empty coldness swept over Wayne.

The silence settled around them, broken only by the whinny of the horses in the corral. As much as Wayne's heart cried out for Loraine to stay, he was anxious for her to leave him alone.

"I saw you talking to Jake before church started."

She fiddled with the strings on her head covering. "There was nothing to it; Jake and I are only friends."

He shrugged. "Whatever you say."

"It's true, Wayne. We—"

"It doesn't matter. You're better off with Jake than you would be with me. Now if you don't mind, I'd really like to be alone."

She blinked a couple of times, and then with a smile that appeared to be forced, she lifted her hand and bid him good-bye.

A lump formed in Wayne's throat as he watched her walk away. Even though he knew she'd be better off without him, it pained him to think of her being with Jake.

With fingertips pressed against his lips, he closed his eyes and relived the first kiss he and Loraine had ever shared.

CHAPTER 20

Wayne stared out the window of their English driver's van, watching the scenery go by and noting that many of the trees had dropped their leaves. It had been six weeks since he'd lost his leg, and this morning, he'd been given a new leg. The doctor had told him that the sooner he started to feel like the prosthesis was a part of him, the sooner he'd be able to adjust to the stride in his steps. He'd given Wayne instructions on how to attach the new leg, and then Wayne had been forced to take several agonizing steps between some parallel bars. He'd left the hospital with a pair of crutches, which he would use for support until he got used to walking with the new leg.

As Wayne stepped out of the van a short time later, he wobbled and gritted his teeth. Walking with his new prosthesis was no easy task.

"I'll probably never adjust to the artificial leg," he mumbled as Pop grabbed hold of his arm.

"Sure you will," Pop said. "Just give yourself some time."

"Would you prefer to ride up to the house in your wheelchair rather than trying to walk?" Mom asked.

Wayne shook his head and gritted his teeth. "I've got to get used to walking with this, so I may as well begin now."

As soon as they entered the house, Mom pulled out a chair

131

for Wayne. "You can sit here and rest while I get a pot of coffee going," she said, motioning to the kitchen table.

"I don't want any coffee," he mumbled.

"You look tired. Why don't you go to your room and rest awhile? I'll call you when I get lunch on the table."

Irritation welled in Wayne's soul. She was doing it again—smothering him. Truth was, he did feel pretty tired and was experiencing some pain. "Guess I'll go to the living room," he said. "I can rest on the sofa there." He hobbled out of the room before Mom said anything more.

～❦ ❦～

"You need to quit smothering him," Crist said after Wayne left the room.

Ada pursed her lips and glared at him. "How many times are you going to tell me that?"

"As many times as it takes." Crist helped himself to a cup of coffee and took a seat at the table. "If our son's ever going to adjust to his new leg, then he'll need to learn to do things on his own, and he doesn't need your suggestions."

Ada frowned. "I just wish—"

"Don't start with the wishing, now. All the wishing in the world won't change a thing. That young lamb Wayne's been taking care of for the last few weeks had to learn to adapt to its handicap, and Wayne's trying to do the same."

"Have you talked to him any more about becoming a taxidermist?"

He shook his head. "He knows the offer's open. I don't want to push him into something he'd rather not do."

"But he's got to do something. I mean, he can't spend the rest of his life taking care of a crippled sheep and feeling sorry for himself."

"I'm sure he won't—as long as we allow him to make his own decisions. Remember, it's his life, not ours, Ada."

Ada fiddled with the napkin beside her cup, finally crumpling it into a tight little ball. If she could have her way, she'd somehow make sure that Fern Bontrager was in Wayne's future. But she knew that wasn't possible, so she'd have to be happy taking care of Wayne for the rest of her life.

❧ ❧

"Have you decided yet whether you're going to stay in Indiana and join the church?" Jake's mother asked him during their evening meal.

Jake gave a noncommittal shrug and poked his fork into a thick slice of ham.

"Your mamm asked you a question, and I think she deserves an answer," Dad spoke up from his seat at the head of the table. "For that matter, I'd like to hear the answer to that question myself."

Jake chewed the piece of ham, then looked over at Mom. "I haven't made up my mind yet what I'm gonna do. I just know I'm where I'm supposed to be right now."

"You're right about that," Dad said with a nod. "And if you want my opinion, you should never have left home in the first place."

Jake ground his teeth. Not another lecture from Dad. Since he'd returned to Indiana, he'd had too many of them already.

"Jake's only hanging around because he's in love with Loraine," Elmer spoke up. "If she gets back with Wayne, he'll leave home again; you'll see that I'm right about that."

Jake glared at his twelve-year-old brother. "You think you know everything, don't you?"

Elmer took a drink and set the glass down so hard that some of the milk spilled out. "Do not. I just know you, that's all. When you set your sights on somethin', you go right after it and don't stop till you've got what you want." He swiped his tongue over his lip. "And when you don't get what you want, you run away."

Jake shook his head. "You don't know what you're talking about. When I went to Montana, it had nothing to do with me

133

not getting something I wanted."

"Are you sure about that? As I recall, you wanted to quit shoeing horses and expected me to loan you the money to buy a herd of horses." Dad leaned his elbows on the table and stared at Jake so hard it made his toes curl inside his boots. "When I said if you wanted to start your own business you'd have to save up the money and do it on your own, you headed for Montana to play cowboy with a bunch of English fellows."

"That was different," Jake said in his own defense. "I knew I could make money quicker working at the horse ranch there than I could shoeing horses here."

Mom touched Jake's arm. "But you promised you'd be back, and you said you'd keep in touch." Her voice quivered, and she blinked a couple of times. "You didn't keep either of those promises."

"How'd that make you feel, Jake?" Dad asked. "Didn't you care that your family missed you and were worried because you didn't write or call?"

Jake's face heated up. "We've been through all this before, and I said I was sorry for not keeping in touch. Can't we just leave it at that?"

"We could if we had a guarantee that you were gonna stay here and join the church," Dad said.

"There are no guarantees in this world. That's evident by what happened to my friends when their van ran off the road and hit a pole."

"Can't we talk about somethin' else?" Jake's sister Marilyn spoke up. "All this arguing is making my stomach hurt."

"Well, don't let me stop you from eating in peace!" Jake pushed his chair aside and stood.

"Where are you going?" Mom asked.

"Outside to be with the horses!"

"But you haven't finished your meal."

"I've lost my appetite." Jake plunked his hat on his head and hurried out the door. He had some serious thinking to do.

Loraine's bare feet tingled as she hurried across the hay-strewn floor of their barn. There stood Jake leaning against one of the horse's stalls, a tender smile on his handsome face.

"I'm so glad you're here," she murmured. "I've been hoping you'd come."

Jake tipped his head and stared at her with such intensity that her toes curled. "I'm here forever and always." He reached for her hand and pressed it against his chest. "I promise never to leave you again, Loraine. I've always loved you, and I was a fool to leave the way I did. Will you please forgive me?"

Loraine's pulse hammered in her head. She tried to speak but couldn't get the words past the lump in her throat. How could she not forgive Jake? It wasn't right to carry a grudge.

Jake slipped his arms around Loraine's waist and held her so close that she could hear the steady beating of his heart.

She smiled, feeling all the tension in her body melt away. It felt right to be with Jake. He made her feel, not think.

His thumb stroked the top of her head with deliberate slowness, and her skin tingled with each light touch.

The barn door creaked open and slammed shut, shattering the pleasant moment.

"I should have known I'd find the two of you together! I'm so disappointed in you, Loraine."

Loraine pulled away from Jake and whirled around. Wayne hobbled toward them, shaking his head. "You'd rather be with him than me; isn't that right?"

Loraine opened her mouth to reply, but only a wordless squeak came out.

"I was a fool for believing you loved me." Wayne's eyes narrowed as he turned to look at Jake. "I thought you were my friend, but I was so wrong about that. Guess I was wrong about everything."

Stunned, and confused, Loraine waited for Jake's response. She could almost feel the sparks between the two men.

"You had your chance," Jake said, taking a step forward. "You pushed Loraine away because you lost your leg, and now she's with me."

Wayne's face turned bright red as rivulets of sweat beaded on his forehead. "I've changed my mind. Loraine belongs with me, and I want her back!"

Jake pulled Loraine to his side. "I think we should let her decide which one of us she wants."

Wayne's piercing eyes seemed to bore a hole right through her. "Who do you choose, Loraine?"

She looked at Jake, then back at Wayne, her heart beating furiously. Suddenly, her head jerked forward, as though she was a rag doll, and she toppled to the floor....

Loraine's eyes snapped open. As the dim morning light filtered through the window, she lay on her bed, trying to shake off the dream that had left her sheets drenched with sweat. *"I love you, Loraine,"* she heard Jake's voice through the mist of her memory.

It had only been a dream, but it was a revelation. The thought that she might be in love with two men terrified her. How could she feel this way? How could she have allowed it to happen?

Loraine clambered out of bed and padded over to the window. She opened it quickly and drew in a couple of deep breaths. The only thing she knew for sure was that she couldn't let either Jake or Wayne know how she felt.

CHAPTER 21

"Y ou look awfully *mied* this morning," Mom said when Loraine entered the kitchen. "Didn't you sleep well?"

"I am tired. I had a bad dream, and it woke me up." Loraine yawned and stretched her arms over her head. "I couldn't get back to sleep after that."

"I'm sorry to hear it. Do you remember what the dream was about?"

"It's. . .uh. . .kind of vague." Loraine reached for her choring apron. She didn't want to talk about her conflicting emotions or the disconcerting dream she'd had—especially not with her mother. It would only bring about more questions—questions she wasn't ready to answer, questions she had no answers to.

"What would you like me to do to help with breakfast?" Loraine asked.

"Why don't you set the table while I keep an eye on the oat-meal cooking on the stove?"

"Okay." Loraine opened a drawer and took out the silverware.

"So you can't remember any of your dream?"

Loraine grimaced. Apparently Mom wasn't going to let this subject drop. "It was about Wayne." *At least part of it was.*

"Oh, I see." Mom took a box of brown sugar down from the cupboard. "Wasn't he supposed to get his prosthesis yesterday?"

137

Loraine nodded. "I think I might drop by there on my way to work this morning. I'd like to see how he's doing."

"Oh, Loraine, do you think that's really a good idea? Wayne did ask you not to go over there anymore."

Loraine didn't need that reminder—especially when she knew how Mom felt about Wayne's handicap and the pensive mood he'd been in since the accident. "I don't think he'll mind if I check on him," she said. "I just need to be careful what I say while I'm there."

"Because he's moody, you mean?"

Loraine replied with a shrug.

"Have you seen Jake lately?" Mom asked suddenly.

Loraine's face flamed. Did Mom suspect she might have some feelings for Jake? Not that Loraine was sure what those feelings were at this point.

She pulled three plates from the cupboard and placed them on the table. "I saw him for a few minutes the other day."

Mom smiled. "I always did like Jake. He seems so easygoing and is always full of humor and so polite."

Loraine couldn't argue with that, but then up until the accident, Wayne had been easygoing, full of humor, and polite, too. It was like he'd undergone a complete personality change.

"Is Jake planning to stay in Indiana and join the church?" Mom asked.

"I don't know what his plans are." Loraine took out some juice glasses and set them on the table. *But I do know that if Wayne and I don't get back together soon, I might succumb to Jake's attentions.*

❧ ❀

"Could you come in here a minute?" Pop asked as Wayne hobbled past the taxidermy shop.

With a muffled grunt, Wayne stepped into the room. "Did you need something?"

"Jah, I need another pair of hands."

Wayne shuffled over to the workbench where Pop sat on a

wooden stool. He'd help because Pop asked, but he really didn't want to. "What exactly do you need help with?"

Pop motioned to a deer hide stretched out on the bench. "I could use your assistance slipping this onto the molded form that'll become the deer's body."

"Can't you do it without my help? You've done deer bodies before, right?"

"Jah, but this one's bigger than most."

"Okay." Wayne sighed. He took a seat on the other stool, resigned to the fact that he was going to have to help Pop whether he liked it or not.

Pop handed Wayne one end of the hide, and he noticed how soft and pliable it felt. As they worked together getting it stretched over the mold, Wayne decided to ask a question.

"I've been wondering about something."

"What's that?"

"Did you give up farming and open this business because you thought I couldn't plow and plant anymore?"

Pop's face turned red as a radish. "That was part of the reason, but I really do enjoy this kind of work and have always wished I could do it full-time." He motioned to the deer hide. "For me, taxidermy work is a lot more enjoyable than farming ever was."

"Guess I never realized you were unhappy being a farmer."

"Oh, I wasn't, really. I just like this a whole lot more." Pop nudged Wayne's arm. "And you know what else?"

"What's that?"

"It wasn't so easy for us to visit when we were out in the fields. I rather like spending time with you like this."

"I enjoy spending time with you, too." Truth was, Wayne would rather be with Pop all day than spend five minutes in the same room with Mom. It wasn't that he didn't love her. He just couldn't deal with her constant hovering. It seemed that she was either trying to do everything for him or telling him what to do. It was enough to keep him on edge.

Pop picked up a pair of glass eyes that would be used in the deer's head. "These little things remind me of a joke I heard the other day."

"What was it?"

Pop scratched the side of his head and blinked. "You know—I can't remember it now."

"Don't let Mom hear you say that. She's likely to start accusing you of being forgetful."

Pop chuckled. "She already has—many times, in fact. And speaking of your mamm, our anniversary's coming up soon. I've been thinkin' I might like to take her on a trip to Sarasota."

"That's a good idea. Mom's been kind of edgy lately. A trip to Sarasota might be good for her." Wayne shifted on the stool, trying to find a comfortable position, and studied the deer hide. "Loraine's cousin Katie has been dealing with depression and fearful thoughts, and from what I hear, it's changed her disposition. That's the reason her folks sent her to Sarasota. They're hoping when she comes home she'll be her old self again."

"If going to Sarasota would change your mamm's disposition, I think I'd move us there permanently."

Wayne's head came up. "Would you want to live in Florida?"

"Not really. I like it here in Indiana." Pop gave Wayne's arm a light tap. "Don't worry, son. If we go to Sarasota, we'll only be gone a week or so."

"Who's going to Sarasota?" Mom asked, sticking her head into the room.

"You and me—for our anniversary." Pop grinned like a boy with a new toy. "What do you think of that idea, huh, Ada?"

Her lips compressed tightly as she stepped into the room. "There's no way we can go to Sarasota right now. I can't believe you'd even suggest such a thing!"

Pop raked his fingers through the ends of his beard. "Why not?"

Mom motioned to Wayne. "Our son just came home with his new leg, and you're asking why not?"

"I'll be fine on my own while you're gone," Wayne was quick to say. He wasn't so sure about that, but he didn't want to stand in the way of his folks taking a trip for their anniversary.

Mom shook her head so hard the ribbon ties on her head covering whipped around her face and into her eyes. "I wouldn't dream of running off to Florida and leaving you here alone." She flipped the ribbons to the back of her neck. "What if you needed something? What if—"

"You're smothering him, Ada." Pop frowned. "Can't you see that you're doing it again?"

She smacked her hand against her hip with a grunt and glared at him. "I'm not smothering him. I just think it's too soon for him to be at home by himself."

"I don't agree. He's got to learn to be independent and do things on his own. He'll never do that as long as you're hovering around trying to do everything for him."

"But I'm his mother, and I think—"

Unwilling to listen to any more of his parent's disagreement, Wayne grabbed his crutches and made his way quickly out the door. Once outside, he drew in a couple of deep breaths to help steady his nerves. It was bad enough that he had to deal with his handicap and Mom's smothering. Did he have to deal with his folks' bickering, too? Ever since the accident, his nerves had been frazzled, and listening to Mom and Pop arguing set his teeth on edge.

Guess I'll head over to the barn and check on Tripod, he decided. *That ought to help calm me down.*

Wayne was halfway there when he noticed a horse and buggy coming up the driveway. He recognized it right away: it was Loraine's. He clenched his fingers until his nails dug into his palms. *What's she doing here? I thought I told her not to come. This isn't doing either of us any good.*

He moved over to the hitching rail, and when her rig approached, he secured the horse for her. Maybe she had a good reason for being here. Maybe it had nothing to do with him.

"Wie geht's?" Loraine asked when she stepped down from the buggy. Her voice was sweeter than a bird calling to its mate.

"As well as can be expected, I guess." Wayne's heart pounded when she smiled at him, and that bothered him a lot. How was he ever going to let her go if she kept coming over here all the time, looking at him with such a sweet expression?

Loraine's gaze moved from Wayne's face to the pant leg that hid his artificial limb. "It looks like you got your new leg."

"Jah. Got it yesterday." Wayne lifted the end of one crutch. "I'm still pretty unsteady on my feet, so I'll be using these for a while, I guess."

"That's probably a good idea." She offered him another sweet smile, and his heartbeat picked up speed. He missed that smile. Missed their long talks. Missed going places with her. If only things could be different for him. If he just hadn't lost his leg.

"You look like you're in pain," Loraine said. "Would it help if we sat down?"

"I took something for the pain when I ate breakfast, so I'm doing okay." Wayne motioned to the barn. "I was heading in there to check on my lamb."

"Oh, how's she doing?"

"Would you like to go in with me and see for yourself?"

She nodded. "I can't stay very long, though. I'm on my way to work and don't want to be late."

"I understand." Wayne sucked in his breath. He understood why she couldn't stay long. What he didn't understand was why he'd invited her into the barn. How was he ever going to sever the ties between them if he kept weakening like this? He'd have to be on his guard from now on. He couldn't let her think there was even a chance of them getting back together.

Wayne entered the barn and led the way over to the stall where he kept Tripod during the night.

Loraine stepped up beside him and gasped. "Ach, that poor little thing! How does she manage to hobble around on three legs?"

"She just does. Tripod has a very determined spirit."

"But how's she ever going to make it with the other sheep in the pasture?"

"I guess she'll make it the same way I will—one step at a time."

Her forehead creased. "Do you really think she'll adjust to walking with only three legs?"

He grunted. "She's got two more'n me."

"That's true, but you have your prosthesis now, and that's going to help you get around much better than being in a wheelchair all the time."

"Maybe so." Wayne motioned to a bale of straw. "Should we sit a few minutes?"

When she nodded, he leaned his crutches against the stall door and lowered himself down, being careful not to lose his balance. It was bad enough Loraine had to see him limping around with a pair of crutches. He didn't want to make a complete fool of himself in front of her.

They sat quietly, watching Tripod bump around in her stall and nibble on the hay in her feeding trough. It was hard to come up with anything to say. What did they really have to talk about anymore? Wayne's missing leg? The pain medicine he'd been forced to take? How miserable he felt because they couldn't be together?

He gazed up at the beams overhead and pondered it some more. In the days before the accident, he and Loraine had always had plenty to say to each other. They used to talk about their future—who they'd invite to their wedding, who they'd ask to be their main attendants, how many children they might have. Even when they didn't talk—just sat quietly watching a sunset or took a walk to the pond—there had been a sense of peace between them. Now, everything seemed tense and unnatural, like they were just going through the motions of visiting with one another.

"Have you heard from Katie or Jolene lately?" Wayne thought to ask.

"I got another note from Jolene the other day, but Katie hasn't answered any of my letters."

"Guess some folks just don't like to write."

"I'm afraid with Katie it's a lot more than that." Loraine leaned her head against the barn wall and sighed. "When Katie's mamm came home from Sarasota, she said Katie had been shying away from riding in a car. She also doesn't want to go out—not even for shopping—and the only time she speaks is when she's asked a question. I'm concerned that if she doesn't snap out of it soon, she might never be the same."

"I guess that's possible." Wayne grabbed a piece of straw and snapped it in two. "I know I'll never be the same."

"I'm sorry," she murmured. "I hope what I said about Katie didn't upset you. I'm sorry for your loss, Wayne, really I am."

"Jah, well, I don't need your pity."

"I didn't mean it that way. I just meant that—"

Ma-a-a! Ma-a-a!

Wayne jerked his attention back to Tripod. The poor little critter had somehow managed to get one of her back feet stuck between a loose board and the wall in her stall.

"Guess I'd better see about getting Tripod set free from that board that's holding her captive." Wayne rose to his feet, and forgetting to use his crutches, he headed for the stall. He'd only made it halfway there when he stumbled and fell flat on the floor.

Loraine rushed forward. "Ach, Wayne! Did you hurt yourself?"

"I'm fine. Just lost my balance is all."

She bent down and placed her hands around his waist. "Here, let me help you up."

Wayne shrugged her hands away as his face heated up. "I'm fine. I can manage on my own." Gritting his teeth and using the wall for support, he rose, wobbled, and fell back down.

Loraine rushed forward again. This time he swallowed his pride and allowed her to help him. With Loraine's assistance, he made it over to the stall.

"If you have no objections, I'll try to get the lamb's leg free," she said, looking up at him with compassion on her face.

Wayne wanted to argue, but his hands shook so badly, he wasn't sure he could do what needed to be done. "Jah, okay," Wayne mumbled, flopping onto the bale of straw. He sat there feeling like a helpless little baby while Loraine freed his lamb.

"Now do you see why we can't be together?" Wayne asked when she returned to his side. "If you and I got married, you'd always feel obligated to help me, just like my mamm does now."

"I wouldn't mind helping at all."

"Well, I would mind!"

A look of bewilderment spread across her face. "I try to reach out to you, and what do I get? You look at me with anger and push me away. Why, Wayne? Why?"

He tried to speak but couldn't make his lips move. He wished he could run and hide, but he didn't know where to go. Loraine deserved so much more than he could offer. She deserved a man who could take care of her, not a one-legged cripple who couldn't even walk without falling on his backside.

With her gaze fixed somewhere near the center of his chest, Loraine whispered, "I love *you*, Wayne."

A vein in Wayne's temple began to throb. His arms ached to hold her. His lips yearned for the taste of hers.

Refusing to lose himself in the depths of her eyes, he stared at his hands, clasped tightly in his lap. "Why won't you let this go? I've told you and told you that it won't work for us anymore. You need to find happiness with someone else." He paused for a second. "You need someone like Jake. I'm sure he still loves you. That's why he came home, you know."

"No. No, he didn't. He said he came back because he heard about the accident and felt concern."

"Then why is he still here? He's seen how we all are and offered everyone his sympathies. He should have been gone by now—back to his horse ranch in Montana, don't you think?"

"Well, I don't know. I—"

Wayne pointed at Loraine. "You're the reason Jake is still here."

She slowly shook her head. "I don't think so."

Wayne shrugged. "Think what you want. I just know it's over between us, and you need to get on with your life—with or without Jake Beechy."

When tears pooled in Loraine's eyes, it was almost his undoing. He clasped his fingers tighter as he struggled with the urge to take her hand. He wished she would go before he said or did something really stupid.

"You can't mean that it's over between us, Wayne." She sniffed deeply. "I know you don't."

"Jah, I do mean it. I don't love you anymore." As the lie rolled off Wayne's tongue, a bitter taste was left in his mouth. Until the accident happened, he'd always been honest with Loraine. Now, he was not only a cripple, but a terrible liar as well.

Loraine stood there a moment, staring at Wayne as though in disbelief. With a deep moan, she whirled around and dashed out the door.

Wayne's head pounded as he watched her disappear. He knew he had hurt her, and it tore at his heart. Maybe someday when she was happily married to someone more deserving, she would realize he'd been right to end things as he had.

"She might even thank me for it," he mumbled.

"Jah, I think you're right."

Wayne's head snapped up. He was surprised when Mom stepped out of one of the empty horse stalls.

"How long have you been there?" he asked.

"Long enough to hear what you told Loraine about not loving her."

Anger boiled in him like hot coals on the fire. "You were spying on us?"

She shook her head vigorously. "No, of course not. I came into the barn to see what you were doing out here, and when I heard you talking to Loraine, I ducked into the stall."

"Why?"

Her face flamed. "Well, I—"

"You didn't want to make your presence known because you were spying on us."

She stared at him like he'd lost his mind, then she slowly shook her head. "This isn't about me, son. This is about you and Loraine."

"There is no me and Loraine anymore." Wayne grimaced. "I'm sure after me telling Loraine that I don't love her anymore, she finally believes it's over between us."

Mom nodded. "You did the right thing by being honest with her. A relationship built on pity would never last anyway."

Wayne tipped his head. "You think she pities me?"

"Jah, I sure do. I also think she feels guilty for talking you into going to Hershey Park. She knows if you hadn't gone along with her foolish idea that you'd still have both of your legs." Mom took a seat beside him. "If Loraine really loved you, she wouldn't be spending so much time with Jake." She patted his knee. "You're better off without her, son."

Wayne pressed his hands against his stomach, hoping he wouldn't get sick. He didn't know if the churning in his stomach was from the pain medicine or because he felt like such a heel for lying to Loraine. "I don't want to hear any more about Loraine! I just want to be alone."

Mom blinked several times. "Are you asking me to leave?"

He gave a quick nod.

She hesitated a minute, then fled from the barn.

Wayne remained on the bale of straw with his head in his hands. He had lied to himself, as well as to Loraine. He'd yelled at Mom and told her to go. He really was a poor excuse for a man!

CHAPTER 22

Loraine's horse stamped nervously and blew a burst of steam from its nostrils as she fumbled with the reins. Her hands shook so badly she could barely make them work.

Wayne's words resounded in her head: *"I don't love you anymore. You'd be better off with Jake."* The finality of his tone could have etched the words in steel.

A tremor shot through her body. It really was over between them. How could she go to work and put a smile on her face when her whole world was falling apart?

"This isn't how I wanted things to turn out!" she murmured tearfully as she guided her horse and buggy down the road.

How did you want them to turn out? an inner voice asked.

The buggy hit a pothole that jarred her, and she winced. "Jake and I are not supposed to be together! We're just good friends. I'm supposed to be with Wayne. I promised him I would always be his."

Loraine gripped the reins tighter, hoping to gain control of her swirling emotions, more than guiding the horse. No way could she allow herself to love Jake again. She couldn't let her guard down. She couldn't allow him to sweep her off her feet the way he'd done before. Wayne might not realize it, but he needed her now more than ever. Surely he couldn't have meant it when he said he didn't love her anymore.

148

A film of tears clouded Loraine's vision. Soon they started running down her cheeks. She sniffed and wiped them away. "Things have to get better," she mumbled, hoping to make herself feel more secure. "Wayne's bound to come to his senses, and I can't give up on him just because he said he doesn't love me anymore."

More tears fell, until Loraine couldn't see well enough to drive anymore. She guided Trixie to the side of the road, knowing she needed to get herself under control before she went any farther.

She reached for her handbag and fumbled inside until she found a tissue, and then she blew her nose. Leaning forward, and closing her eyes, she began to pray.

"Dear Lord, please give me some direction and a sense of peace. I know I can't keep pestering Wayne to change his mind about us, but should I give up and let him go? If Wayne and I are meant to be together, then help him see that. If we're not, then I need some assurance and confirmation."

❦

"Whoa!" Jake called to his horse after he spotted a horse and buggy parked along the side of the road. He wondered if the driver might have encountered some kind of problem. He pulled in behind it, climbed down from his buggy, and raced around to the driver's side of the other rig. When he saw Loraine sitting in the driver's seat with her head bowed, his heart gave a lurch. Had something happened to her? Could some impatient driver have run her horse and buggy off the road? He knew it happened at times when some wild teenagers decided it would be fun to have a good time at someone else's expense.

He jerked the door open, and her head snapped up. "Ach!" she gasped. "You scared me, Jake!"

"You scared me! When I saw you sitting here with your head down, I was afraid something terrible had happened to you."

"No, no. I'm fine." Her eyes glistened with tears, and her chin trembled like the petals of a flower on a breezy day.

"You're obviously not fine, or you wouldn't be crying." Jake flapped his hand at her. "Move over and let me come in."

Her eyes widened. "What for?"

"So we can talk about whatever made you cry."

With a wordless shrug, Loraine scooted to the passenger's side, and Jake climbed in beside her.

"So what's wrong?" he asked.

She sniffed and dabbed at her eyes with the tissue she held in her hand. "I. . .I've just come from seeing Wayne."

"Is he worse?"

"Not physically, but he's so negative, and he seems determined to push me out of his life."

"What do you mean?"

Sniff! Sniff! "He said he doesn't love me anymore, and—" Her voice cracked, and she sniffed a couple more times. "I just can't accept the idea that things are over between us. It doesn't seem right."

She blew her nose and put the tissue in her purse, bumping Jake's arm in the process.

Jake felt a jolt of electricity zip from his arm to the tips of his fingers. He wished he could tell Loraine how he felt about her—that he'd never stopped loving her, that he wished he could stay here in Indiana and ask her to marry him. He swallowed hard and resisted the urge to pull Loraine into his arms. "I can see how unhappy you are," he said gently. "Is there anything I can do to help?"

She shrugged.

"Would you like me to talk to Wayne—see if I can get him to rethink his decision?"

Her chin quivered. "You—you would do that?"

I don't want to, but I'd do it for you. He nodded. "If you want me to, I will."

Her lips curved into a smile. "Danki, Jake. You're such a good friend."

Good friend, Jake fumed. *Is that all I'll ever be to you?* "I'll do my best to get through to Wayne," he said with a nod.

She touched his arm, sending another jolt of electricity all the way to his fingers. "Before you stopped, I was praying for some direction. I think you might be the answer to my prayers."

He ground his teeth. *Maybe so, but I don't think it's the same answer I'm hoping for.*

～≫ ≪～

As Jake headed down the road in his buggy awhile later, he rehearsed in his mind what he was going to tell Wayne. Should he come right out and say that he'd spoken to Loraine and knew that Wayne had cut her out of his life? Or should he engage Wayne in idle conversation for a while and see if he volunteered anything himself?

Jake knew if there was any chance of getting back with Loraine, he'd have to figure out a way to win her trust again. He also needed to be sure things were really over between her and Wayne before he made a move. If things were to work out like he hoped, he could end up staying in Indiana for good. Between what he made shoeing horses and what he'd saved up working at the horse ranch, he might be able to buy a couple of standard-bred racing horses that could be trained to pull Amish buggies. At least it would be a start, and once he got his business going good, he'd be ready to join the church and felt sure he'd be able to support a wife.

Jake flicked the reins to get his horse moving faster. The sooner he talked to Wayne, the sooner he'd know which direction to take with Loraine.

～≫ ≪～

Wayne had just put Tripod in the pasture with the other sheep and was preparing to head back to the house, when a horse and buggy pulled up next to the barn. He was surprised to see that it was Jake.

"It's good to see you walking," Jake said after he'd climbed down from the buggy and secured his horse to the hitching rail.

"Got my new leg yesterday." Wayne pulled up his pant leg to reveal the prosthesis and lifted the end of one crutch. "My goal is to learn how to walk without using these for support."

Jake smiled. "I'm sure you will once you've gotten used to the prosthesis."

"I lost my balance in the barn awhile ago and ended up flat on my back. Had to rely on Loraine to help me get up." Wayne grimaced. "If she hadn't been there, I'd probably still be lying on the barn floor, feeling like a helpless invalid."

"It's good that Loraine was there. Does she come over to see you often?"

"She used to, but she won't be anymore."

"How come?"

"I told her to go—said things won't work between us, so she may as well get on with her life." Wayne leaned his crutches against the fence and wobbled a bit as he lowered himself to a wooden stool.

Jake took a seat on another stool. "Are you sure you really want to break up with her? I mean, don't you want to reconsider that decision?"

Wayne folded his arms and shook his head. "I made it clear that there's no future for us. Told her she ought to find someone else." He bumped Jake's arm. "I'm thinkin' that someone oughta be you."

Jake gave his earlobe a tug. "Wh–what makes you think that?"

"You and Loraine used to date. Fact is, if you'd come back from Montana sooner, you two might be married by now, and I wouldn't even be in the picture."

Jake popped a couple of knuckles on his left hand, and then he did the same to the knuckles on his right hand. "Wouldn't you be jealous if Loraine and I started dating again?"

Of course I'd be jealous; I'd hate seeing the two of you together. I'd hate the reminder that I'll never be with the woman I love.

Wayne forced a smile. "All I want is for Loraine to be happy. If she stayed with me, I'd only drag her down." He pointed to Jake. "I think you, on the other hand, have just what it takes to make her happy."

"How do you know that?"

"Because you're all she ever talked about when you first left home. She thought you were coming back. She thought you planned to marry her."

Jake's gaze dropped to the floor. "I did plan to come back and marry her, but then I met Roxanne."

"Who's Roxanne?"

"My boss's daughter. I thought for a time that I was in love with her, but after she went away to Bible college, I realized what I'd felt for Roxanne had only been an infatuation. To tell you the truth, I didn't even miss her that much."

"Then why didn't you come back for Loraine then?"

Jake shrugged his shoulders. "I don't really know. Guess I got so caught up in working with the boss's horses and tryin' to put money away that I lost track of my original goal."

"How do you feel about Loraine now that you're back at home? Could you begin a relationship with her now?"

Jake's face turned crimson. "Are you absolutely sure there's no chance of you and Loraine getting back together? Because if there is—"

Wayne held up his hand. "Things will never be the same for me and Loraine. It's over between us."

"Can you honestly say you don't love her anymore?"

"Jah, that's how it is." Each lie Wayne told seemed to get easier than the last. "Given a little time," he said, "I'm sure Loraine will come to realize that she's not in love with me, either."

Just then, Wayne's father stepped out of his shop and hollered, "Wayne, could you come here a minute? I need your help with something!"

Wayne reached for his crutches and grunted as he pulled himself up. "Guess I'd better go see what Pop wants." He bumped Jake's arm. "Think about what I said, okay?"

"Sure, I'll give it some thought." Jake stood and sprinted for his buggy.

As Wayne made his way up to Pop's taxidermy shop, a wave of nausea washed over him. He'd literally given Loraine over to Jake with his blessings. As much as it had hurt him to do it, he was convinced that it was for her own good.

CHAPTER 23

"Are you sure you don't want to take your wheelchair with you today?" Wayne's mother asked as they prepared to leave for the benefit auction on Saturday morning.

He shook his head and kept walking toward the buggy Pop had rolled out of the buggy shed. "I need to get used to walking with my artificial leg, and that won't happen if I sit around in my wheelchair all day."

She stepped in front of him and pursed her lips. "I understand that, but it's going to be a long day. If you get tired of standing or walking, you might wish you had your wheelchair."

"I won't be walking around that much. I'll find a seat and stay put most of the time."

"Even so, I think it would be good if you—"

"I'll be fine! Would you just stop mothering me?"

If Wayne thought the direct approach would put an end to his mother's nagging, he was sorely mistaken. "I'm your mudder, and I care about your welfare—even if you don't!" She pointed her bony finger at him. "I insist that you take your wheelchair!"

Despite the chilly fall morning, Wayne's face heated up. If he and Mom kept going on this way, they'd both be so upset that neither of them would want to go to the auction. Since Wayne was one of the benefactors of the money that would be taken in, he figured he ought to at least put in an appearance. He also knew that he should try to be in a halfway decent mood when he spoke to his friends who would be there.

Forcing a smile he didn't really feel, Wayne looked at his mother and said, "I'll ask Pop to put my wheelchair in the back of the buggy, but I won't use it unless I have to."

She smiled in return and gave a quick nod. "Danki. That's a wise decision."

I hope the rest of the day goes better than this, Wayne thought as he made his way to the buggy. *And I hope I can keep my emotions in check when I see Loraine, because I'm sure she'll be there.*

❧ ❧

"I figured I'd find you here," Loraine said when she entered the room inside the auction barn where baked goods were being sold and found Ella behind one of the tables.

Ella motioned to the tray of pumpkin bars in front of her. "You know how much I like to bake, so where else would I be but in a room full of baked goods?"

Loraine smiled, despite the misgivings she felt about being at the auction today. She dreaded seeing Wayne yet looked forward to it at the same time. "Are you working in here?" she asked Ella. "Or did you come in to buy something sweet to eat and get roped into working?"

"I came here to work—at least for the first half of the day, which I'm sure will be the busiest time."

Loraine moved closer to the table. "I'd be happy to help if you need me."

"We can always use another pair of hands," Ella's fourteen-year-old sister, Charlene, spoke up.

Ella bumped her sister's arm. "Why don't you work at that table over there?" She pointed across the room. "Then Loraine can take your place and be here with me."

Charlene wrinkled her nose and glared at Ella a few seconds before she finally moved away. It was obvious that she didn't like being told what to do by her older sister.

"I'd better go to the restroom and wash my hands before I start helping," Loraine said.

Ella nodded. "That's a good idea."

Loraine scurried off toward the women's restrooms. Halfway there, she spotted Wayne sitting in the big room where the auction had already begun. His parents sat on either side of him.

Loraine was tempted to go over there and say hello, but after the things Wayne had said to her the other day, she decided against it.

Just then, Wayne turned his head and looked in her direction. Their gazes locked for a few seconds, and then he quickly looked away.

A sense of hopelessness welled in Loraine's soul, causing her shoulders to droop. She bit her bottom lip in an effort to keep from crying. She ought to be a married woman by now, not a frustrated *maedel* forced to avoid the man she had promised to marry. She ought to be sitting beside Wayne right now, not standing on the sidelines, watching Ada fuss over her son.

～※ ※～

"Looks like there's quite a crowd here today," Jake said as he and his family entered the auction barn.

Dad nodded. "Not only is there a good crowd from our Amish community, but many of our English neighbors have come out as well."

The air rang with the sound of the auctioneer's booming voice mingled with the murmur of the crowd sitting or milling about. Mom motioned to the items at the front of the room—dressers, chairs, tables, quilts, and a whole lot of miscellaneous. "If most everything goes, there should be plenty of money brought in today, and that will help with everyone's hospital and doctor bills."

Jake nodded as he caught sight of Wayne and his folks across the room, sitting behind Bishop Hershberger and his wife, Sadie. He knew Wayne probably had a lot of medical bills and would

156

likely have a lot more bills mounting up in the days ahead.

Jake shifted his gaze to the other side of the room and scanned the crowd. When he turned his head to the right, he saw Loraine walking toward the area where the baked goods were sold.

Mom nudged Dad's arm. "Should we have a seat or walk around and look at some of the things that'll soon be up for bid?"

"Let's walk around a bit," he replied. "If I sit too long, my back might cramp up on me."

"Can we get somethin' cold to drink?" Jake's brother Kyle asked, tugging on Mom's hand.

"Jah, sure we can." Mom looked over at Jake. "Are you coming with us, son?"

"Not right now. Think I'll get myself a doughnut or something else to eat. You and the rest of the family go ahead. I'll catch up to you later on."

"When we decide we're ready to bid on something, should we save you a seat?" she asked.

"No, that's okay. After I get my doughnut, I might wander around outside and see what kind of farm machinery's being auctioned off."

Dad's eyebrows shot up. "Why would you need any farm machinery?"

Jake shrugged. "I don't. Just thought I'd nose around. Besides, it's already hot and crowded in here. I don't like being stuck in a stuffy building with a bunch of noisy people."

Jake's brother Elmer poked Jake's arm with his stubby finger. "You never minded noise when you lived with us before you went to Montana."

"That was then; this is now," Jake mumbled.

"Maybe you just don't wanna be with us. Maybe—"

"Never mind, son." Dad gathered the other children together and hurried them in the direction of where the cold drinks were being sold. Mom shuffled behind them, unable to keep up with Dad's long strides.

Jake headed for the baked goods. As soon as he entered the

room, he saw Loraine behind one of the tables. Her cousin Ella stood beside her, making change for an elderly English woman who'd bought two loaves of bread.

"How's it going?" Jake asked, stepping up to Loraine.

"It's going okay. How are things with you?"

"Can't complain, I guess." He smiled. "Being at this benefit auction is a reminder for me that I have a lot to be thankful for. A day like this is a reminder that, but for the grace of God, it could be any of us in need of financial assistance."

She nodded. "I think we all tend to take life for granted at times."

Jake leaned against the table as he studied Loraine. She really was beautiful—inside and out.

She must have realized that he was staring at her, for her cheeks turned pink and she quickly averted his gaze. "Did you want to buy something?" she asked in a near whisper.

"Uh—jah. I'll take a couple of doughnuts."

"What kind would you like—sugar doughnuts, lemon-filled doughnuts, powdered sugar doughnuts, or doughnuts covered with chocolate icing and sprinkles?"

"I'll take a lemon-filled and one dipped in powdered sugar." Jake held up two fingers. "Better make that two powdered sugar doughnuts. I might save one for later."

Loraine snickered. "I guess some things never change. You always did have a sweet tooth, Jake Beechy."

He wiggled his eyebrows and grinned. "You know me so well. Or at least, you used to."

Loraine's face flamed, and when she picked up a powdered sugar doughnut, she gripped it so hard that it broke right in two. "Sorry about that. I'll pick out another one for you."

Jake dug around in his pocket for the money while she gathered up his doughnuts and put them on a paper plate.

"Here you go." He handed her a one-hundred-dollar bill.

"Oh, I'm not sure I have enough change for a bill that size."

"No problem; keep the change. You can call it my donation to the benefit auction, 'cause I probably won't bid on anything here today."

She smiled. "That's so nice of you, Jake. *Danki.*"

"It's the least I can do to help out my friends." Jake turned and started to walk away; then, gathering up his courage, he turned back around. "I thought I might go outside and walk around for a bit. Would you like to walk with me?"

"She's busy helping me," Ella cut in.

The color in Loraine's cheeks deepened. "I did say I'd help sell the baked goods."

Jake bumped her arm with his elbow. "We won't be gone very long."

"We need her help here." Ella shot Jake a look that could have stopped a runaway horse.

Loraine's cousin doesn't like me anymore, Jake thought. *Come to think of it, maybe she never did. Even before I left for Montana, she was never all that friendly toward me. I wonder if I've done something to offend her.*

"How long do you need to help out here?" Jake asked, directing his question to Loraine.

"For as long as we need her." Ella motioned to a group of English people who had just entered the room. "Looks like we're going to be busy for quite a while yet."

Jake looked back at Loraine, and when she said nothing, he decided it was probably time to head outside. "See you later, Loraine."

He made his way quickly through the crowd and was almost to the door when he heard a shrill voice.

"Wait a minute, Jake!"

He spun around with a feeling of dread. "What do you want, Ella?"

"I want to talk to you about Loraine."

"What about her?"

"I hope you have no ideas about you and Loraine getting back together."

"Well, I—"

"She's still in love with Wayne, and once he realizes they can work things out, they'll get married, just like they'd planned."

"You need to get right in your thinking," Jake said through clenched teeth. "Wayne broke up with Loraine, so he has no plans to marry her now."

"That doesn't mean he won't change his mind." Ella's forehead puckered. "If you start seeing Loraine again, everything will get all messed up. Loraine thinks—"

"Fire! Fire! Someone—put out the fire!"

Jake whirled around. He spotted several of the women who'd been selling baked goods running out of that room. With heart pounding and sweat rolling down his face, he tore across the building.

CHAPTER 24

By the time Jake arrived at the baked good's room, all the women were gone. Some of the men were leading the women and children from the main part of the auction barn outside, where they would be safe should the fire start to spread.

As sparks and shooting flames exploded from the light fixture hanging above one of the tables, Jake jumped into action.

"What's going on?" Andrew Yoder asked as he dashed into the room.

Jake pointed upwards. "Looks to me like it's an electrical problem. We need to get the fire out as quickly as possible!"

By this time, the sparks had ignited a pile of cardboard boxes that had now begun to burn. Jake feared if they didn't get the fire out soon, it would become uncontrollable. He looked frantically around the room. "Andrew, do you know where there might be a fire extinguisher?"

"Maybe there's one in the kitchen!" Andrew shouted. "I'll hurry and check!" He rushed out of the room.

"I'd better call 911!" Jake reached into his pocket and pulled out his cell phone.

By the time he'd finished making the call, Andrew was back with a fire extinguisher. Several other men had arrived on the scene, as well.

Once the fire was out and the power had been turned off, Jake breathed a sigh of relief. Everyone had been evacuated from the building, which meant the auction would have to be put on hold until the fire department had arrived and made sure it was safe to resume.

"Maybe we should check the conduit pipe in other parts of the building to be sure that there aren't any hotspots," Jake said to Loraine's father, who'd come into the room to see if his help was needed.

Amos nodded. "It's a dangerous thing when a fire starts like this."

"I'm just glad no one was hurt and that we didn't lose the building," Jake said.

"My daughter was in here selling baked goods, so I appreciate what you did in getting the fire out so quickly." Deep wrinkles formed across Amos's forehead. "Last year during the Mennonite Relief Sale in Goshen, there was a fire. Two of the buildings at the fairgrounds went up in smoke because it wasn't caught in time."

"I didn't know about that," Jake said.

"Guess you wouldn't, since you weren't living here at the time and didn't keep in touch with anyone."

Jake winced at the remark. He wondered if Loraine's dad thought he was a terrible person because he'd taken off to Montana and had quit writing to Loraine.

Just then, a group of firemen swarmed into the building. Jake quickly explained what had happened and suggested they check for possible hotspots in other parts of the building.

"We appreciate the information, and we'll take it from here," one of the firemen said with a nod.

Jake, Amos, and the other Amish men joined the crowd waiting outside. A light rain had begun to fall, and many of the people hovered under umbrellas or one of the tents that had been set up to house some of the farming equipment.

Jake scanned the area until he spotted Loraine. She was talking to Ella and her mother. As much as Jake wanted to speak with Loraine, after the encounter he'd had with Ella awhile ago, he figured he'd better not engage Loraine in conversation in front of her take-charge cousin.

He glanced in another direction and noticed Wayne sitting in his wheelchair across the way. *I think I'll go talk to him,* he decided.

~ ❦ ~

"I wonder if they'll let us back in the auction barn soon," Wayne's mother said as she pushed his wheelchair under one of the tents.

"I don't know, but I'm glad I took your advice and brought my wheelchair along. I wouldn't want to have to stand out here all this time while we wait to find out."

She nodded soberly. "All the chairs are inside, too. Guess we should have thought to bring some out with us."

"There was no time for that," Wayne said. "It wasn't safe to stay in the building."

Mom glanced over her shoulder. "I see your daed's talking to some of the men in charge. Maybe he has some news to report. I think I'll go find out." She opened her umbrella and scurried away.

Wayne was about to follow when he saw Jake heading his way, so he decided to stay put.

"I hear you're the one who put out the fire," Wayne said when Jake approached.

Jake nodded. "Andrew Yoder helped by getting the fire extinguisher, and then we turned off the power." He motioned to the fire trucks lined up in the parking lot. "Now the firemen are checking things over in other parts of the building, looking for hotspots."

"Guess that makes good sense."

"I saw you walking earlier, but I see that you're in your wheelchair now," Jake said. "Does that mean you haven't adjusted to your new leg yet?"

"No, I haven't. It's a struggle to get my balance, but I'm forcing myself to wear it several hours every day." Wayne frowned deeply. "If I could hobble around on one leg as well as my lamb does on three, I'd have no need for a prosthesis."

"I guess not."

"Have you talked to Loraine today?" Wayne asked, taking their conversation in a different direction.

"I spoke with her for a few minutes when I went into the room where she was selling baked goods. Why do you ask?"

"I was wondering if you've given some thought to what I said the other day about asking her out."

"I didn't talk to her long enough for that." Blotches of red erupted on Jake's cheeks. "Besides, I'm still a little concerned that things aren't really over between you two."

"I told you before, Loraine and I are—"

"I just spoke with some of the firemen," Wayne's father said, stepping between them. "It looks like the auction is over for the day. They want to call in an electrician to check things out and make sure everything in the barn is up to code." He tapped Wayne's shoulder. "It's probably for the best, son. You look really tired, and I've come down with a sore throat, so I think we ought to head for home."

Wayne nodded. "Where's Mom? Does she know we're leaving?"

"I spoke with her a few minutes ago. She's saying good-bye to some of her friends and will meet us out by the buggy." Pop swallowed a couple of times and grimaced. "I can't remember the last time my throat hurt this bad. Sure hope I'm feeling better by Monday, because I've got a lot of work to be done in my shop, and this is no time for me to be getting sick."

"I'm sorry to hear your throat hurts, Pop." Wayne motioned to Jake. "As soon as Jake and I have finished our conversation, I'll meet you and Mom at the buggy."

"Oh, okay." Pop hurried off, and Wayne turned to face Jake again.

"As I was saying before my daed showed up—Loraine I are

not getting married, so you have free rein to ask her out whenever you choose."

Jake hesitated a moment, but then, what Wayne could only classify as a look of relief spread over his face. "All right, I just might ask her out."

"Since that's all settled, I'd better get going. Don't want to keep my folks waiting any longer." Wayne forced a smile and turned his wheelchair toward the opening of the tent. He had to get out of here quick, before Jake saw the look of regret that no doubt showed on his face.

Wayne was almost to the area where the horses had been tied, when Ella rushed up to him, waving her umbrella.

"Hold up a minute, would you, Wayne? I need to talk to you about something!"

Wayne halted and waited for her to catch up to him. "What's up, Ella?"

She stopped in front of his wheelchair and bent down so her umbrella covered both of them. "I need to talk to you about Jake Beechy."

"What about Jake?"

"He's been hanging around Loraine a lot lately. I think he wants to date her again."

Wayne shrugged. "So, what's that to me?"

Her eyes widened. "Are you kidding? Up until the day of our accident, you and Loraine were a happy couple looking forward to your wedding, and—"

"Things are different now. I'm not the man Loraine needs anymore."

"How can you say that? Don't you know how much she loves you?"

"I'm not sure she ever really loved me." Wayne couldn't keep the bitterness out of his tone. "As I'm sure you already know, she used to love Jake. I was only her second choice."

"It may seem that way, but—"

"Loraine feels sorry for me now that I'm a cripple, and she

165

thinks she has to keep her promise to marry me." He shook his head. "But she doesn't. I've released her of that promise and told her that she's free to get back with Jake."

"What if she doesn't want Jake? What if she wants you?"

"Then she'll have to make *him* her second choice, because we're not getting back together so we won't ever be getting married!"

Ella released an exasperated sigh. "I see your mamm's waving for you to come, but I just want to say one more thing before you go."

"What's that?"

"If you want my opinion, you're full of *hochmut*."

"I am not full of pride; I'm just doing what I think is best."

"Jah, well, if you don't wake up and come to your senses soon, you're going to live to regret it!"

Ella dashed off, and Wayne sat in the pouring down rain, shaking his head and feeling sorry for himself. "I already do regret it," he mumbled, "but it's the only way."

CHAPTER 25

"How's your throat feel today?" Ada asked when Crist entered the kitchen on Monday morning.

"Not so good. It's even worse than it was two days ago." He touched his throat and winced. "I can barely swallow."

"Open your mouth and let me have a look-see," she said, standing on her tiptoes.

He shook his head. "No need for that; you're not a doctor."

"I just want to see if your throat is red or swollen. If there are any white patches, it could mean that you have an infection." Ada hurried across the room and opened a kitchen drawer. She returned, holding a flashlight. "Now, open real wide."

Crist stood like a statue for several seconds, but finally grunted and opened his mouth.

Ada squinted as she shined the flashlight inside. "Umm. . . .I'm afraid your throat doesn't look good at all. After breakfast, you'd better go on back to bed while I run out to the phone shed and call the doctor's office."

"Does my throat look that bad?"

She gave a slow nod. "You'll probably need some antibiotics to get it under control."

He groaned. "Oh, great. This is just not what I need this morning."

"What's not what you need?" Wayne asked, wheeling into the room.

"Your daed's throat is still sore, and I think he needs to see the doctor."

Wayne looked over at Crist. "That's too bad, Pop. I was hoping you'd feel better this morning."

"You and me both."

Ada motioned to Wayne's wheelchair. "How come you're not wearing your prosthesis?"

"My leg's kind of sore from where the appliance rubs, so I decided not to wear it today."

"Maybe you need to have it adjusted," Ada said. "Want me to see if Dr. Bower can take a look at it if I'm able to get an appointment for your daed today?"

"That's okay," Wayne said. "I have an appointment to see the specialist next Monday, so I'll talk to him about my problem when I go in then."

"You mean you're not going to try that silly tapping method?" Ada still couldn't believe her son thought something like that could actually work. But then, maybe it was a mind over matter kind of thing, and if that was the case, then he could have talked himself out of the pain.

Wayne shook his head. "The tapping method helped my phantom pains, but I don't think it'll take the place of an adjustment on my prosthesis."

"So what are you going to do until next Monday—sit around in your wheelchair all the time?" Crist asked, giving Wayne a look of disapproval.

"I'll try wearing the prosthesis again later today or tomorrow at the latest. It might feel better by then." Wayne rolled his chair up to the table. "Is breakfast ready yet, Mom?"

"Not quite. The bacon's still frying, and I have to do up some eggs."

"No bacon for me," Crist said. "I'd never be able to eat it."

"How about some oatmeal?"

"That sounds good."

She touched his arm. "If I do get an appointment for you, would you like me to go along?"

"No, thanks. I'll probably run a few errands while I'm in town, so I might be gone awhile."

"I wouldn't mind running some errands with you," she said.

He shook his head. "Thanks anyway, but I'll go alone."

"Whatever you say." Ada shuffled over to the stove. It was obvious that Crist didn't want her to go with him. Could he still be upset because she'd refused to go to Sarasota to celebrate their anniversary? Or was he worried that she might embarrass him by asking too many questions of the doctor?

She looked over at Crist and then at Wayne. *Men can be so hard to figure out at times.*

⊶ ⊷

"Are you feeling okay this morning?" Ella asked her mother as they cleared the breakfast dishes from the table. "You look really tired, and I noticed during breakfast that your hands were shaking."

"I think it's all the excitement of the weekend. I was feeling pretty keyed up when we left the auction on Saturday, and then, with Sunday services being held here, it left me a bit drained." Mom placed the plates she was holding into the kitchen sink. "I had a hard time sleeping last night, too, which didn't help, either."

"I'm sorry to hear that. Why don't you go rest while Charlene and I do the dishes?"

"I really should go to Shipshewana this morning. I need to get some sewing notions at Spector's."

"Just give me a list of what you need, and I'll run to town for you," Ella said.

Mom smiled wearily. "Oh, I'd appreciate that. You're such a thoughtful *dochder.*"

"Ella can go to town right now if you want her to," Charlene spoke up as she brought the rest of the dishes to the sink. "I can manage to wash and dry the dishes on my own."

169

"Are you sure you don't mind?" Ella asked.

"Don't mind a bit."

Mom patted Charlene's back. "Danki. You're a thoughtful daughter, too." She yawned noisily. "Now, I think I'll go rest."

"I'm worried about her," Ella whispered after Mom had left the room. "She hasn't been the same since Raymond died."

Charlene wrinkled her nose. "Of course she hasn't. What mother could be the same after one of their kinner passed away?"

Ella gave her sister a little nudge. "When did you get to be so *schmaert*?"

"I've always been smart," Charlene said with a smirk. "You've just been too busy to notice."

"Jah, maybe so." Ella grabbed her sweater and black outer bonnet and hurried out the door.

After the heavy drizzle they'd had for the past two days, a thick layer of fog covered much of the land. Ella shivered and quickened her steps. She didn't look forward to going anywhere in this chilly weather but figured the sooner she got it over with, the better it would be.

She hitched her horse to the buggy and was preparing to back away from the hitching rail when—*whack!*—something bumped the rear end of her buggy. Her head snapped forward and she gasped. "What on earth was that?"

She jerked the door open and was just getting ready to climb down, when Jake stepped up to her buggy. Ella squinted at him. "Did you have anything to do with that jolt I just felt?"

Jake nodded. "Afraid so. The front of my rig caught the back of your rig as I was pulling in. You ought to take a look behind you before you pull out."

"Well, you shouldn't have snuck up behind me like that. What are you doing here, anyway?"

"I wasn't sneaking. I came to shoe one of your daed's horses. Didn't he tell you I was coming?"

"No, he sure didn't." Ella wrinkled her nose. "You shouldn't have come barreling in here, smashing into my buggy."

"I didn't barrel or smash your buggy. It was only a little tap." Jake thumped the spot where his chin dimple was and scowled at her. "Who gave you driving lessons, anyhow?"

"My daed, that's who."

"Well, he must have been wearin' blinders."

Refusing to let Jake get the best of her, Ella folded her arms and glared at him.

He motioned to the back of her buggy. "I don't think any damage was done, so you needn't look at me as though I'm your enemy."

"There better not be any damage," Ella said through tight lips. She rushed around to the back of the buggy and was relieved to see that there was no dent. Even so, she was irked at the way Jake kept smirking at her.

"You're very inconsiderate, you know that, Jake?"

His eyebrows lifted. "You think I'm inconsiderate because I accidentally bumped your buggy?"

"I'm not just talking about the fact that you bumped my buggy."

"What then?"

"I think you were very inconsiderate when you took off for Montana two years ago and left Loraine in the lurch. Don't you know that it almost broke my cousin's heart?"

Jake opened his mouth as if to defend himself, but Ella rushed on. "Your lack of consideration proves what kind of a person you are. I hope Loraine never believes anything you have to say, because I sure don't!"

Ella thought she would feel better for spouting off like that, but all it had done was leave her with a sick feeling in the pit of her stomach. She had watched Loraine mope around for months after Jake left Indiana. When he'd quit writing and didn't return home, Ella was afraid Loraine might never get over being jilted by her first love. But then Wayne, bless his heart, had become Loraine's good friend. Ella had been real pleased when the couple had fallen in love and become engaged to be married. She just wished Wayne hadn't ruined things by breaking up with Loraine.

Couldn't he see that she would be better off with him than she would be with self-centered, selfish Jake?

Jake cleared his throat a couple of times and stared at the ground. "I know what I did was wrong, but I've grown up and changed since then."

"Have you really? From what I heard, the only reason you came home at all was because you heard about the accident my cousins and I were in. If it hadn't been for that, I'll bet you'd still be in Montana playing cowboy."

"Well, I—"

"You'd better not break Loraine's heart again. I mean it, Jake." Ella's hand shook as she pointed at him. "Because if you do break my cousin's heart, then you'll have to answer to me!"

"I won't break Loraine's heart. I care about her a lot."

"If you care about her so much, then you'll leave her alone. She and Wayne are meant to be together, and if you'll just stay out of the picture, I'm sure in time they'll get back together."

Jake looked like he was going to say something more, but Ella's father showed up just then.

"Glad to see you made it here early," he said, thumping Jake on the back. "I have a chiropractor's appointment this morning and have to be there soon, and I'd like to get my horse shod before I go." He looked over at Ella and smiled. "Your mamm said you were going to pick up some things for her in town, but I can do it if you'd rather stay home."

Ella shook her head. "Since today's my day off from working in your shop, I don't mind going. In fact, getting away from here for a while might be just what I need." She glanced over at Jake, but he shrugged and walked away.

Ella climbed into her buggy again, gathered up the reins, and headed down the driveway at a pretty good clip. She wished Jake would leave Indiana for good!

❦

"Where are you going?" Wayne's mother called as he headed for the back door, wearing his prosthesis.

"I'm sick of sitting around. I'm going outside to check on my lamb."

"But I thought your leg was bothering you. You said earlier that you weren't going to wear the prosthesis today."

"I said I might try it later on, and I've decided to give it a try now." Wayne hurried out the door before Mom could respond.

Once outside, he drew in a couple of deep breaths. The air felt clean and fresh after the rain they'd had. Even though the rain had stopped, the sun had tried all morning to make an appearance but never quite overcame the low-hanging clouds. He guessed that was better than chilling rain.

Wayne hobbled out to the fence that separated their yard from the pasture and stood watching the sheep graze. He couldn't help but smile when Tripod let out a loud *baa* and headed straight for him. He bent over and reached through the fence so he could pet the sheep's head. "You've accepted your plight in life, haven't you, girl?" he murmured. "Sure wish I could do the same."

Tripod turned and rubbed her side against the wooden boards on the fence.

"What's the matter, girl? Have you got an itch?" He rubbed her wooly back and sides and snickered when she closed her eyes, obviously enjoying the attention.

He glanced over at the watering trough and noticed that it was almost empty. "Guess I'd better give you and the other sheep some fresh water to drink."

Tripod let out a loud *baa* as Wayne moved away from the fence.

"Don't worry, girl; I'll be back."

Wayne made his way over to the hose, turned on the water, and then hauled the hose back across the yard. That seemed easier than having to walk back to the spigot and turning the water on after he'd placed the hose in the trough.

Poking the hose through the fence slats, he let it drop into the trough. He then stood back and watched as Tripod and the other sheep eagerly drank their fill.

One of the more aggressive rams pushed two ewes out of the way and bunted the hose with his nose. The next thing Wayne knew, the hose was on the ground with water shooting into the air.

"Oh, great," Wayne moaned. He reached through the slats to grab the hose, and at the same time his hat fell off his head and landed in the pasture on the other side of the fence.

He winced as he hobbled over to the gate and stepped into the pasture. The part of his leg where the prosthesis was attached had begun to throb.

Wayne leaned down to retrieve the hat, when—*whoomp!*—the rambunctious ram butted him from behind, sending him into the watering trough with a *splash!*

Wayne gasped as the chilly water hit his body. Gritting his teeth, he grabbed the edge of the trough and tried to pull himself up. *Splash!*—he fell right back in.

He tried two more times to get out of the water, but with no success. He realized that he had no other choice but to call for help and hope that Mom would hear him hollering from inside the house.

Just then, a van pulled into the yard and stopped near the fence. A middle-aged English man got out.

"Looks like you're in need of some help," he said, stepping into the pasture.

Wayne accepted the man's hand, despite the humiliation he felt over being found in such an awkward, embarrassing position.

"Thanks," he mumbled as the man pulled him to his feet. "I was stuck in there and couldn't get out."

The man chuckled. "If it was a warm summer day, I might have thought you were trying to cool off, but since winter will be coming soon, I'm guessing you didn't purposely take a dip in that old water trough."

"No, I sure didn't." Wayne shook his head, spraying water everywhere. "One of our rams knocked me into the trough when I was trying to pick up my hat. I never even saw it coming."

The man's gaze traveled around the pasture. "Say, did you know that one of your ewes is limping real bad?" he asked, pointing to Wayne's crippled lamb.

"That's Tripod. She had one of her legs amputated not long ago." Wayne pulled up his pant leg, exposing his prosthesis. "See, just like me."

A look of shock registered on the man's face. "I didn't realize you had only one leg."

"Lost it in an accident a few months ago. If you live around here, I'm surprised you didn't hear about it."

"Actually, I'm new to the area," the man said. "One of my friends told me that an Amish man runs a taxidermy shop here, so I brought over a couple of pheasants I'd like to have stuffed."

"It's my dad's business, but he's not here right now," Wayne said. "You can leave the birds with me if you like, and I'll see that he gets 'em." He motioned to the house. "If you'd like to put the pheasants on the back porch and come inside with me, I'll take down your information and give it to Pop as soon as he gets back."

"Oh, okay."

The man followed Wayne up to the house. When they stepped into the kitchen, Mom greeted them with a frown. "What happened to you, Wayne? Your clothes are sopping wet!"

"I fell in the watering trough, and this nice man was kind enough to help me out."

Mom regarded the Englisher with a curious stare. "I don't believe I've met you before."

He extended his hand. "My name's Howard McKenna. I brought some pheasants by to have them stuffed."

"Oh, I see. Well, my husband's not here right now."

"Yes, I know. I'm going to leave the pheasants, as well as my name and phone number. He can call me whenever they're done."

Mom nodded. Then she turned to look at Wayne. "I'll take care of getting the details from Mr. McKenna. You'd better get out of those wet clothes before you end up sick like your daed."

Wayne didn't argue with her. His teeth had already begun to chatter.

❧ ❧

When Wayne returned to the kitchen, the man was gone, and Pop was sitting at the table holding a cup of tea.

"What'd the doctor say about your sore throat?" Wayne asked as he took a seat beside his dad.

Pop grimaced. "Said it's strep."

"Ach, no!"

"He gave me a prescription for an antibiotic, but I was feeling so rough, I didn't even go to the pharmacy; just came straight home."

Mom reached over and touched Pop's forehead. "You're running a fever, Crist, and you don't look well at all! I insist that you go right to bed. I'll head to town and get the medicine for you."

"My horse is in the pasture, and the buggy's put away, so you'll have to get them both out again."

Mom shook her head. "That'll take me too much time. I'll just ride my bike to the pharmacy. It shouldn't take long at all."

❧ ❧

As Loraine sifted flour into a bowl and added some sugar, her thoughts carried her back to the auction on Saturday. Even though they hadn't been able to resume the auction after the fire was put out, she'd learned that they'd taken in a pretty good sum of money that morning, and it had been decided that another auction wouldn't be necessary at this time. Loraine was glad for that, because she didn't think she could go to another auction any time soon and watch Wayne at a distance, feeling that she couldn't even speak to him. It was ridiculous for him to think they couldn't be together just because he'd lost his leg. And him saying he didn't love her anymore made no sense at all. How could a person love someone one day and not the next?

Loraine stirred the cookie batter so hard that her fingers began to ache. *Why, God, why? Why did Wayne have to lose his leg? Why can't he accept the fact that I still love him and want to be his wife?*

An image of Jake flashed into her mind. She had wanted to be his wife once, too. Had she loved him more than she did Wayne? Could she let herself love Jake again?

"You'd better let me take that job over for you," Mom said when she stepped into the kitchen. "It's almost time for you to go to work, and if you don't leave now, you'll probably be late."

Loraine glanced at the clock on the far wall. She'd been asked to work the afternoon shift today, and it was nearly one o'clock. She did need to get going.

She handed Mom the wooden spoon she'd been using and removed the apron she wore to do her household chores. "I guess I should have started the cookies sooner," she said. "I don't know what I was thinking."

"It's all right; I'll do them. You run along and have a good day at work."

"Danki, I'll try." Loraine slipped into her jacket and outer head covering and headed out the door. When she stepped outside, the cold, damp air sent a shiver through her body. She pulled her jacket tightly around her neck, hurried to the barn, and took out her horse.

A short time later, she was headed down the road toward Shipshewana. She'd only gone a short ways when she spotted Ada Lambright pedaling her bicycle along the shoulder of the road. Suddenly, Ada's bike started to wobble. It looked like she had hit a patch of loose gravel. Loraine shrieked when the bike toppled over and Ada fell to the ground.

"Whoa!" She halted the horse and clambered out of the buggy. Then she raced over to Ada.

A thin, wordless cry tore from the poor woman's lips as she looked up at Loraine.

Loraine dropped down beside her. "Are you hurt, Ada?"

"I think my leg's broken. I've never had such horrible pain." Ada's voice sounded muffled, as if she were trying to talk under water.

That's when Loraine noticed that Ada's left leg was bent at a very odd angle.

She knew she needed to make Ada as comfortable as possible, and the hard ground was anything but comfortable.

"I'm going to my buggy to get some blankets," Loraine said. "Just hold real still and I'll be right back." She hurried off, and returned with two blankets. She folded one and put it under Ada's head and draped the other one over Ada's shivering body.

"Can you hang on here while I'll go to the nearest phone shed and make a call for help?" Loraine asked, touching Ada's shoulder.

Ada nodded, as tears seeped out from under her lashes. "Guess I don't have much choice."

"I'll be back as quick as I can." Loraine hurried to her buggy and tore off down the road.

CHAPTER 26

Loraine paced from the row of chairs in the hospital waiting room over to the window and back again. It wasn't that long ago that she'd been in another hospital waiting room, waiting to hear how Wayne and the others were doing after their accident. Now she waited impatiently for some news on Ada's condition.

Loraine had called the paramedics from Sandy and Glen Pritchard's house, then left a message on the answering machine in the Lambrights' phone shed. The Pritchards had dropped Loraine off to wait with Ada until the ambulance came and had taken Loraine's buggy home to their house, where she would pick it up later. If she hadn't been in such a hurry to get back to Ada, she might have stopped at the Lambrights', but the Pritchards' place was a lot closer, and Loraine knew she needed to get back to Ada as quickly as possible.

During the time Loraine and Ada had waited for the ambulance to arrive, Ada had told her that Crist was in bed with a bad sore throat and that Wayne had been having trouble with his prosthesis. Loraine figured it wasn't likely that either Wayne or Crist would check for phone messages today, so they'd have to be told about Ada when Loraine brought her home.

After they'd arrived at the hospital emergency room in Goshen, Loraine had called her boss and explained what had happened, asking if she could be excused from work today. She was pleased that Esther had said yes and had seemed so understanding. Then she'd called Marge Nelson and alerted her to the fact that they would need a ride home once Ada's leg had been taken care of.

If things had gone as Wayne and I had originally planned, we'd be married now, Loraine thought painfully. *I'd be here at the hospital waiting for news on my mother-in-law, not my ex-fiancé's mother, who didn't even tell me thanks for seeing that she got help today.*

Tears sprang to Loraine's eyes. *I shouldn't expect any thanks for what I've done. It's my Christian duty to help others, whether they thank me or not.*

"You look tired," Marge said, when she entered the room. "Have you had any news on Ada yet?"

"No, and I'm beginning to worry. It's been over an hour since they took her back to be examined." Loraine sighed and flopped into a chair. "I wonder what could be taking so long. I hope it's not a bad sign."

"I'm sure everything will be fine," Marge said in her usual positive tone. "You just need to sit there and relax."

Loraine plucked a magazine off the table and pretended to read it. She wasn't just worried about Ada; she was worried about Wayne and how he would manage with both of his parents laid up.

"Maybe I should have gone over to the Lambrights' and told them about Ada instead of coming here," Loraine said. "I'm sure Wayne and his dad are wondering why she hasn't returned home, and I doubt that either of them has checked their answering machine."

Marge opened her purse and removed her cell phone. "I'll give my husband a call and ask him to stop by their place on his way home from work and explain things to them."

"Thanks. That's a real good idea."

Marge punched in a few numbers and lifted the cell phone to her ear. Several seconds went by before she clicked off the phone and dropped it back in her purse. "I should have remembered."

"Remembered what?"

"Brian didn't answer because he left his cell phone at home this morning, so it wouldn't make any sense for me to leave a message on his voice mail."

"I'm Dr. Gaylord," a middle-aged man announced as he stepped into the room. "Are you a relative of Ada Lambright?" he asked Loraine.

She shook her head. "I'm just a friend of the family, and I'm waiting to take Ada home."

"I'm afraid she won't be going home until sometime tomorrow," the doctor said. "She's suffered a bad break in her leg, and we're going to have to do some surgery before we can set it."

"I'm real sorry to hear that. Her family has no idea she's here, so I think we should let them know right away." She looked over at Marge.

Marge nodded. "I'll drive you there now if you like."

"I appreciate that, but I'd like to see Ada first and let her know that I picked up Crist's prescription and will stop by the house and let her family know what's happened to her."

"Mrs. Lambright's being prepared for surgery right now," the doctor said, "but I'll see that she gets your message."

"Thank you." Loraine stood and moved toward the door. Marge joined her.

"With Ada being laid up for the next several weeks, she's going to need a lot of help," Loraine said as she and Marge headed down the hall toward the exit.

"I'm sure the women in your community will chip in and do whatever they can."

Loraine nodded. "I'll help out as much as possible, too."

❧ ❧

Wayne glanced at the clock on the kitchen wall and frowned. Mom had been gone several hours already. It shouldn't have taken her this long to pick up Pop's prescription.

Maybe she stopped off to visit one of her friends, he thought as he peered out the window. *Maybe I should go to the phone shed and check the answering machine. If she did stop somewhere, she might have called and left a message.*

He slipped into his jacket, grabbed his crutches for support, and headed out the door.

<hr>

As Loraine neared the Lambrights' house, her heartbeat picked up speed. She had wanted to see Wayne again, just not under these circumstances.

She clucked to her horse and guided him off the road and onto the Lambrights' driveway. Smoke curled from the chimney of the house, so she figured either Wayne or his dad must be tending the fire.

She spotted Wayne on the porch, with a pair of crutches under his arms. He stood motionless until she pulled her rig up to the hitching rail, and then he headed her way. By the time he reached her, she was out of the buggy and had tied the horse to the rail.

Deep wrinkles formed in Wayne's forehead when he stepped up to her. "What are you doing here? I thought I told you—"

"I came to let you know that your mamm's been in an accident. She's in the hospital in Goshen with a broken leg."

Wayne's eyebrows shot up. "What happened?"

Loraine quickly explained the details of how she'd seen Ada fall off her bike and had then gone to call for help. "When Marge and I left the hospital, I asked her to drop me off at my house so I could tell my folks what was going on and let them know I was coming over here. I figured you'd be worried about your mamm."

"Jah, I sure was."

"I also came over to fix you some supper," she said.

"You're here to fix supper?" His mouth gaped open.

She nodded. "Your mamm told me about your daed being sick, so I figured since you—"

"I may be handicapped, but I'm not an invalid! I'm perfectly capable of fixing Pop and me something to eat."

Loraine cringed, and the pressure behind her eyes signaled

that tears were forthcoming. Until the accident had occurred, Wayne had never been so sharp with her. Now, he always seemed to be full of anger and resentment.

With a sigh of resignation, Loraine turned toward her buggy. "If you don't want me to fix supper, then I'll just take the chicken and potatoes I was planning to prepare and head for home."

Wayne stepped in front of her, and she noticed that his expression had softened a bit. "Did you say, 'baked chicken'?"

Loraine nodded. She knew baked chicken was one of Wayne's favorite dishes, so hopefully, he might change his mind.

She wasn't disappointed when he gave her a bird dog look and said, "I've. . .uh. . .changed my mind. If you're still willing, then I'd appreciate having you fix my supper."

"I'm more than willing." Loraine reached into the buggy and pulled out a cardboard box.

"I'd help you with that, but I don't think I could manage it and hold onto my crutches, too," he said.

"It's not heavy. I'll do fine on my own."

Wayne started moving toward the house, and she walked beside him. They were halfway there when he halted and drew in a quick breath.

"Are you okay?" she asked with concern.

"I've been wearing my prosthesis most of the day, and the stump of my leg is really sore."

"Do you need my help, because if you do, then I'll just—"

"I can manage fine on my own!"

Loraine bristled. "Why must you always be so defensive?"

"I just don't need you treating me like a boppli. I get enough of that from my mamm."

"I'm not your mamm."

"Never said you were. Just said you were treating me the way she does."

Loraine kept walking. There was no use arguing with him; it wouldn't solve a thing.

When she stepped into Ada's kitchen, she was surprised to see that the dishes were done and the room looked clean and orderly. *Of course,* she reasoned, *Ada probably cleaned it this morning. It's not likely that Wayne cleaned the kitchen—not with his leg hurting.*

"I'm going to let Pop know about Mom, and see if he feels up to eating anything for supper," Wayne said.

Loraine reached into the box and withdrew the container of cut-up chicken. "I can fix him some soup if his throat's too sore to deal with baked chicken."

"Okay, I'll tell him that." Wayne hobbled out of the room, and Loraine set right to work in Ada's kitchen.

Wayne didn't return until the chicken was almost done. This time he was in his wheelchair. "Pop's throat still hurts real bad, so he'll just have some soup," he said.

"That's fine. Oh, I almost forgot." Loraine reached into the cardboard box and pulled out a paper sack. "At your mamm's request, I picked up your daed's prescription. If you'd like to take it to him, I'll bring in the soup as soon as it's ready."

Loraine's fingers brushed Wayne's as she handed him the bottle of pills. The innocent contact brought warmth to her cheeks.

Apparently unaffected by her touch, Wayne placed the bottle of antibiotics in his pocket and rolled out of the room, mumbling something under his breath that she couldn't understand.

Oh, how Loraine wished things could be as they once were. The tension she felt between her and Wayne and the anger and despondency she heard in his voice made it difficult not to be snappish with him in return. It grieved her to realize that, unless God brought a miracle, things would never be the same between her and Wayne.

CHAPTER 27

Rivulets of sweat poured off Wayne's forehead as he tossed and turned in his rumpled sheets. It would be time to get up soon, and if he didn't get a few more hours' sleep, he wouldn't be worth anything all day. He'd had trouble falling asleep, thinking about Loraine and how wonderful the supper she'd fixed had tasted. He hated to admit it, but he'd enjoyed being with her. As they'd shared a meal at the table, it was a taste of what it would be like if they were husband and wife. Wayne had been careful to keep his distance, however, and spoke only when she'd asked a question. No point in letting her think there was even a chance of them getting back together.

If only I felt capable of supporting her and being able to meet all of her needs, he thought with regret. *That fall I took in the water trough only confirms that I'm not able to care for myself, much less look after a wife and children.*

He punched his pillow and rolled onto his side. *I love Loraine too much to let her spend the rest of her life taking care of a cripple. She needs a whole man—one she can count on to always be there for her. She needs to get back with Jake.* He gave his pillow another good punch. *I need to keep after Jake and make sure that it happens.*

❧ ❧

"You're up earlier than usual this morning," Priscilla said when she

185

stepped into the kitchen and found Loraine in front of the sink.

"I want to stop by the Lambrights' and check on Wayne and his daed before I head to work, so I need to get an early start on my day." Loraine placed the last of her dishes in the dishpan and dried her hands on a clean towel. "I've already eaten, so unless you need my help fixing breakfast for you and Dad, I'll be on my way."

Priscilla shook her head. "I don't need your help with breakfast, but I don't see why you have to go over to the Lambrights' again this morning."

Loraine's forehead creased. "With Ada being laid up with a broken leg, Crist having strep throat, and Wayne dealing with the loss of his leg, they need someone to help out over there."

"I realize that, but does that *someone* have to be you?"

"Maybe not, but since they have no other family members living nearby, I thought—"

"There are others in our community who I'm sure will help." Priscilla pulled the pot of coffee off the stove and poured herself a cup. "I'm wondering if the real reason you're going over there isn't just so you can spend more time with Wayne. Are you hoping you can get him to change his mind about marrying you?"

Loraine's face flamed. "I do want to be with him, and I'm hoping that he will change his mind about marrying me, but that's not the reason I said I would help."

"Are you hoping Ada will become friendlier toward you if you do all her chores? Is that the reason you're overextending yourself?"

"I'm not overextending myself, Mom, and I'm not helping out in order to impress Ada or anyone else."

"You don't plan to go over there every day, I hope."

"I'll go before and after work, and on my days off, I'll probably be there most of the day. That way, I can wash clothes for them, and also clean their house."

"As I said before, I'm sure someone else can do all that." Priscilla took a drink from her cup and winced when it burned her lips. "It doesn't have to be you!"

"But I want it to be me. I still care about Wayne, and I want to help him and his family."

Priscilla lowered herself into a chair. She knew if she said too much, she would only drive her daughter away. "You can do whatever you like; just don't expect any thanks from Ada. She's been in a foul mood ever since Wayne's accident, and I doubt that your helping out there will change her attitude any."

"I don't care about that. I'm not helping to make Ada like me." Loraine slipped into her jacket and picked up her purse. "See you later, Mom. Have a good day."

When the back door clicked shut, Priscilla ambled over to the window. "What a dreadful day," she mumbled, peered out at the dismal-looking gray sky. It looked like there was more rain coming, which she could certainly do without. The dreary day clearly matched her mood.

⁓ஜ ஜ

As Loraine headed to the Lambrights', a sense of excitement welled in her soul. She was anxious to see Wayne. He'd been awfully quiet during supper last night, but at least he'd seemed to enjoy the meal she'd prepared and had even thanked her for it. When she'd said she would be back this morning to fix his breakfast, she was grateful that he hadn't argued with her. At least that was a step in the right direction.

As Loraine neared the crossroad leading to the Lambrights', she spotted another buggy up ahead. When she drew closer, the driver pulled to the side of the road and stopped. Jake climbed down and signaled her to pull over.

"I thought that was you behind me," he said after he'd come around to the driver's side of her buggy. "Where are you heading so early this morning?"

"I might ask you the same thing."

"I have a horse to shoe for an English fellow who lives nearby. He wanted it done right away this morning, so I'm heading there now." Jake offered Loraine a sincere-looking smile. "You can't be heading to work this early. Am I right?"

"I'm going over to the Lambrights' to fix Wayne and his daed some breakfast. When I'm done, I'll be going to work."

"Why would you be fixing breakfast for the Lambrights?" Jake asked. "Isn't that Ada's job?"

"Ada's not there. She fell off her bicycle yesterday and broke her leg. She won't be going home from the hospital until sometime today."

"Too bad about her leg. That family's sure had their share of troubles, haven't they?"

Loraine nodded. "Since Ada won't be able to do much for the next several weeks, I've decided to help out whenever I can."

"That's real nice of you, but can't Wayne or his daed fix their meals?"

"Under normal conditions they probably could, but Crist has strep throat, and Wayne's having a hard time adjusting to his prosthesis."

Jake thumped his chin a few times. "I'll bet they could probably use some help with the outside chores. Maybe I'll swing by there after I finish shoeing the horse and see what needs to be done."

"I'm sure they'd appreciate it." Loraine started to turn away but turned back. "By the way, have you talked to Wayne yet about his decision to break up with me?"

Jake scuffed the toe of his boot in the dirt, and his cheeks turned pink. "Well, I tried to once, but Wayne didn't give me much chance to say a whole lot, and what I did say didn't seem to be appreciated."

Loraine dropped her gaze to the ground. "Oh, I see."

"I can try again if you like."

She lifted her gaze to meet his. "No, don't bother. If Wayne thinks he's being pushed, he might never change his mind."

"I guess you're right." Jake gave the dirt another pass with his toe. "Guess I'd better go. See you later, Loraine." He gave her a quick smile and sprinted for his buggy.

As soon as Jake pulled out, Loraine got her horse moving again. *Despite what Ella says, Jake really does seem to care about other people,* she thought. *I just wish I knew whether he'll be sticking around this time or not.*

CHAPTER 28

Loraine had just returned to the kitchen after taking Crist some poached eggs on a tray and was getting ready to serve Wayne a plate of eggs, when a knock sounded on the back door.

"I'll get it!" Wayne wheeled his chair out of the room before Loraine could respond.

He returned a few seconds later with Jake at his side.

"I heard that your mamm broke her leg and your daed's down with a sore throat," Jake said to Wayne. "Thought I'd come by and see if you need my help with anything."

"Guess I could use some help feeding the livestock, but I'm feeling so hungry it's making me a bit shaky, so no chores will be done till after I've eaten." Wayne motioned to the table. "Would you like to join us for breakfast?"

"My mamm fed me a decent breakfast before I left home, but I worked up an appetite shoeing Milo Watkin's horse, so if you've got enough to go around, I think I could eat a bit more." Jake looked over at Loraine, as if needing her approval.

"There are plenty of eggs," she said with a nod. Maybe with Jake here, Wayne would be more talkative than he had been last night.

"How bad is your daed's sore throat?" Jake asked Wayne.

"Still pretty sore, and he's got about as much energy as an old hound dog on a hot summer day."

Jake chuckled. "Speaking of hound dogs, one of the fellows at the ranch where I worked in Montana told me a story about a very smart hound dog. Want to hear it?"

Wayne shook his head. "Not really."

"I'd like to hear it," Loraine said as she placed a platter of scrambled eggs and some bacon on the table. She took a seat between the two men. "Let's pray first; then Jake can tell us his story."

All heads bowed, and when their prayers were done, Loraine handed the platter of eggs to Wayne. "I hope these are the way you like them."

"I'm sure they're fine." Wayne spooned some onto his plate and handed the platter to Jake.

"Mmm, these sure do look good." He helped himself and passed the eggs to Loraine. "Now about that story.... An Englisher had a sign in his front yard that read: TALKING HOUND DOG FOR SALE—$5.

" 'Who do you think you are, advertising a talking dog?' the man's neighbor asked. 'There's no such animal!'

"Just then the dog looked up at the man and said, 'I used to be the richest dog in the world, but my owner took all my money and won't buy me any food.'

"The neighbor's mouth dropped open. 'Well, what do you know? That dog really can talk!' He looked at the dog's owner and said, 'How come you're selling this remarkable dog for only five dollars?'

" 'Because,' said the dog's owner. 'I'm gettin' real tired of listening to all his lies!'

"The hound dog looked up at the neighbor, tipped his head back, and howled. 'I'm not a liar; I just remember real big!' "

Loraine laughed and was pleased when Wayne actually snickered. It was good to see him relax a bit and respond to Jake's humor.

Jake told a couple more jokes, and they visited about the weather and various other things as they ate. When the meal was over, Loraine cleared the table and ran warm water into the sink. She was surprised when Jake followed her across the room.

"Why don't you wash, and I'll dry?" he suggested.

Loraine glanced at the clock on the far wall. "I need to leave for work soon, so I appreciate your offer of help." She turned to face Wayne. "Is there anything else you'd like me to do before I have to head out?"

He shook his head.

"Okay, then. I'll come back after work and fix your supper." Loraine smiled. "Hopefully, your mamm will be home from the hospital by then."

Wayne nodded. "Our main driver isn't available right now, but I called Marge Nelson last night. She said she'll go to the hospital and get Mom whenever she's ready to come home. She'll be checking with the hospital sometime this morning."

Loraine smiled. "Marge is usually available whenever we need a driver."

"I still have my truck," Jake put in. "So I could drive you, or anyone in your family, anywhere you need to go."

"I thought you'd been driving a horse and buggy since you came home," Wayne said without commenting on whether he'd accept a ride.

Jake nodded. "I have been driving a horse and buggy most of the time, but I still have my truck. Until I'm ready to join the church, I plan to keep it."

"I'll bet your folks aren't too happy about that," Wayne said.

"You're right. My daed's been giving me a hard time about joining the church, but I told him I won't do it until I feel ready."

You were ready once, but you ran off to Montana and never looked back, Loraine thought with regret. The sponge she held slipped from her fingers and plopped into the water, splashing water and soapy bubbles onto the front of her dress.

Jake chuckled. "You'd better be careful or you'll be washin' yourself instead of those dishes."

She laughed, and swatted his arm with her wet, soapy hand.

"You'd better watch it now, or this could get ugly." The twinkle in Jake's eyes let Loraine know he was only teasing. It was nice to have someone to kid around with again. Wayne sure wasn't in the mood to tease her these days. In fact, the last time she remembered him teasing her was the day they'd been riding in Paul Crawford's van, heading for Hershey Park.

With a grunt, Wayne pushed his wheelchair away from the table. "I'm going down the hall to check on Pop, and then I guess I'll head outside to feed the sheep."

"I'll be leaving as soon as I'm done with the dishes, but I'll see you later today," Loraine called as he went out the door.

"Wayne seemed kind of edgy during breakfast, don't you think?" Jake asked.

She nodded. "I wonder if he's in pain."

"That could be, or maybe watching the two of us together made him feel uncomfortable."

"Do you think he's jealous?"

"Could be." Jake shrugged. "You know how it is—people always take for granted what they have until they don't have it anymore."

Hope welled in Loraine's soul. "If Wayne is feeling jealous, do you think that might be enough to make him realize he and I are supposed to be together?"

Jake grabbed a glass from the dish drainer and dried it with the towel before he replied. "I think he wouldn't have called off your wedding if he really cared. Makes me wonder if you two were ever supposed to be together."

Loraine nodded slowly. As much as she hated to admit it, Jake could be right. What if she and Wayne had gotten married, and then he'd decided he didn't love her? It hurt to know he didn't love her anymore, but it was better to find that out now than to find out after it was too late.

❧ ❧

"I was hoping I'd find Loraine here today," Ella said to Esther

Lehman when she entered the hardware store in Shipshewana and found her moving several things around on one of the shelves.

Esther turned to Ella and smiled. "Loraine is scheduled to work today, so she should be in soon, I expect. Is there anything I can help you with?"

Ella shook her head. "I need to talk to Loraine about something."

"You're welcome to wander around the store and wait, or you can have a seat on one of the benches outside the store."

"I think I'll wander around awhile." Ella moved away and busied herself looking at the various wind chimes her father had made and sold to the store. They were very well built and had a much prettier sound than any of the other wind chimes she'd seen for sale in town.

She was getting ready to head over to the book rack when Loraine showed up.

"I'm glad to see you," Ella said, clasping Loraine's arm. "I came in early, figuring you'd be here already."

Loraine shook her head. "My shift begins now, and I work until three; then I'm going over to—"

"I wanted you to know that I put Jake Beechy in his place during the auction the other day."

Loraine's eyebrows furrowed. "What did you say to Jake?"

Ella pulled Loraine off to one side and lowered her voice. "I let him know what I thought about him running off to Montana the way he did. I said I didn't trust him, and that I didn't want him hanging around you so much. I also made it clear that I didn't want him trying to come between you and Wayne."

Loraine's lips compressed into a thin, tight line. "You had no right to say those things, Ella—especially when they're not even true."

"Do I need to remind you that when Jake ran off to Montana, he left you in the lurch?"

"I don't need the reminder. Besides, Jake's back now, and he's trying to be a good friend to Wayne and to me. I'm sure he's not trying to come between us, either."

"Oh, really? Then how come he hovers around you all the time?"

"Jake doesn't hover around me!"

"Jah, he sure does. I've seen that hound-dog look he gets whenever he's anywhere near you."

Loraine turned away, and Ella, determined to make her cousin see the truth for what it was, moved in front of Loraine. "I'm only saying these things because I care about you. I don't want Jake to hurt you again."

Loraine's eyes filled with tears. "I couldn't be hurt any more than I already am."

"You mean because of Wayne breaking up with you?"

"Jah."

"That's why I'm concerned. If Jake keeps hanging around, Wayne's bound to see it, and then the two of you will never get back together."

"I don't think Wayne cares about getting back together." Loraine sniffed. "At least he's changed his mind about me coming over to his house, though."

"That's a real good thing. What brought about that change?"

"His daed's down with a bad sore throat, and his mamm broke her leg yesterday. I'm planning to go over there and help out before and after work every day."

"Now that is good news!" Ella's face heated up. "I don't mean Ada's broken leg or Crist being sick is good news." She grinned widely. "Ada's probably going to be laid up for several weeks, which means if you go over to their place every day, you'll see Wayne a lot, and he might finally come to his senses before it's too late."

"That would be nice, but it's not the reason I'm doing it. I just want to do the right thing and be helpful." Loraine smiled. "Jake's promised to help out, too. He came over this morning to do some of the outside chores, and he's going back there again this evening."

Ella grimaced. "That's just great. Now he'll have even more

of a chance to hover over you. Can't you discourage him from helping out?"

"I doubt it. He seemed determined, and Wayne was more than willing to accept his help." Loraine shrugged. "Besides, it's not my place to discourage Jake. The Lambrights need all the help they can get right now."

"I'm sure there are others in our community who will help."

"That may be so, but there's no reason for Jake not to help if he wants to."

"Then *you* ought to stay home." Ella smiled as an idea popped into her head. "I know what—I'll go over to the Lambrights' in your place. I'm only answering the phone and doing some paperwork in my daed's business, and I'm sure he wouldn't mind if I took a few hours off every day to help out at the Lambrights'."

"But you've said several times before that your mamm needs you around at home to help her out."

Ella nodded. "That's true, but she's got Charlene to help, and I'll be around most of the time, so I'm able to go over to the Lambrights' whenever I'm needed."

Loraine shook her head. "But you said a few minutes ago that my helping out would be a good way for me to spend more time with Wayne. How am I going to do that if you're taking my place?"

"I know what I said, but that was before I realized Jake was going to be there messing things up between you and Wayne."

"He's not messing things up. He's going to talk to Wayne, and hopefully he'll get him to change his mind about us." Loraine grunted and picked up a box of nails that had been sitting on the floor. "I need to get busy working, so let's drop this discussion!"

Ella felt like a glass of cold water had been thrown in her face. In all the years she'd known Loraine, she'd never spoken to her in that edgy tone of voice. It appeared that Jake was not only coming between Loraine and Wayne, but he was coming between two cousins who used to be such good friends.

CHAPTER 29

As Loraine headed to the Lambrights' that evening, she thought about her conversation with Ella. Could it be true? Was Jake trying to worm his way back into her life? Could he have offered to help at the Lambrights' just so he could be near her?

She shuddered as the thought shook her clean to her toes. Did she want to get back with Jake? Would she be happier with him than she had been with Wayne?

No, no, I mustn't think like that, she chided herself. *It would hurt Wayne too much if Jake and I got back together.* Her fingers gripped the reins until they began to ache. *At least, I think Wayne would be hurt. If he really doesn't love me anymore, then he might be relieved if I found someone else.*

The multitude of confusing thoughts continued to swirl in Loraine's head like a windmill turning at full speed in a heavy wind. As she approached the Lambrights' driveway, she directed the horse to turn in and, at the same time, reined in her thoughts. She was here to help Wayne and his family and needed to keep her focus on that.

As Loraine drew closer to the house, she saw Marge's van parked in the driveway. Ada was obviously home from the hospital, hopefully in less pain than she'd been in yesterday.

"Does your leg hurt much?" Wayne asked as Mom hobbled over to the sofa, using the pair of crutches she'd come home with.

She nodded and gritted her teeth. "Never had such pain before. Even childbirth was less painful than this."

Wayne had no firsthand experience with the pangs of childbirth, but he was no stranger to pain. "Maybe you ought to try the tapping method I've used for my phantom pains," he suggested.

"Puh!" Mom flapped her hand like she was shooing away a pesky fly. "Like that's going to help with anything!"

"It might, and you'll never know if you don't give it a try."

"I won't be doing any tapping because I'm just not interested in anything of that nature." She collapsed against the sofa pillows, then pointed to Wayne's empty pant leg. "I see you're not wearing your prosthesis again. Are you still having pain?"

"Not the phantom pain; just the spot on my stump where the prosthesis has rubbed it sore," he replied. "When I see the doctor on Monday, he'll probably suggest some adjustments be made to the appliance."

"I'm free on Monday," Marge spoke up, "So if you need a ride, I can take you to your appointment."

"I appreciate that," Wayne said, "but Jake was here earlier today, and he said he'd be glad to take me there."

"I can't believe you'd go anywhere with that fellow!" Mom's eyes narrowed. "If you ask me, Jake Beechy's not to be trusted!"

Before Wayne could comment, a knock sounded on the back door. "I'll see who that is," he said, wheeling quickly out of the room.

When he opened the door, he found Loraine on the porch, holding a cardboard box. "I wasn't sure what your mamm had on hand for supper, so I picked up a few things at the grocery store after I got off work." She scurried into the kitchen and set the box on the table. "Does stew and dumplings sound good to you?"

Wayne's mouth watered with anticipation. "Next to baked

chicken, stew and dumplings is one of my favorite meals."

Loraine snickered. "I can think of lots of things you've told me that you like to eat, so I'm sure you have more than one or two things you'd like to call your favorite meal."

He nodded. "I've gotta be careful how much I eat now, though. Since I'm not farming anymore, I don't get the exercise I used to get, so it would be easy for me to put on some extra pounds."

Marge stepped into the room just then. "I'm heading for home now, Wayne. You know my number, so give me a call if you need anything."

"I will, thank you."

Marge smiled at Loraine. "Are you here to fix supper?"

"I am, and you're welcome to join us if you like."

"I appreciate the offer, but Brian should be home from work by now. I don't think he'd be too pleased if I ate supper here and he had to fend for himself."

"I suppose not. Most husbands I know want their wives cooking for them when they come home from work." Loraine glanced at Wayne, but he looked away. He couldn't risk her seeing the look of longing he figured must be on his face.

"I'd better go back to the living room and check on Mom," Wayne said, wheeling quickly away. If he didn't get out of the kitchen soon, he might say or do something he would later regret.

"I'll get the stew going," he heard Loraine call over her shoulder. "Then I'll be in to say hello to your mamm."

When Wayne returned to the living room, he found Mom stretched out on the sofa with her eyes closed. Figuring she needed to sleep, he started to leave, but her eyes snapped open.

"You looked so comfortable there, I thought you might be sleeping," he said.

"Not yet, but I am kind of drowsy." She yawned. "I think it must be from the pain medicine they gave me at the hospital."

"Maybe I should leave so you can sleep."

She shook her head. "No, stay and keep me company."

"Okay, Mom." Wayne maneuvered his wheelchair close to the

sofa and tried to relax. It was hard to think about anything other than Loraine in the next room, making supper.

"Loraine came over. She's making stew and dumplings for our supper." He smiled at Mom.

"With all this pain I'm having, I hope I can eat," she said, making no reference to Loraine's good deed.

"She fixed supper for Pop and me last night, too."

A deep wrinkle formed above Mom's nose as her eyebrows pulled together. "And what do you suppose her motive was for that?"

Wayne shrugged. "Because she knew we'd be hungry?"

"Humph! I'm guessing her coming over here to fix supper last night and then coming back again this evening has more to do with her wanting to get you to change your mind about marrying her than it does with the fact that she knew you'd be hungry."

Wayne's skin prickled. He didn't understand why Mom was always so quick to criticize Loraine. Even though he'd done what he felt was right by breaking up with Loraine, he figured her motive for helping out was pure and right.

When Wayne looked over at Mom, prepared to tell her what he thought about her comment, he noticed that her eyes were closed again. This time, however, Mom's heaving breathing and soft snoring indicated she'd fallen asleep.

It's probably for the best, he decided. *If I said what I really thought, we'd only have ended up in an argument. I may as well go back to the kitchen and see if Loraine needs my help with anything. It'll be better than sitting here, watching Mom sleep.*

Wayne wheeled into the hallway and halted just outside the kitchen door, watching as Loraine took a kettle out of the cupboard, set it on the stove, and put the meat inside. His chest tightened as he continued to watch her. He marveled at her easy, efficient movements. She was capable, intelligent, and a hard worker. She also looked pretty good in the face. He wanted to melt in the warmth of Loraine's ebony eyes, but cold reality stabbed him before he allowed his thoughts to carry him away. He gripped the arms on his wheelchair. Loraine really would make a wonderful wife. Just not his wife.

Loraine turned toward him just then, and the seconds ticked by as they stared at each other. What was going through her mind? Did she know what was going through his?

"I didn't realize you were there," she said, touching her flushed cheeks.

Wayne's face heated up as well. The chemistry between them was still there, although he wished it wasn't. "I was wondering if you needed my help with anything," he mumbled.

She hesitated a moment, then shook her head. "I've got the meat going now, and after I've said hello to your mamm, I'll add in the vegetables."

"Mom's asleep right now, and my daed was sleeping the last time I checked on him, too, so you'll have to wait awhile to say hello."

"Oh, I see. I guess there's really no hurry. I just wanted to see how she's doing today." Loraine headed for the pantry, and when she bent down and lifted the bulky sack of potatoes sitting on the floor, her face turned red and she grunted.

Wayne grimaced. He wished he'd been able to lift the sack for her. If he had two good legs, he surely could have. If he was wearing his prosthesis, he might have been able to lift the heavy sack, too. But no, he was stuck in a wheelchair, unable to do much at all.

"You look tired. Why don't you go back to the living room and relax?" Loraine suggested. "I'll call you when supper's ready."

"If that's what you'd prefer."

She nodded. "I think it would be best."

Wayne whipped the wheelchair around and rolled quickly out of the kitchen. Maybe Loraine didn't want to be alone in the same room with him. Maybe she was sickened by seeing him in his wheelchair. She seemed to be pulling away from him more all the time.

Isn't that what you were hoping for when you broke up with her?

his conscience reminded. *Jah, I just didn't know it would hurt this much.*

～ ✿ ～

Jake smiled when he pulled his horse and buggy up to the Lambrights' barn and saw Loraine's rig. She'd no doubt come to fix supper.

Jake hated the inner battle he'd been fighting since he'd come home—one minute anxious to make some headway with Loraine, the next minute feeling guilty for wanting the woman who had fallen in love with and planned to marry his best friend. It gave him no pleasure to feel happy at his friend's expense, but he felt a sense of relief and had to keep reminding himself that Wayne had given his permission for him to pursue a relationship with Loraine. That must mean Wayne actually wanted them to get back together. Or at least, it seemed that way. Maybe Wayne was hiding behind the mask of self-pity and depression he seemed so determined to wear. Maybe one of these days, he would wake up and wish he hadn't foolishly pushed Loraine away.

Despite all the misgivings running through his head, Jake knew that, if he really wanted to get back with Loraine, he'd have to get past the guilty feelings and work up the nerve to ask her to go out with him. He just hoped she wouldn't turn him down when he finally did.

Jake eased his horse up to the hitching rail, climbed out of the buggy, and unhitched the horse. He figured he'd probably be awhile, so it would be best to put Midnight in the corral.

When that was done, Jake sprinted to the house and rapped on the back door.

"We're in the kitchen, so come on in!" Wayne called from the other side of the door.

When Jake stepped into the room, he was surprised to see Wayne, Loraine, and Ada sitting at the table. He figured they would have been done with supper by now.

A delicious aroma filled the room, and Jake sniffed deeply.

"Did I interrupt your supper?" he asked.

Wayne waved a hand. "Not so much."

"If you want to tell me what chores need to be done, I'll just head back outside and let you eat your meal in peace."

"No, no. Why don't you join us?" Wayne motioned to the large bowl of stew sitting on the table. "Loraine made plenty, and I'm sure you'll work a lot harder if your belly's full."

Jake chuckled and rubbed his chin. "You've got a good point there." He looked over at Loraine and grinned. "That stew does smell mighty *gut*."

Her cheeks reddened. "It's just an ordinary stew; nothing fancy, that's for sure."

"Stew always sounds good to me—especially on a chilly evening such as this." Jake pulled out the chair next to Wayne and sat down.

When Jake had finished his silent prayer, Loraine passed him a bowl of stew, topped with two plump dumplings. He smacked his lips and took a bite. "Mmm, this is sure tasty."

"Danki," she said, without glancing his way. He wondered if having him here made her nervous. Maybe she felt uncomfortable eating supper with her two ex-boyfriends. Come to think of it, she'd seemed a lot more relaxed this morning. But then, Wayne's mother hadn't been sitting at the table with them.

"I was sorry to hear about your broken leg," Jake said, looking over at Ada. "Is it causing you much pain?"

Ada nodded and reached for her glass of water. "I never knew anything could hurt so bad. The doctor gave me something for the throbbing, but it doesn't help that much."

"I'm sure in a few days you'll be feeling better," Loraine spoke up.

Ada shot her a look of obvious displeasure. "How would you know that? Have you ever broken a bone?"

Loraine slowly shook her head.

"I didn't think so."

The room got deathly quiet. Jake didn't care for the serious expressions he was seeing. He figured it was time to ease the awkward tension, so he quickly launched into the talking hound-dog story he'd told during breakfast, hoping he might get at least one smile from someone around the table.

When Jake finished the story, Ada sat, stony-faced, without uttering a word. To Jake's surprise, however, Wayne leaned his head back and roared. "Ha! Ha! Ha! That sure was a good one, Jake! It was even funnier hearing it tonight than when you told it this morning. You're sure good at making people laugh, and you're such a hard-working fellow. I'll bet you'll make a good daed someday."

Now where did that come from? Jake wondered. *Is Wayne trying to make a point, or is he just making polite conversation, hoping to take his mother's mind off the pain in her leg?*

"Speaking of daeds, how's your daed feeling?" Jake asked, looking at Wayne.

"Crist's throat has improved some from what it was two days ago," Ada said before Wayne could even open his mouth. "But he's still hurting and doesn't feel up to being out of bed much yet."

"Sorry to hear that." Jake reached for a hunk of celery from the vegetable platter and took a bite. He was beginning to think Wayne had done Loraine a favor by breaking their engagement. Putting up with an irritable busybody like Ada Lambright would have been hard on Loraine and probably wrecked havoc on her and Wayne's marriage.

They ate in silence for a time; then Jake, unable to stand the quiet, spoke again.

"I told Wayne that I'd help out for as long as it's needed," he said, looking at Ada, "so Crist won't need to be in a hurry to get back to his chores."

Ada nodded. "I'll be sure and tell him that." She glanced at the calendar across the wall. "Looks like Crist and I are going to be laid up on our anniversary tomorrow."

"When you're both feeling better, maybe you can go to the Blue Gate or one of the other nice restaurants for a meal," Loraine suggested.

"We'll have to wait and see how it goes," Ada mumbled around a mouthful of stew.

"Say, Jake," Wayne spoke up, "when Loraine's ready to go home, would you mind following her in your rig? The last time I looked outside, it had started to rain real hard, so the roads might be kind of slippery, not to mention that it'll be pitch dark."

Jake looked over at Loraine to gauge her reaction. He was relieved when she offered him a little smile and nodded.

"Jah, sure. I'd be happy to see that Loraine gets home."

CHAPTER 30

Jake squinted against the pouring rain, and turned on his battery-operated windshield wipers. If not for the flashing red lights up ahead, he wouldn't have known Loraine's buggy was ahead of his. He'd never cared much for rain, but since it was a common occurrence during the fall, he'd just have to deal with it. He guessed he shouldn't complain. If he was still in Montana, he might be dealing with bitter cold, snowy weather by now.

I wonder if Loraine will invite me in when we get to her house. That would be nice, but if her folks are around, it won't give us the chance to be alone. Jake had been hoping for the opportunity to ask her out and thought maybe tonight would work out.

Swish! Swish! The noise of the wiper blades pulled Jake's thoughts aside. It was raining harder, and he squinted to see out the window.

Blink. . .blink. Blink. . .blink. . . At least he could still see the lights on Loraine's buggy up ahead.

When the headlights of a car that had decided to pass shone on Loraine's buggy, Jake noticed that one of the back wheels on her rig was wobbling. After making sure that no other cars were coming, he eased his horse into the other lane, passed her buggy, and pulled onto the shoulder of the road. As soon as she pulled in behind him, he hopped out and sprinted around to the driver's side of her rig.

"What's wrong?" she asked when he opened her door. "Why'd you pass me like that?"

"Your left back wheel seems to be loose. It's been wobbling really bad."

"I did notice the buggy bumping, but I thought it was just the rough road."

Jake shook his head as he swiped at the raindrops splashing on his face. "It's the wheel all right, and if I don't fix it now, you'll never make it home."

"Oh, okay." She stepped out of the buggy. "What can I do to help?"

"I don't know yet. Let me get a flashlight, and then I'll take a look and see whether a nut fell out or if something might have broken."

Jake sprinted back to his buggy and got a flashlight, then he handed it to Loraine. "Shine it right there," he said, pointing to the hub of the wheel.

She did as he asked, and he squatted down to inspect things. "The wheel nut's missing all right, and—"

Whack! They bumped heads as he stood.

"Are you okay?" A jolt of electricity shot through Jake's fingers as he reached out and touched Loraine's forehead.

"I'm fine. How about you?" Loraine's voice trembled, and Jake wondered if she'd felt the same connection between them as he'd felt.

"I'm okay." He laughed. "Don't think any permanent damage was done."

"None for me, either."

They stood staring at each other for several seconds. Jake was on the verge of taking Loraine in his arms and kissing her, when she turned her head away. "If the nut's missing, how are we going to fix my wheel?"

"I could look for it along the road, but since we don't know when or where it fell off, that wouldn't make much sense. Especially

207

since it's dark and raining." Jake motioned to his own rig. "I've got some extra wheel nuts in my toolbox."

"I guess you'll need this then." She handed him the flashlight.

Jake hesitated a minute, then ran back to his rig. A few minutes later, he was back with the nut and necessary tools.

Loraine held the flashlight while Jake worked, and in short order he had it fixed. "There you go; it's good as new."

"Danki, Jake."

He smiled. "You're welcome." *Should I ask her out now? Would this be a good time?*

"Well, we'd better get going. It's raining harder, and I'm really getting wet standing out here like this."

Jake nodded and swiped a hand across his damp face. Maybe he'd have a chance to ask Loraine out when they got to her place.

~❦ ❦~

As Loraine climbed back in her buggy and took up the reins, she thought about the way Jake had looked at her after they'd bumped heads. Had he been about to kiss her? Did she want him to?

Pushing her thoughts aside, she focused on the road ahead and concentrated on keeping her horse from losing its footing on the slippery, wet pavement. She'd have time to think about all this later on—after she was home safely and had changed out of her wet clothes.

Loraine was glad Wayne had suggested that Jake follow her home. She didn't know what she would have done if she'd been all alone when the nut had fallen out of the buggy wheel. If she'd gone much farther with it that way, the wheel would probably have fallen off, and she might have ended up in a serious accident.

As Loraine approached her folks' place, she clicked on the right-turn blinker and guided the horse up the driveway. She halted it near the barn, and when she climbed down, she was surprised to see Jake pull his rig in beside hers. She figured he would have gone on his way home once he'd seen her turn up the driveway.

"Danki for seeing me home," she said when he stepped up to her. "And again, I appreciate your help with the buggy wheel."

"No problem. Glad I could do it." He fiddled with the flashlight in his hands, turning it over and over a couple of times. "Uh, Loraine, there's something I want to ask—"

"What are you two doing out there in the rain?"

Loraine looked toward the house. There stood Mom with her hands cupped around her mouth.

"Jake followed me home from the Lambrights'!" Loraine called back.

"Bring him in for some hot coffee!"

Loraine looked over at Jake. "What do you think?"

"I think a cup of coffee sounds pretty good about now," he said with a nod. "If you want to get in out of this cold, I'll take care of putting your horse away, and then I'll be up as soon as I'm done."

"I appreciate that." Loraine shivered. "I really do need to get out of my wet clothes."

"You go ahead then, and I'll be in shortly."

Loraine hurried into the house, shivering all the way.

When she stepped into the kitchen, Mom handed her a towel. "Where's Jake? Isn't he coming in for coffee?"

Jake? Was he all Mom could think about? Didn't she even care that Loraine was sopping wet and shivering from the cold?

"Jake's putting Trixie away for me, and he'll be in as soon as he's done." Loraine turned toward the door leading to the stairs. "I'm going up to my room to change out of these wet clothes."

"That's a good idea. I'll set things out and have them on the table by the time you get back." Mom motioned to the living room door. "Your daed's in there reading the newspaper. I'll go see if he wants to join us in the kitchen."

"Okay." Loraine hurried from the room.

When she returned sometime later, she found Mom, Dad, and Jake sitting at the kitchen table, eating thick slices of apple pie and drinking coffee.

Mom motioned to the chair next to Jake. "Have a seat, Loraine."

Loraine hesitated a minute, then pulled out the chair and sat down.

"I told your mamm I was awfully wet and probably shouldn't sit at her table," Jake said, smiling at Loraine. "But she just plopped a towel down and told me to take a seat and that between the fire in the wood burning stove and a hot cup of coffee, I'd warm up and dry off real quick."

Loraine smiled. "The heat from the stove does feel good."

Mom handed Loraine a piece of pie. "Jake explained about the missing wheel nut on your buggy."

Loraine nodded. "It was Wayne's idea for Jake to follow me home."

"It's a good thing he did," Dad said. "Otherwise you might have had a serious problem out on the road by yourself. I'll have to keep a better check on our buggy wheels from now on. Wouldn't want to see an accident happen because I was negligent about checking."

Mom poured more coffee into Jake's cup. "Would you like another piece of pie?"

He nodded with an eager expression. "Jah, sure, why not?"

"Jake was also telling us that he plans to raise and train horses," Mom said as she cut a large piece of pie and handed it to Jake.

"What kind of horses did you say you want to raise?" Dad asked.

"Standard-bred racing horses, because they're good for pulling our buggies." Jake took a drink of coffee and swiped his napkin across his lips. "When my business gets going good, I may want to raise some Percheron workhorses, too."

Loraine ate her pie and drank her coffee as she listened to Jake talk about horses and answer all of Mom and Dad's questions. Every once in a while, Mom would compliment Jake on something—how much he knew about horses, how helpful he was, and what an easygoing, pleasant person he seemed to be.

Jake's cheeks reddened, and he quickly launched into a couple of humorous stories, which Mom especially seemed to enjoy.

Finally, Jake pushed back his chair and stood. "Guess I'd better get home before my folks start to worry." He looked over at Mom and smiled. "Danki for the pie and coffee, Priscilla. It was just what I needed."

She grinned at him. "You're quite welcome. Come by and see us anytime."

Jake looked over at Loraine. "Guess I'll see you soon."

She nodded. "Jah, probably so."

When the door clicked shut behind Jake, Mom turned to Loraine and said, "I think that young man likes you."

"What makes you think that?"

"The way he kept looking at you and telling those funny stories. I think he was trying to make you laugh."

"You seemed to be enjoying Jake's stories more than Loraine." Dad nudged Mom's arm with his elbow.

She smiled and nodded. "I think an encouraging, positive thinker like Jake would make a real good husband."

Loraine couldn't argue with that. She just wasn't sure she'd want Jake to be *her* husband.

⚜ ⚜

"You look mied," Wayne said when he entered the living room where Ada sat on the sofa with her leg propped on a pillow.

She yawned. "I am tired, but I dread going to bed."

"How come?"

"The cast on my leg is so cumbersome, and it's hard to find a comfortable position." She leaned her head against the sofa cushion and sighed. "I can't wait until my leg's healed and I can finally get this cast taken off. It's so heavy and awkward."

Wayne lowered himself into a chair. "This prosthesis I'm expected to wear weighs about four pounds, and since it doesn't feel like my own leg, I wonder if I'll ever fully adjust to walking with it."

"Just give it some more time and try to be patient." Ada stretched her arms over her head and released another noisy

211

yawn. "One of the biggest reasons I can't wait to get my cast off is so I can take over my household chores again. It's hard to sit around and watch someone else come in here and do everything the wrong way."

"Who's doing things the wrong way?" Wayne asked.

"Loraine."

"What did she do that was wrong?"

"For one thing, she put my frying pans and kettles in the cupboard on the left-hand side of the sink." Mom grunted. "They're supposed to go in the drawer beneath the stove."

"It's not the end of the world, Mom. Once you're able to take over in the kitchen again, you can put the frying pan and kettles back exactly where you want them to be."

Ada pursed her lips and folded her arms. "She left dust on the bookcase, too—which she said she had cleaned, and then she—"

"I think Loraine's doing the best she can," Wayne interrupted. "She doesn't have to take time out of her busy day to come over here and help, you know. I think you ought to appreciate what she does instead of complaining and finding fault all of the time."

"I'm not complaining or finding fault; I'm just stating facts." Ada wrinkled her nose. "If you want my opinion, I think Loraine only comes over here so she can make you jealous."

Wayne's eyebrows furrowed. "Jealous of what?"

"Not what—*who*. Haven't you seen the way Loraine hangs on Jake's every word? I think she's using him to try and get to you. And Jake's no better," she quickly added. "He hovers over Loraine all the time, and hangs on her every word. He's out to get her back as his girlfriend. Mark my words, before this year's out, they'll be announcing their engagement."

Wayne shrugged. "That's fine with me. Fact is, I'm hoping Loraine and Jake get back together."

"You. . .you are?"

He nodded. "Why else would I have suggested that Jake follow Loraine home tonight?"

As Wayne's words set in fully, Ada smiled to herself. *It's amazing how when you want something badly enough, it all works out for the good. And to think, I didn't even have to make this happen myself.*

CHAPTER 31

For the last two weeks, Loraine had gone over to the Lambrights' every morning before work and every afternoon on her way home. She still hadn't won Ada over, but at least the difficult woman was willing to accept Loraine's assistance. Some of the other women, including Loraine's mother, took turns helping out, too.

Wayne's father was feeling better, so he'd taken over his chores again. For some reason, Jake thought his help was still needed, though, so he came over nearly every day. When he was finished with the chores, he hung around Loraine. That made her nervous.

On Saturday, Loraine had the day off from her job at the hardware store, so she was free to spend most of the day at the Lambrights'. She'd just begun baking some bread when Jake entered the kitchen.

"I'm done cleaning the barn, and Wayne's in his daed's shop helping him with some taxidermy stuff, so I thought I'd see if you needed my help with anything." He stopped and sniffed the air. "Whoa! Something sure smells good in here!"

"I'm baking bread."

"What kind?"

"I've already made one loaf, using the basic recipe for friendship bread, but I'm planning to add some nuts and chocolate chips to this next batch, hoping to make it more interesting for finicky taste buds."

Jake snickered. "Can't imagine who'd have finicky taste buds in this family."

Loraine put her fingers to her lips. "*Shh. . .*she'll hear you."

He glanced around. "Where is the old grouch?"

"In her bedroom, resting her leg. She was up on it quite a bit yesterday, and I'm afraid she's paying the price for it today."

"She's had you and several other ladies from our community helping out, so why was she doing too much?"

"It's her home, and she wants to help. You can't really blame her for that."

"No, I guess not." Jake frowned deeply. "I sure can't figure out why Ada's so grouchy all the time. You must be a saint for helping someone who doesn't even appreciate it. For all the mean things that woman has said to you, I'd think you'd want to stay as far away from her as you possibly can."

Loraine shook her head. "I'm no saint; I just care about people and want to help whenever I see a need. Even if Ada never comes to like me, I won't regret having helped during her time of need." She stood on her tiptoes, reaching for the jar of nuts on the top shelf of the cupboard.

"Here, let me get that for you." Jake rushed forward and grabbed the jar at the same time as she reached for it. Their heads collided, the jar slipped out of his hands, and it tumbled to the floor. Crushed walnuts scattered everywhere!

"Rats!" Jake dropped to his knees and picked up the jar. "Well, at least it's not broken."

Loraine sighed. "No, but now I have no nuts to add to the bread dough."

"Sorry about that. Guess that's what I get for trying to help you get the jar down. I should have minded my own business."

Jake's sheepish look brought a smile to Loraine's lips. He'd always been a bit accident prone. "If you really want to help," she said, motioning to the utility room, "you can get a broom and dustpan and sweep up this mess while I finish mixing my bread dough."

"Sure, I can do that."

Loraine turned back to the counter and had just begun adding the chocolate chips when she heard a *crunch*, then a *crash!*

She whirled around. Jake sat on the floor in the middle of the scattered nuts, wearing a bewildered expression.

"I can't believe it," he groaned. "I really am a big *dummkopp!*"

"You're not a dunce. You're just a little clumsy at times, but that doesn't mean you're stupid." She held out her hand. "Here, let me help you up."

Jake reached out his hand, and as their fingers touched, Loraine felt a tingle shoot all the way up her arm. A familiar longing crept into her heart as she remembered how she used to feel when she and Jake had been dating. *Why does his touch send my heart flying up to my throat?* she wondered. *It's over between us and has been for some time.*

With Jake standing so near, Loraine could feel his warm breath on her neck and smell a minty aroma. It made her light-headed. Jake's face was so close to hers that she noticed the fine lines etched around his eyes and saw a look of longing on his face.

She drew back, her heart hammering fiercely in her chest. "I'd better get busy on the bread or it'll never get baked." She couldn't let him know how being this close to him had affected her. She couldn't—wouldn't—admit it to herself.

"I'd better try once more to get this mess cleaned up. Sure wouldn't want Ada to come in here and see her kitchen floor littered with nuts. She might have a conniption." Jake wiggled his eyebrows and gave her a playful wink.

Loraine quickly turned her back on him. Was he flirting with her? Worse yet, did she want him to? Jake had such a pleasant way about him, and he'd always been able to make her laugh. But the look of longing she'd seen a few minutes ago frightened her.

She braced herself against the counter, her pulse hammering in her head. *Dear God, please make me strong. Help me not to lose my heart to Jake and forget the promise I made to Wayne.*

"What's going on in here?" Ada asked, hobbling into the room on her crutches. "I was napping in my room, until I heard a crash, and then—" Her mouth opened wide. "Ach, my! Why are those nuts scattered all over my kitchen floor?"

Loraine quickly explained what had happened and said that Jake was getting ready to sweep the floor.

"If you're the one who dropped the jar, shouldn't you be the one cleaning up the mess?"

"She didn't drop the jar, Ada. I did," Jake was quick to say.

"Whatever." Ada's eyes flashed as she stared angrily at Loraine. "I thought you came here to help, not wreck havoc with my kitchen!"

Loraine opened her mouth, ready to spew out angry words, but a verse of scripture, Matthew 5:44, came to her mind: *"But I say unto you, Love your enemies, bless them that curse you, do good to them that hate you, and pray for them which despitefully use you, and persecute you."*

I need to pray for Ada, she reminded herself. *I'll never win her over with angry, spiteful words.*

Forcing a smile to her lips, Loraine looked at Ada and said, "It was an accident, and I'm sorry about the mess. Jake and I will get it cleaned up as quickly as we can, so why don't you go back to your room and rest?"

Ada stood staring at the floor several seconds, then with an undignified grunt, she turned and hobbled out of the kitchen.

Jake poked Loraine's arm with his elbow. "I don't care what you say, you really are a saint."

She grinned and poked him right back. "You'd better hurry and get that broom before Ada decides to come back in here and chew me out some more."

❧ ❧

As Jake carried the broom and dustpan into the kitchen, he glanced back at Loraine. The memory of the way she'd smiled at him earlier sparkled like a moment in a pleasant dream. When he'd smiled at her in return, he'd seen a flicker of something. There'd been a flush on her cheeks and a sparkle in her heavily fringed eyes that he hadn't seen for a long time. Was it a look of longing, or was it merely his own wishful thinking?

Jake leaned against the doorjamb, watching as Loraine poured the bread dough into two pans. For the nearly two years Jake had been living in Montana, he'd been running from what he wanted most and hadn't even realized it. He couldn't deny his feelings—he was still in love with Loraine. The question was, what should he do about it?

Ask her out, prompted a little voice in his head. *Do it now, before you lose your nerve.*

He quickly swept up the nuts, deposited them in the garbage can, and put the broom and dustpan away. The whole time, he rehearsed what he should say to Loraine. *I've never stopped loving you. I think we're meant to be together. Would you go out with me?* No, it would be too bold to declare his feelings right out. If he said he loved her too soon, it might push her away.

He wiped his sweaty palms on the knees of his trousers and stepped up beside her. "Loraine, I was wondering—"

"Oh, look, there's Wayne and that cute little ewe of his." Loraine pointed out the window. "I can't get over how well that sheep gets around on only three legs."

"Jah, and the critter likes to follow Wayne everywhere he goes."

"Have you noticed that Wayne seems to be walking better with his prosthesis now?"

Jake nodded. "Since he had it adjusted a few weeks ago, he's walking more normally and, from what I can tell, with less pain." Jake transferred his weight from one foot to the other and moistened his lips with the tip of his tongue. *Ask her now, before you lose your nerve. What are you waiting for, anyway?*

"This bread's ready to go in the oven now," she said, picking up the two pans. "And I think it'll be good, even without the nuts."

"Anything you make is bound to be good."

Her cheeks reddened, and she looked away.

"Sorry if I embarrassed you. I was just remembering how you used to make ginger cookies for me when we were going out together, and they were always so good."

Loraine moved over to the stove and put the bread pans in.

"Do you remember how much fun we used to have when we were together?"

She gave a slow nod and closed the oven door.

Jake grabbed a glass from the cupboard, filled it with water, and took a drink. As he let the cool liquid trickle down his throat, he contemplated what to say next. "Uh. . .I was wondering, would you like to have supper with me on Friday evening?" There, it was finally out.

Loraine's eyes widened as she turned to face him. "Are you asking me out on a date?"

"Jah, I am. I thought we could go to Tiffany's in Topeka. We used to like going there to eat, remember?"

"I do remember, but—" She slowly shook her head. "I couldn't go out with you, Jake. It wouldn't be fair to Wayne."

"You've been working real hard here these last few weeks, and I think you should go."

Jake whirled around. He hadn't realized Wayne had come into the house, much less had entered the kitchen. "Are you sure you don't mind? I mean, if—"

"Don't mind at all."

A look of shock registered on Loraine's face. "But, Wayne, we're—"

"Just friends. That's all we'll ever be, Loraine." Wayne's words were crisp and to the point. Apparently, he'd meant what he'd said to Jake about dating Loraine. Could it be that Wayne had been telling the truth when he'd said that he really didn't love her anymore? Jake wondered. Or was he only giving Loraine over to Jake because he no longer felt like a man?

"We're more than friends, Wayne." Doubt tinged Loraine's voice, and there was no sparkle in her eyes. She'd been clearly hurt by Wayne's remark.

"We used to be more than friends, but not anymore." Wayne moved over to the refrigerator and took out a gallon of apple cider.

Then he grabbed two paper cups from the pantry and turned them upside-down over the lid on the cider. "My daed sent me in to get us something cold to drink, so I'd better get back out to his shop with this." Without so much as a backwards glance, he shuffled from the room.

Loraine looked at Jake like she couldn't quite believe what had just happened. Then, with a smile that held no sparkle at all, she said in a voice barely above a whisper, "I'd be happy to go out to supper with you on Friday night."

Jake stood there, too stunned to say a word. As much as he wanted to take Loraine out, he'd really expected her to say no. *I guess I have Wayne to thank for her change of heart, but I hope she's not going out with me just to spite him. I'd feel a lot better if I knew she really wanted to be with me.*

"I'll pick you up at your house at five o'clock," he said. "Does that sound all right?"

She nodded slowly. "Five o'clock is fine for me."

~❧ ❧~

A raw ached settled in the pit of Wayne's stomach as he headed to his dad's shop. Even though he'd convinced himself that breaking up with Loraine was for her own good, he felt miserable. It was obvious from the look on Jake's face whenever Loraine was near that he'd never stopped loving her, but he wasn't sure how Loraine felt about Jake.

Wayne stopped walking and rolled his shoulders in order to loosen his stiff muscles and erase the tension he felt. Loraine had been happy with Jake once; she could be happy with him again.

He kicked at a fallen tree branch with the toe of his boot and groaned. *I love her too much not to let her go. I just wish I didn't have to see her and Jake together.*

As Wayne started walking again, an idea popped into his head. After their accident in Paul's van, Katie and Jolene had left home in order to find healing. Maybe he should go away, too.

CHAPTER 32

"You seem to be having a hard time keeping your mind on the job at hand," Pop said, nudging Wayne's arm. "Are you bored with working on animal skins?"

Wayne shook his head. "Not really. I thought I'd hate it at first, but after working here awhile, I realize it's not so bad."

Pop's face broke into a wide smile. "I'm real happy to hear that. Someday, when I'm too old to do this anymore, maybe you can take over the business."

Wayne shrugged his shoulders. "I don't know about that. I've been thinking I might want to do something else."

Pop's eyebrows furrowed. "Are you still wishing you could farm? Because if you are, and you think you're up to it, I can let you have a few acres of land and see how it goes."

Wayne shook his head. "I'm thinking I might want to move to Arthur, Illinois, and stay with Uncle Ezra and Aunt Evelyn awhile. Maybe Uncle Ezra would be willing to teach me something about the woodworking trade."

Pop's mouth formed an O. "I had no idea you were thinking of leaving home. I thought you were happy here."

Wayne gripped the piece of deer hide in his hands so hard his fingers began to ache. "Happy? Pop, I haven't been happy since I lost my leg!"

"You need to give it more time, son. Healing, emotionally and physically—that's gonna take some time."

"That's why I want to move away and leave all the memories behind."

"What about your leg? Don't you think you need to stay close to your doctors until it's sufficiently healed?"

"I'm sure there are plenty of good doctors in Illinois who can take over my case."

Pop dropped the piece of deer hide he'd been working on onto the workbench and massaged the bridge of his nose. "You can't run from your past, son. It won't solve a thing."

"I wouldn't be running. I just need a fresh start."

"What about Loraine and your plans to be married? Have you spoken to her about the idea of moving to Illinois?"

Wayne shook his head. "I've told you this before, Pop—Loraine and I will not be getting married. She's moving on with her life. In fact, she'll be going out to supper with Jake this evening."

Pop continued to rub his nose. "So that's the reason you want to go away. You're still in love with Loraine and can't stand the thought of her seeing someone else."

Wayne offered no reply.

"If you're in love with her, then you shouldn't let her go." Pop made a sweeping gesture of the room. "If you keep working here with me, you can make enough money to support a wife. There's no reason you and Loraine can't be married like you'd planned."

"Even if I could provide a decent living for a wife and family, I'll always be handicapped, and I don't want to be a burden."

"I'm sure Loraine wouldn't see being married to you as a burden. For goodness' sake, Wayne, there are folks with worse handicaps than yours, and many have gotten married and lived a normal life."

"There's nothing *normal* about losing a leg." Wayne couldn't keep the bitterness from his tone. "Besides, Loraine doesn't love me anymore. She used to love Jake before he went to Montana, and I've seen the way the two of them look at each other." He slowly shook his head. "I won't stand in the way of their happiness, and I won't hold Loraine to her promise to marry me just because she feels sorry for me now. I've made up my mind to leave, and I plan to contact Uncle Ezra next week."

Pop clasped both of Wayne's shoulders and turned him so they were eye to eye. "I can't keep you from going to Illinois, but I think it would be best if you waited until your mamm gets her cast off and is able to take over the cooking and household chores again."

"Loraine and some of the others in our community are helping out. Mom doesn't need me here for that."

"That's true, but your mamm's been an emotional wreck ever since your accident, and breaking her leg has only added to her frustrations." Pop blew out his breath as he whacked the edge of his workbench with his knuckles. "I think it would put her over the edge if you took off for Illinois right now."

Wayne stared at the workbench, contemplating his father's words. As much as he needed to get away, he didn't want Mom to feel any worse than she already did. Pop was right; she hadn't been the same since the accident. No one had, really.

"All right then, I'll wait until Mom gets her cast off and is getting around well enough on her own, but then I'll be heading for Illinois."

"You won't say anything about these plans to her now, I hope. It would really upset her, you know."

Wayne shook his head. "For the time being, I'm not going to mention it to anyone else."

᠁

Loraine peeked out the kitchen window, watching for Jake's buggy to come into the yard. She could hardly believe she'd agreed to go out with him this evening. Would it be like old times, or would she feel stiff and uncomfortable eating supper with him at Tiffany's? They used to go there a lot when they were dating— sometimes with other couples, sometimes just the two of them.

Their times together had always been relaxed yet exciting. Back then, Loraine had believed that she and Jake would eventually marry. Now she wasn't sure what she wanted or how she felt about much of anything.

Is going out with Jake tonight what I really want to do? she asked herself. *Or am I only going out with him because Wayne wants me to? Why does Wayne want me to go out with Jake, anyway? Could he really have stopped loving me, or is he just feeling sorry for himself and thinking this is the best thing for me?*

"Are you watching for Jake?" Mom asked, stepping up to Loraine.

"Jah, and I'm feeling a bit *naerfich* about going out with him this evening."

Mom gave Loraine's arm a gentle squeeze. "Don't be nervous. Jake's so pleasant and easygoing; I'm glad you're seeing him again."

"He is easy to be with, but I can't forget the promise I made to Wayne."

"He broke up with you, Loraine. That means you're no longer bound by your promise."

Loraine blinked against the tears that threatened to spill over. "Can we please change the subject? I'd rather not talk about this anymore."

"Jah, sure. I need to get supper started for me and your daed anyway." Mom went to the refrigerator.

"I think I'll wait out on the porch for Jake," Loraine said.

"Oh, okay. Have a good time, and tell him I said hello and to come by again soon for more pie and coffee."

Loraine nodded, grabbed her jacket and bonnet, then scurried out the door. She'd no more than taken a seat on the porch swing when a horse and buggy rolled into the yard. Only it wasn't Jake who climbed down from the buggy—it was Ella.

"I went over to the Lambrights', thinking you'd be there," Ella said when she stepped onto the porch. "I found Aunt Leah there, fixing supper for them instead." She scowled at Loraine. "I was shocked when Ada said you weren't there because you were having supper with Jake this evening."

Loraine nodded. "That's right. He's taking me to Tiffany's, and he should be here any minute."

Ella grunted as she plopped down beside Loraine. "After the way Jake hurt you before, I don't understand how you could even consider going out with him now."

Loraine gripped the armrest of the swing, hoping to gain control of her emotions. It seemed that every time she spoke to Ella these days, they ended up in an argument over Jake.

Ella bumped Loraine's arm. "Can you explain why you've ignored my advice and accepted a date with Jake?"

"I enjoy being with him. And he's apologized for what he did."

"Puh!" Ella's nose crinkled as though some foul odor had permeated the air. "I've said it before, and I'll say it once more, that fellow's not to be trusted. How do you know he won't run off again?"

"I don't know that. There are no guarantees in this life."

"What about Wayne? Does he know you're going out with Jake?"

"Jah, he knows, and he seems to be perfectly fine with the idea." Loraine blew out her breath. "In fact, he actually said I should go."

"What?" Ella's eyes widened. "You've got to be kidding!"

"No. Not only has Wayne said several times that it's over between us, but the other day, he came right out and said he thought Jake and I should get back together."

Ella sat several seconds, rubbing her chin and tapping her sneaker against the weathered porch floor. "I can't believe it. It doesn't make sense that Wayne would want you and Jake to get back together."

"It makes sense if Wayne doesn't love me anymore." Loraine swallowed hard, hoping she wouldn't break down in tears. "And he obviously doesn't, or he wouldn't be trying to push me and Jake together, now would he?"

"I don't know. I mean—"

A horse whinnied, and Loraine turned to look toward the driveway. A buggy rolled in. The door on the driver's side was open, and she could see Jake sitting inside with one foot hanging out the opening. He had always liked to ride in his buggy like that, even in colder weather.

She watched as he pulled alongside the barn, but instead of getting out and tying his horse to the rail, he just sat there.

"Jake's here now, so I'd better go," Loraine said, rising to her feet.

Ella jumped up from the swing. "Look at him—he's just sitting there like a bump on a log. Isn't he coming up to the house to get you?"

"Maybe he thinks there's no need since I'm out here waiting for him."

"That's baremlich! If he wants to take you on a date, then the least he can do is come up to the house and get you."

Loraine started off the porch, but Ella grabbed her arm. "Don't you dare go out there!"

"Why not?"

"You'll look overanxious, and it won't teach Jake anything about proper manners." Ella's nose wrinkled. "That fellow is so into himself, which I just don't understand, since it's not the way he was raised!"

Irritation welled in Loraine's soul as she looked Ella in the face. "I am not Jake's mamm, and it's not my place to teach him good manners. Besides, I think you're wrong about Jake. He's kind and helpful and not at all into himself."

Ella's eyes squinted into tiny slits. "If you go out there, I'll never speak to you again!"

Loraine sighed. "Don't be *lecherich*. When we were little girls and you didn't get your way, you used to threaten not to speak to me. Don't you think it's time for you to grow up and stop trying to control every situation?"

Ella's face flamed. "I'm not being ridiculous or trying to

control every situation. I just care about you too much to stand by and watch you get hurt by the likes of him." She stared across the yard, where Jake still sat in his buggy. "But if you want to ruin your life, then go ahead; don't let me stop you."

Loraine took a step forward, but halted. She didn't want Ella to be mad at her, but at the same time she didn't want to keep Jake waiting. Maybe if she didn't rush out to his buggy, he would take the hint and come up to the house to get her. On the other hand, if she did go out to him, she'd never hear the end of it from Ella, even if she had threatened not to speak to her again.

❧ ☙

Jake shifted on the buggy seat, trying to decide what to do. He wanted to go up to the house and see if Loraine was ready for their date, but with Ella standing there, it might be best to let Loraine come to him. The last time he'd talked to Ella, they'd ended up in an argument. He didn't want to risk that again. At the same time, he didn't want to offend Loraine. He'd worked too hard at gaining her trust to ruin things now.

Gathering up his courage, Jake hopped down from the buggy and started for the house.

When he stepped onto the porch, he smiled at Loraine and said, "Are you ready to head to Topeka?"

She smiled. "I'm more than ready."

Jake glanced over at Ella and forced a smile. "Wie geht's?" he asked.

"I'm doing fine. I was at the Lambrights' and decided to stop by here and see Loraine for a few minutes before I went home." She turned to Loraine and gave her arm a little squeeze. "Think about what I said, okay?"

Loraine gave a quick nod, stepped off the porch, and hurried toward Jake's buggy. It made him wonder if she was as anxious to get away from Ella as he was. At least this time Ella hadn't said anything mean to him.

He helped Loraine into his buggy and went around to untie

227

the horse. When he climbed into the driver's seat, he noticed Loraine looking over her shoulder with a worried expression.

"Is everything all right?" he asked.

She nodded. "I'm just worried about Ella. She's been trying to be everything to everyone ever since her bruder died, but sometimes she's just too pushy."

"You won't get any argument from me there." Jake snapped the reins and directed his horse onto the main road. "Now, can we forget about Ella and concentrate on the two of us having a good time this evening?"

Loraine smiled. "That's exactly what I plan to do."

CHAPTER 33

The fried chicken here at Tiffany's is sure good," Loraine said, then took another bite and savored the delicious taste.

Jake smiled. "Jah, but not nearly as good as yours."

Loraine's cheeks warmed. "Danki."

"I mean it, Loraine, you're really a good cook. That bread you baked for Ada the other day was real tasty."

"I think Ada must have liked it, too, because she ate most of one loaf." Loraine's eyebrows squeezed together. "Of course, she'd never say it was good or give me a compliment for anything. I've come to accept the fact that she's probably never going to like me."

"That's too bad. I guess she doesn't know when she's met a good person."

Loraine shrugged and forked some mashed potatoes into her mouth.

As they continued to eat their meal, Loraine listened with interest while Jake told her more about the horse ranch in Montana where he'd worked and how he'd purchased a couple of thoroughbred horses the other day and hoped to breed them.

"I've worked with horses ever since I was a buwe, and I've had the dream of owning my own business since I turned sixteen." Jake leaned forward, his elbows resting on the table and a serious expression on his face. "That's the reason I went to Montana—so

I could make more money."

"Money isn't everything," she said with a catch in her voice. "Being with family and friends—that's what's important."

"I agree, but a fellow can't provide for a wife and family if he doesn't have enough money."

"Weren't you making a decent living working for your daed?"

Jake shook his head. "Not enough to save up much money. Besides, I don't want to shoe horses for the rest of my life. It's hard on the back and not nearly as much fun as training them."

Loraine took another bite of chicken and washed it down with a swallow of water. "Your daed must enjoy shoeing horses. He's been doing it for quite a few years."

Jake nodded and swiped his napkin across his chin where some juice from the chicken had dribbled. "That doesn't mean I want to follow in his footsteps."

"Who's going to take over the business when your daed retires?"

"Maybe my younger brother Elmer. He's only twelve, but he's already taken an interest in helping Dad." Jake reached for his glass of water and took a drink. "I just know it won't be me takin' over my daed's business."

"I guess if you don't like it that well, then it's not something you should do for the rest of your life."

"How about you?" he asked. "Do you enjoy your job at the hardware store in Shipshewana?"

"I like it well enough, but it's not something I'd want to do forever," she replied.

Jake jiggled his eyebrows. "Nothing's forever. Nothing here on earth, at least."

"That's true. We won't know eternity until we get to heaven."

Jake's gaze shifted to the other side of the room. "Say, isn't that Fern Bontrager sitting over there? I haven't seen her in a good long while."

"I don't think so. Fern and her folks moved to Ohio a few months after you left for Montana, and they've not been back since."

Jake continued to stare. "Sure does look like her. Same mousy blond hair and turned-up nose. Jah, that's gotta be Fern."

Loraine's head snapped to the right, and her breath caught in her throat when she saw the young woman Jake was referring to.

"It's her, isn't it?"

Loraine nodded slowly. "I wonder what she's doing here, and who's that young man sitting with her?"

"Maybe she's gotten married since she moved to Ohio."

"Or maybe he's a friend or a relative."

"There's only one way to find out. Let's go over there and ask." Before Loraine could respond, Jake pushed his chair away from the table and started across the room.

With a sigh of resignation, Loraine rose from her seat. The idea of talking to Wayne's ex-girlfriend held no appeal, but it wouldn't be right to remain at the table while Jake went over to say hello. Besides, Loraine was curious as to what had brought Fern back to Indiana.

By the time Loraine reached the table, Jake had already pulled out a chair and taken a seat next to the young man with a thick crop of sandy brown hair.

"Hello, Fern," Loraine said, forcing a smile. "I'm surprised to see you here. I thought you were living in Ohio."

"We have been, and my folks are still there, but I've been asked to teach the older grades at the schoolhouse where your cousin Jolene used to teach, so I'm moving back here."

Loraine's heart started to pound. "Y–you're going to be teaching here now?"

"That's right." Fern motioned to the young man sitting across from her. "My brother Freeman came along to see about opening a bicycle shop here similar to our Uncle John's bike shop, where he's worked for the past several years." She smiled at her brother. "Freeman misses Indiana and wants to get settled in here. Since our Grandma Sara is widowed and has plenty of room, we'll be staying with her, at least for now."

Jake thumped Freeman on the back. "Wow, you've sure grown

up since I last saw you. I didn't even realize it was you."

"I'm almost twenty-two years old now," Freeman said with a grin.

Fern motioned to the empty chair beside her. "Would you like to have a seat, Loraine?"

Loraine shifted uneasily, wishing Jake would say they ought to return to their table. He made no move to get up, however, because he was deeply engaged in conversation with Freeman.

Reluctantly, Loraine pulled out the chair and sat down. Other than the fact that she and Fern had both dated Wayne, they really had nothing in common. She didn't have a clue what to talk about, either.

Fern seemed equally uncomfortable, as she fiddled with the fork beside her plate. "I. . .uh. . .heard about the accident you, Wayne, and the others were in. It must have been horrible for him, losing a leg like that."

"Jah, it was quite a shock."

"How's Wayne getting along now?"

"As well as can be expected." Loraine saw no need to tell Fern how depressed Wayne had been or that he'd called off their wedding. Since Fern was moving here, she would probably hear all about that soon enough anyway—especially if she talked to Ada.

I wonder how things will be once Ada finds out Fern's moving back? Loraine wondered. *It would be just like Ada to try and get Wayne and Fern together again. But then,* she reasoned, *if Wayne thinks he's not capable of taking care of a wife and family, it's not likely that he'd start going out with Fern—especially since he was the one to break up with her.*

"I'll try to get over and see Wayne sometime this week," Fern said, scattering Loraine's thoughts. "I'd like to see how he's doing and offer a few encouraging words."

"I'm sure he'd appreciate that." Loraine looked over at Jake again, silently begging him to say that they needed to return to their table. If he didn't say something soon, maybe she'd say it herself.

After what seemed like an eternity, Jake rose to his feet. "I guess Loraine and I should get back to our table before our food gets cold." He smiled at Fern and her brother. "It's been nice seeing you both. If you ever have a horse in need of some shoes, just give me or my daed a call."

～❧ ❧～

Jake glanced at Loraine out of the corner of his eye. She hadn't said more than two words since they'd left Topeka. In fact, ever since their brief visit with Fern and her brother, Loraine had been quiet.

"It was sure strange seeing Fern again, wasn't it?" he said, hoping to break the silence between them.

Loraine nodded.

"Her brother's sure changed. I wouldn't have recognized him if Fern hadn't said his name."

"Uh-huh."

"While Freeman and I were gabbing, what'd you and Fern talk about?"

"Not much. Just said a few things about the accident."

"It's good that the school board's found someone to take your cousin's place, don't you think?"

"I suppose, although the older scholars are doing okay with their temporary teacher, and I know from what I've heard that they really do miss Jolene." Loraine sighed. "She was a good teacher, and it's a shame she won't be able to teach school again because of losing her hearing."

"Maybe she'll find something else to do—something that doesn't require her to hear."

"Jah, maybe so."

"Getting back to Fern," Jake said, "as I recall, she always had an easygoing way about her. Hopefully, she'll get along well with her students."

"Time will tell, I guess."

"I overheard her say something to you about visiting Wayne. Are you bothered by that?"

233

Loraine shook her head. "Why should I be?"

"I just thought since he and Fern used to date that you might—"

"Wayne and I aren't engaged anymore, so he can see whomever he pleases."

Jake decided to drop the subject. From the responses Loraine had given, he figured she wasn't too excited about Fern moving back, and he had a hunch she hadn't gotten over Wayne yet, either. Could she be jealous of Wayne's old girlfriend? Or could Loraine's coolness toward Fern have something to do with the fact that she'd be taking over Jolene's teaching position?

"Are you warm enough?" Jake asked. "Because if you're not, there's a buggy robe under the seat."

"It is a little chilly." She reached under the seat but came up empty-handed. "There's no buggy robe there, Jake."

He scratched the side of his head. "Maybe my mamm washed it and forgot to put it back. She said something about washing all the buggy robes the other day." He patted the empty space beside him. "You could move closer to me if you're cold. There's nothing like a little body warmth to chase away the chill."

Loraine didn't make a move at first, but then to Jake's surprise, she scooted a little closer. So close, in fact, that their shoulders touched.

Jake smiled. The warmth of her arm against his brought back memories of their courting days. They'd been so happy and carefree. It felt good to be out with her again—almost like old times. He wished the evening never had to end. He wished they could get back to where they'd once been. Well, given some time, maybe they could.

"Look at that starry sky." Loraine pointed out the front window. "It almost seems as if the stars are hung on invisible threads."

Jake nudged her arm gently. "Listen to you now. All those flowery words make you sound like a poet."

She nudged him back. "For your information, I have written a few poems."

"Oh, really? Why don't you let me hear one of them?"

"Are you sure? I mean, some people aren't interested in poetry."

"Well, I'm not *some* people. I'm interested in any poem that was written by you." Throwing caution to the wind, Jake reached for her hand and was pleased when she didn't pull it away.

"All right then. . ." Loraine cleared her throat. "My poem goes like this:

"I looked up at the sky one night;
　　across the horizon, clouds were bright
with streaks of red and pink hues,
　　and the sky was a brilliant blue.
I gazed upon this glorious sight,
　　and knew the Artist had done it all right.
God had painted the sky for everyone to behold,
　　so that His glory could always be told!"

Jake gently squeezed Loraine's fingers. "That was really good. I think you have a talent for making up poems."

"Really?"

He nodded. "Maybe you ought to quit your job at the hardware store and become a poet."

She snickered. "Jah, right."

"No, I mean it, Loraine. You ought to at least try to get some of your poems published."

She shook her head. "I'm not interested in that. I only write poems when the mood hits, and I doubt that anything I've written would be considered good enough to publish."

"You'll never know unless you try. Want me to check at the library and see if there's any information available about where you could send your poems?"

She shook her head. "I appreciate the offer, but I think not."

He shrugged. "If you change your mind let me know."

They rode in silence the rest of the way home, but Jake found that words weren't needed when he was with Loraine. It felt so natural and pleasant, sitting here beside her like they were meant to be together.

"I wish I'd thought to bring my harmonica along," he said, breaking the silence. "It would have been fun to play it on the drive home."

"You'll have to bring it next time," she said.

He nodded. *Next time. Why did that sound so good?*

"I had a nice time tonight. Danki for inviting me to have supper with you, Jake." Tenderness laced Loraine's words like a soft blanket against rough, calloused skin.

"You're welcome; I had a good time, too."

Jake smiled to himself. If Loraine's response on this drive home was any indication of how she felt toward him, then he was confident that they were making some headway toward getting back together. The expression he'd seen on her face during supper and the way she'd listened so intently to his description of Montana and life on the horse ranch had made him think she still cared for him, too. She'd seemed happy and relaxed while they were eating—at least until they'd talked to Fern and her brother.

Jake guided his horse and buggy up the driveway leading to her place and stopped it on the side of the barn, facing the pasture, where he knew they couldn't be seen from the house.

His stomach lurched with nervous anticipation as he slid his hand under Loraine's chin. Should he tell her about Roxanne, and how they'd almost become engaged? Was there any reason she needed to know? Pushing the thought aside, he slowly lowered his head and captured Loraine's lips with a kiss that stole his breath away.

She leaned closer and placed both hands around his neck.

Caught up in the moment, he moaned and deepened the kiss.

With a sudden gasp, she pulled away, trembling like a blade of grass shaken by the wind. "I'd better go." Without waiting for

Jake's reply, she hopped out of the buggy and made a beeline for the house.

"Maybe I shouldn't have done it," Jake mumbled. "I hope that kiss won't keep Loraine from going out with me again."

CHAPTER 34

Loraine's legs shook like a newborn colt as she stumbled into the house. She could hardly believe Jake had kissed her. She could hardly believe she'd let him.

She leaned against the door, her heart racing so hard she feared she might pass out. Gulping in several deep breaths, she tried to calm herself.

Should I have agreed to go out with Jake tonight? Am I falling for him again? Oh Lord, how could I have let this happen? If I allow myself to fall in love with Jake, how can I ever face Wayne?

Loraine remained slumped against the door, breathing deeply and replaying Jake's kiss in her mind. At first it had taken her by surprise, but then she'd begun to relax, and had found the kiss to be comforting and kind of nice. Then, when he'd deepened the kiss, it had taken her breath away. That frightened her a lot!

She stayed at the door for several more minutes. Once she'd calmed down enough to walk without shaking, she tiptoed up the stairs and into her room. Thankfully, Mom and Dad's bedroom door was shut, so she assumed they were asleep. Good. She didn't feel up to engaging in any small talk or answering anyone's questions about her date with Jake. She needed to be alone to think, pray, and read her Bible.

Loraine found the Bible lying in the drawer of her nightstand.

She'd been negligent in reading it regularly, using the excuse that she was too tired by the time she went to bed each night. Tonight, however, she needed some answers and knew they'd best come by filling her mind with God's Word.

She took a seat on the bed, opened the Bible, and turned to Psalms, one of her favorite books. She thumbed through a few pages, until her gaze came to rest on verse 4 of chapter 37. It was the same verse that had been attached to a loaf of friendship bread she'd gotten from Ella several weeks ago. "Delight thyself also in the Lord: and he shall give thee the desires of thine heart."

I don't know what my desire is, Lord, Loraine silently prayed. *I used to think I wanted to be married to Jake, but after he left, I fell in love with Wayne. Now Jake's back, and I'm having some feelings for him again. Yet whenever I see Wayne, I long to be with him. Is what I'm feeling for Jake really love? Or am I merely attracted to Jake because Wayne's pushed me away? If I continue to see Jake, will he think we're back together? Do I want us to be? Wayne says he doesn't love me anymore, but I can't seem to let go of what we once had. Oh Lord, what do I want? What should I do?*

No answers came; just the steady *tick-tock* of the clock by her bed.

She stood and moved over to the window. The bright, full moon she'd seen earlier was now hidden behind the cloudy night sky. As she stared into the yard, she saw nothing but darkness. Even the stars she'd made comment about on the drive home had disappeared.

She pulled the window open, and a chilly breeze blew in, causing her to shiver. She didn't care. The cold air might help clear her head. Leaning against the windowsill, she drew in several deep, even breaths.

Still, no clear direction as to what she should do.

With a sigh of resignation, she closed the window and returned to her bed.

Flopping against the pillows, Loraine closed her eyes. Almost immediately, an image of Jake popped into her head—playful, teasing, full of laughter and life. Then she saw Wayne in her mind's eye—not the way he used to be, but the way he was now: somber, pessimistic, full of self-doubt.

What happened to you, Wayne? Loraine's soul cried out. *Why'd you have to stop loving me? Have you given up on life? What happened to our plans to live together as husband and wife for the rest of our lives?*

Tears coursed down her cheeks, and she sniffed and swiped them away with the back of her hand. *Maybe I should give Jake a chance. That's what Wayne wants, after all. I may not love Jake in the same way I love Wayne, but I do enjoy being with him more than I care to admit. Maybe it's okay to settle for second best.*

❦ ❧

Feeling a tug at his heart to spend some time in God's Word, Wayne lifted his Bible off the nightstand and took a seat on his bed. He opened it to the book of Proverbs, and his gaze came to rest on chapter 3, verses 5 and 6: "Trust in the Lord with all thine heart; and lean not unto thine own understanding. In all thy ways acknowledge him, and he shall direct thy paths."

Wayne swallowed against the lump in his throat. He knew he hadn't been trusting in God these last few months. He'd been wallowing in self-pity and was full of doubts. His understanding of things had pulled him down to the pit of despair. He hadn't acknowledged God or allowed Him to direct his paths, either. He'd been trying to do everything in his own strength, irritated when others wanted to help. He'd been ashamed of his appearance and embarrassed and concerned about what others thought because he only had one leg. He'd felt incapable of becoming a husband because he thought he was only half a man.

Wayne turned over to the book of Isaiah and read chapter 50, verse 7: "For the Lord God will help me; therefore shall I not be confounded: therefore have I set my face like a flint, and I know that I shall not be ashamed."

He set the Bible aside and closed his eyes. *Maybe my situation isn't hopeless, Lord. Just as the stump of my leg has begun to heal, my emotional wounds need to heal as well. I realize now that You've been with me all the time, helping me to get through each day. Please help me learn to accept my limitations and be thankful for the things I'm able to do.*

Wayne thought about how, for the last few weeks, he'd been helping Pop in his taxidermy business. To his surprise, he'd found that he rather enjoyed the work, and they were making a decent living. He'd adjusted fairly well to the prosthesis, too, so maybe getting married and raising a family wasn't an impossible thing.

He winced as he pulled the covers aside and crawled into bed. *Loraine's the only woman I'd ever want to marry, but it's too late for us now that she and Jake are back together. She deserves to be happy, so I won't come between them. Loraine and Jake will never know how I feel.*

~❧ ❧~

Tears sprang to Ella's eyes as she sat near the fireplace, rocking in her chair, and thinking about Loraine and the things she'd said when Jake had come to pick Loraine up for their date.

I only want to help her, she silently moaned. *I don't want to see her get hurt again.* Ella's tears trickled down her cheeks and splashed onto the front of her robe. She was glad the rest of the family had gone to bed. She was supposed to be the strong one and didn't want anyone to see her give in to her tears.

Loraine and I have always been so close, but since the accident, we've been drifting further and further apart. She squeezed her eyes shut. *Is it my fault, Lord? Am I the reason Loraine's been pulling away?*

When Ella opened her eyes, she saw Dad's Bible lying on the coffee table, where he'd placed it after they'd done their family devotions earlier this evening. *What was that verse of scripture Dad read?* Ella had been so upset with Loraine and Jake when she'd come home, she hadn't really listened to much of anything during devotions.

Ella rose from her chair and picked up the Bible. Then, taking a seat on the sofa, she opened it to the place that had been marked with a narrow piece of ribbon. It was the book of Proverbs, and Dad had underlined verse 24 of chapter 18. "A man that hath friends must shew himself friendly: and there is a friend that sticketh closer than a brother."

The words swam on the page because of Ella's tears. She'd been trying to be a good friend to Loraine, but everything she said seemed to be taken the wrong way. *Why can't Loraine see that Jake isn't the right man for her? Why won't she listen to my warnings? Doesn't she realize she's walking on dangerous ground?*

Ella flipped through a few more pages, until her gaze came to rest on another verse Dad had underlined: "A word fitly spoken is like apples of gold in pictures of silver."

She continued to read several more verses that had been underlined, and swallowed on the sob rising in her throat when she read Proverbs 27:15: "A continual dropping in a very rainy day and a contentious woman are alike."

"I've been a contentious woman and have been going about trying to help Loraine in all the wrong ways," she murmured. "If I want Loraine to remain my friend, then I need to keep quiet about Jake. It's Loraine's life, and she has to make her own decisions without interference from me. From now on, I'll keep my opinions and concerns to myself."

~∗∗~

As Jake headed down the road toward home, he couldn't stop thinking about Loraine and the way he'd felt being with her tonight. He only hoped his unexpected kiss hadn't driven her away. Since he'd recently purchased a couple of thoroughbred horses, he figured if things went well with Loraine and he was able to get his business going soon, in a few more months, he might be in a position to ask her to marry him. The question that nagged him the most, though, was whether Loraine might still be in love with Wayne.

Directing his focus on the road ahead, Jake decided he would stop worrying and commit his future to God.

He was almost home when he spotted a couple of horses running down the road. It was too dark to see what color they were, but he had a sinking feeling they were his.

He pulled his horse and buggy onto the shoulder of the road and was about to get out and investigate, when he spotted a semi-truck barreling down the road in the opposite lane.

Jake's heart leaped into his throat. Before he had the chance to react, the truck slammed on its brakes, skidded several feet, and plowed into the first horse, knocking it to the side of the road. The second horse, obviously panicked, reared up, and rammed into the side of the truck.

Jake let out a yelp, jumped from his buggy, and dashed into the road, where the truck had stopped.

The driver got out, and stood there, shaking his head. "I didn't see the horses until it was too late." He looked over at Jake. "Are they yours?"

Jake nodded, as the headlights from the truck made the horses clearly visible. They were his! What a horrible ending to an otherwise perfect day!

CHAPTER 35

I still can't believe my horses got out on the road last night," Jake said as he took a seat at the breakfast table. "One horse is dead, and the other one injured so bad it might never fully recover." He groaned. "I'll never get my business going at this rate."

"Maybe you need to accept the fact that you might not be able to have your horse ranch here," Dad said. "You oughta be thankful you've got a job working for me."

"I've already told you, I don't want to shoe horses for the rest of my life. I want to raise and train horses." Jake looked over at his three younger brothers. "When I left to take Loraine out to supper last night, my horses were both in the corral, and the gate was closed. Did any of you open the gate?"

Vern and Kyle, the two youngest boys, shook their heads.

"I never went near the corral last night, either," Elmer said.

"Well, somebody had to open that gate!" Jake frowned. "It sure didn't open itself and let the horses out."

"Maybe it blew open in the wind," Jake's sister Marilyn spoke up.

Jake shook his head. "That's not likely since there wasn't any wind last night. I'm sure someone in this family opened that gate and they're just sittin' here, afraid to tell." He eyeballed his brothers again.

"That's enough with the blaming," Dad said in a stern voice. "The horses got out, and we don't know how, so let's just leave it at that."

"That's easy enough for you to say," Jake mumbled. "They weren't your horses."

"Even if they had been my horses, I wouldn't be trying to put the blame on someone else for what happened." Dad put both hands on the table, and locked his fingers together. "Now, let's pray."

As Jake bowed his head with the others, all he could think to pray about was his situation with Loraine. He had to see her today. Had to find out if she was upset with him for kissing her last night. Had to know if there was any chance that they might have a future together.

I'll go over to her place later today, he decided. *Or maybe I'll stop by the Lambrights' around five o'clock. Loraine might be fixing dinner for them.*

❧ ❧

"I'll be going over to the Lambrights' after I get off work again today," Loraine told her mother as she set the table for breakfast.

"I wish you wouldn't go over there so often," Mom said, reaching for her choring apron.

"Ada still needs help." Loraine grabbed three napkins from the basket in the center of the table.

"I realize that, since I, too, have been helping out there. Even so, I don't think it's good for you to hang around Wayne so much." Mom sighed. "I know the main reason you keep going over there is because you're hoping he'll change his mind about breaking up with you."

Loraine let the napkins fall to the table and whirled around to face her mother. "I'm not trying to get Wayne to change his mind. Fact is, I've changed *my* mind."

"What do you mean?"

"I've decided to give Jake a chance. If he asks me out again,

I'm going to say yes."

Mom smiled and moved over to the stove. "Now that is good news."

Loraine took a pitcher of grape juice from the refrigerator and set it on the table. She could understand why Mom might like Jake better than Wayne. He was a lot more pleasant to talk to, and he always had a joke or funny story to tell. Still, Wayne had his good points, too—or at least he used to before the accident. Too bad Mom couldn't be more supportive of Wayne. Maybe with a little encouragement, Loraine might not have given up on Wayne herself. Maybe Mom could have even put in a good word with Ada on Loraine's behalf. But no, she just took her turn at helping and never said a thing.

Loraine poured juice into one of the glasses and took a drink, hoping to push down the lump that had lodged itself in her throat. Ella, who was supposed to be one of her best friends, wasn't supportive or understanding, either. Mom wanted her to get together with Jake, and every chance Ella got, she tried to convince Loraine that Jake was no good for her. Well, Ella and Mom could think whatever they wanted. After mulling things over last night, despite the fact that she'd gotten no clear answers from God, Loraine had made her decision.

❦ ❧

Wayne poured the last bit of coffee from his cup down the sink and glanced out the window just as a young Amish woman pedaled up the driveway on a bicycle. He squinted, trying to make out who she was, but she was too far away to know for sure.

He waited at the window until she drew closer, and when she stopped her bike near the house and got off, he realized it was Fern Bontrager.

What's Fern doing here? he wondered. *Last I heard, she was living in Ohio.*

He went to the door and opened it just as she stepped onto the porch.

"Hello, Wayne." Fern smiled shyly. "It's good to see you again."

He gave a nod. "I didn't realize you were in the area. Has your family moved back to Indiana?"

Fern shook her head. "My folks still live in Ohio, but my brother Freeman and I are moving here."

"Oh?"

She nodded. "I'll be teaching at the schoolhouse where Jolene Yoder taught before she lost her hearing, and Freeman hopes to open a bike shop."

"I see." Wayne leaned against the doorjamb, feeling the need for a little support. He remembered how, when he and Fern had been going out together, Mom had said she really liked Fern and hoped she and Wayne might get married someday. He figured Mom would probably be happy to hear that Fern was moving back, but he hoped she wouldn't have any ideas about him and Fern getting together again. He wasn't sure why Mom had always liked Fern so well. Maybe it was because she was such a compliant person and had always agreed with everything Mom said.

"I heard about the horrible accident you and your friends were in," Fern said. "I felt bad when I learned that you'd lost a leg because of it."

Wayne lifted his pant leg enough to reveal his prosthesis. "Thanks to this, I'm able to walk at least."

"It's really good that things like that are made available to people who lose a limb."

Wayne nodded. "They're expensive, though."

"I can only imagine. Did you have help from the community paying for it?" she asked.

"Jah. They held an auction, and even though it was cut short because of a fire in the building, enough money came in to help with everyone's medical expenses."

"That's good to hear." Fern's forehead wrinkled. "I saw Loraine Miller and Jake Beechy at Tiffany's restaurant last night. I was surprised to see them together. The last I'd heard, you and Loraine were engaged to be married, and Jake was living in Montana."

Wayne shrugged. "Loraine and I broke up, and now she's seeing Jake again."

"Oh, I see."

A harsh wind whistled under the eaves of the porch, causing Fern to shiver and pull her jacket tightly around her neck. "The weather sure is unpredictable these days. One day it's too warm for fall, and the next day it almost feels like winter."

Wayne nodded. "Why don't you come in out of the cold? I'm sure my mamm will be glad to see you."

"I'd like to see her as well." Fern stepped into the house, and Wayne shut the door.

"Mom broke her leg a few weeks ago, so she's not up to doing much yet." Wayne motioned to the door leading to the living room. "You'll find her in there."

Fern gave him a curious stare. "Aren't you coming in to visit with us?"

Wayne shifted uneasily. He had no desire to listen to Mom gush over Fern, but he didn't want to appear impolite, either. "Jah, sure," he said, feigning a smile. "I guess I can sit and visit awhile."

When they stepped into the living room, Mom's face broke into a wide smile. "Fern Bontrager! What a pleasant surprise! I had no idea you were back in town."

"I've been hired to teach at the schoolhouse in this district," Fern explained.

"Ach, that's wunderbaar!" Mom patted the sofa cushion beside her. "Come, sit and tell me all about it."

Fern removed her jacket and took a seat beside Mom. Wayne seated himself in the recliner across from them. For the next several minutes he listened to Fern tell about her folks and how much they enjoyed living in Ohio. When Fern finally came up for air, Mom jumped right in.

"Did you hear about the accident Wayne and his friends were in?"

Fern nodded soberly. "My folks found out when they read

about it in *The Budget*. We were sorry to hear that some lost their lives."

"It's been a sad time for all." Mom looked over at Wayne with a doting expression. "We're very grateful that our son is alive, even though his leg had to be amputated because of his injuries."

"She knows about that, too," Wayne said, "But let's not go into the details, okay?"

Mom's pinched expression let him know that she'd planned to do just that, but he was relieved when she nodded and relaxed against the sofa pillows.

"I can't tell you how much I've missed our visits," she said, patting Fern's arm. "As soon as you get settled in, you'll have to come over for supper some evening." She glanced back at Wayne. "It'll give you two a chance to get reacquainted."

Fern said nothing, and Wayne looked around the room, wishing there was a hole in the floor so he could crawl right in it.

"Do you need a place to stay while you're here, Fern?" Mom asked. "Because if you do—"

"My bruder, Freeman, and I will be staying with our grandma, Sara Bontrager."

"Is Freeman moving here with you?"

Fern nodded. "He's hoping to open his own bike shop."

Mom smiled. "That sounds exciting. We can always use another bike shop in the area."

For the next several minutes, Wayne listened to Mom and Fern gab on and on, but when Mom started dropping hints about what a good wife Fern would make for some lucky fellow, he decided it was time to take his leave.

"If you two will excuse me," he said, rising to his feet, "I need to get out to the taxidermy shop. Pop's planning to work on a baby fox that was brought in by one of our English neighbors, so I'd better not keep him waiting."

Mom pursed her lips. "Oh, but I thought—"

"It's been nice seeing you again, Fern." Wayne hurried from the room.

~❧ ❧~

When Ella entered the hardware store, she was relieved to see Loraine behind the counter waiting on a middle-aged English woman. After the decision she'd made last night, she needed to talk to Loraine and make things right.

She waited over by the rack of books until the customer had paid for her purchases and left the store, and then she quickly stepped up to the counter. "I'm glad you're working today, because I need to tell you something," she said, leaning as close to Loraine as the counter between them would allow.

Loraine tapped her fingers along the edge of the cash register. "If you're here to give me another lecture about Jake, you can save your breath; I've already made my decision."

"What decision?"

"About me and Jake." Loraine's voice lowered to a whisper. "Since Wayne has made it more than clear that he doesn't love me anymore, I've decided to give Jake a chance. That is, if he wants to continue seeing me," she quickly added.

Ella leaned against the counter, too dumbfounded to say a word. Even though she'd planned to tell Loraine that she wouldn't say negative things about Jake anymore, she hadn't expected to hear such a declaration.

"Aren't you going to say something?" Loraine asked, nudging Ella's arm. "I'm sure what I said is not what you were hoping to hear; am I right about that?"

Ella slowly shook her head. "It's not what I'd like to hear, but I've been doing some thinking and praying, and I've come to realize that it's your life, not mine." She forced a smile. "So if you think Jake will make you happy, then it's none of my business."

Loraine's mouth gaped open as she stared at Ella in disbelief. "Do you really mean that?"

"Said so, didn't I?" Tears welled in Ella's eyes. "We've been best cousin-friends since we were little girls, and I don't want anything or anyone to come between us. I'm sorry for the things I said before. From now on, I'm behind you one hundred percent."

Loraine stepped out from behind the counter and gave Ella a hug. "You really are my best cousin-friend."

Ella grinned. She might not like the idea of Jake dating her cousin, but she felt good about her decision to stop nagging Loraine and just be her friend.

~≈ ≈~

"Pop's gonna run to town for a few things we need in his shop, and I'd like to go with him," Wayne said when he stepped into the living room where Ada sat on the sofa with a basket of mending beside her. "Will you be okay here by yourself until we get back? I don't think we'll be gone for more than a few hours."

"Jah, sure, I'll be fine." She lifted the pair of trousers she'd been mending. "I'll stay busy with these for a while, and then I may take a nap."

"That's a good idea. I'm sure one of the ladies in our community will be over later with some supper for us, so there's no reason you can't rest until we get back from town."

As Wayne started to leave the room, she called out, "Were you as surprised to see Fern this morning as I was?"

He turned and nodded. "I guess the members of the school board will be happy to have another full-time teacher."

"What about you, son? Aren't you happy to have your girlfriend back in town?"

Wayne's eyes narrowed. "Ex-girlfriend, Mom. Fern and I haven't dated each other in several years."

"That's true, but since she's back now, I thought maybe—"

"You thought you could figure out some way to get us back together?"

Ada's face heated up. "Well, I—"

"If that's what you had in mind, you can forget about it." Wayne shook his head. "I'm not interested in a relationship with Fern or any other woman. I've come to realize that staying a bachelor's the best thing for me."

"Oh, but—"

"I've gotta go. Pop's waiting in the buggy, and the sooner we get going, the sooner we'll be back. See you later, Mom." Wayne hurried from the room, leaving Ada shaking her head.

"I wish men weren't so stubborn," she mumbled as she threaded her needle. "And I wish my son would realize that I only want what's best for him."

Ada's stomach rumbled, and she looked at the battery-operated clock across the room. It wouldn't be suppertime for several more hours, but she was hungry now.

She set the sewing aside, grabbed her crutches, and stood.

When she entered the kitchen, she headed straight for the refrigerator, thinking she'd get a jar of canned peaches.

"Oh, bother," she said when she realized there were no peaches. "I really wanted some of those."

She turned toward the basement door. *There's more downstairs. I wonder if I can get myself down there without breaking another bone.*

With sheer grit and determination, Ada opened the basement door, and using one crutch and the handrail, she started down the stairs. She'd only made it halfway, when she lost her grip on the crutch, and it slipped out from under her arm. With only the handrail for support, she quickly lost her balance. The next thing she knew, she was tumbling down the stairs.

CHAPTER 36

As Loraine headed to the Lambrights' place, she wondered if she would see Jake. He often dropped by when he was done working for the day. Since she'd ridden her bike and not come by horse and buggy, she knew she'd have to get home before it got too dark. Even though she had a battery-operated light on her bicycle, it wasn't good to be out in the dark of night. That meant she'd have to hurry and fix supper for the Lambrights and be on her way.

She pedaled up their driveway, parked her bike near the barn, and hurried up the steps. No one answered the door on her first knock, so she knocked again.

Still no answer.

Maybe no one's at home, she thought. *They could have had errands to run in town, or maybe Ada had a doctor's appointment and Crist and Wayne went with her.*

She was about to head back to her bike when she noticed that the kitchen window was wide open. Since a breeze had come up, and it smelled like rain was coming, she decided to go inside and close the window.

Loraine hurried to the kitchen and had just shut the window when she heard a noise.

She tipped her head and listened. There it was again—a soft

moan. It sounded like it was coming from the basement.

When she discovered that the basement door was partially open, she grabbed the flashlight hanging on a nail near the door and descended the stairs. As her foot touched the bottom step, she gasped. Ada lay in a heap on the floor.

Loraine rushed over to the woman. "Ada, can you hear me? Are you hurt?"

No response.

She touched Ada's forehead and felt something warm and sticky ooze between her fingers. A quick glance with the flashlight, and she knew it was blood. Ada must have fallen down the stairs and hit her head on the floor.

"Ada, can you hear me?"

Ada moaned slightly but didn't open her eyes.

"Oh, dear Lord," Loraine prayed out loud. "Please let Ada be all right. This family's been through so much; they don't need anything more."

Suddenly, Ada's eyes popped open. "You—you were praying for me?"

Loraine nodded as a sense of relief flooded her soul. "I'm so glad you're awake."

Ada tried to sit up, but Loraine kept her from moving by placing a gentle hand on her chest. "Better not move just yet. There's a gash on your head, and it's bleeding. I can't tell how bad it is, but you might have a serious injury."

"I can move my arms and my one good leg, so I don't think I broke any more bones." Ada groaned. "But my head sure hurts. I think I hit it pretty hard when I fell down the stairs."

"What were you doing coming down here, and where's the rest of your family?"

"I came to get a jar of peaches. The menfolk went shopping in Shipshewana."

"Oh, Ada," Loraine said, shaking her head, "you should never have come down here alone. Not with a cast on your leg!"

Ada's chin quivered, and she blinked a couple of times like

she might be on the verge of tears. "I know it was a stupid thing to do, but I was hungry for peaches and there weren't any in the refrigerator."

Loraine glanced around, searching for something she could put under the poor woman's head. When she spotted a laundry basket full of towels, she wrapped a smaller towel around Ada's head where the gash was and put another one under Ada's head as a cushion. "You need to lie very still while I go out to the phone shed and call for help."

Ada clasped Loraine's hand. "Please, don't leave me here alone."

"I promise, I won't be gone long. We need to get you to the hospital so you can be checked over by a doctor."

"What time is it?" Ada asked.

"When I left home, it was two thirty, so it's probably sometime after three."

"Crist and Wayne left around two, and Wayne said he thought they'd only be gone a few hours. I'm sure they'll be here soon. Then Crist can see that I get to the doctor's."

Loraine nibbled on her lower lip as she contemplated the problem. "I don't know, Ada. I'm really worried about you, and—"

"You prayed for me, and now you're worried about me?"

"Jah."

"I can't believe it." A few tears slipped under Ada's lashes and splashed onto her cheeks. "You're the one who got help for me when I fell off my bike and broke my leg, and you're the one who's been coming over here regularly to help out ever since."

Loraine nodded.

"Why, Loraine? Why have you been so nice to me when all I've done is to treat you unkindly?"

Loraine blinked against her own set of tears. "I did it because I care about you, Ada."

"But how could you care when I've been so mean and unappreciative of the things you've done?"

"It's not always easy, but it's our duty as Christians to do what we can to help others, regardless of how they might treat us."

"I'm sorry, Loraine. Sorry for all the nasty things I've said to you and about you. I haven't been thinking clearly since Wayne lost his leg. I was wrong when I blamed you for asking him to go to Hershey Park." Ada sniffed deeply, as more tears fell. "Can you find it in your heart to forgive me?"

Loraine nodded and squeezed Ada's fingers. "I forgive you."

"What can I do to make it up to you?"

"Nothing. I don't expect you to do anything at all."

"But I messed things up between you and Wayne. If I hadn't interfered and said I disapproved of you, he might have—"

"No, Ada." Loraine shook her head. "Wayne broke our engagement of his own free will. He doesn't love me anymore. He thinks I'd be better off with Jake." She swallowed hard and nearly choked on the sob rising in her throat. "It took me awhile, but I've finally come to terms with the way things are. I'm now trying to move on with my life, and I hope Wayne will do the same."

"Are you in love with Jake?"

"I do care for him, but—"

Ada squeezed Loraine's fingers. "You're a good woman. Any man would be pleased to have you for a wife, so I hope Jake appreciates what he's found."

Thunk! Thunk! Thunk! Loraine heard footsteps upstairs. "That must be your men," she said to Ada. She cupped her hands around her mouth and shouted, "We're down here! Ada's fallen and needs to see a doctor right away!"

～⁓ ⁓～

Taking the stairs as carefully as he could, Wayne followed his father to the basement. When they reached the bottom, he saw Mom lying on the concrete floor. Loraine was kneeling beside her.

"What happened here?" Pop hollered as he hurried toward Mom. "Why's my *fraa* lying on the floor?"

"Silly me. I decided to come to the basement to get a jar of peaches. When I was halfway down, my crutch sailed right out from under me." Mom looked up at Loraine and smiled. "Loraine found me here, and she put a towel under my head." *Sniff! Sniff!* "She even prayed for me. Can you believe that, Crist? Loraine actually petitioned God on my behalf."

"I'm glad Loraine came by when she did." Pop knelt on the floor beside Mom and took her hand, and then he looked up at Wayne. "We need to get your mamm to the hospital right away. Would you please go to the phone shed and call 911?"

"Nee," Mom shook her head. "I don't think I'm seriously hurt."

"There's a gash on your head, and it's bleeding. I think you should listen to your husband and let Wayne call for help," Loraine said.

Wayne nodded. "I agree. You need to be seen by a doctor."

"Oh, all right; I can see that I'm outnumbered in this," Mom said. "Go ahead and call for help."

Wayne chuckled, despite the seriousness of the situation. Leave it up to Mom to have the last word, even when she was lying on a cold, hard floor with a cut on her head.

Loraine looked at Wayne. "Once the ambulance shows up, I'll head for home while you and your daed go with your mamm to the hospital."

"Absolutely not!" Mom shouted. "Crist can ride to the hospital with me, while Wayne sees that you get safely home!"

CHAPTER 37

Would you like me to fix you something to eat before I head for home?" Loraine asked Wayne after the ambulance had pulled away.

"I'm not all that hungry." He moved toward the door, feeling suddenly uncomfortable in her presence. He was tempted to ask about how her date went with Jake, but thought better of it. No point in rubbing salt in his own wounds.

"I'll get your bike and put it in the back of my buggy," he mumbled.

"I'm sure it's heavy; you might need some help." Loraine rushed out the door before he had a chance to respond.

Wayne frowned. *Doesn't she think I'm capable of doing anything?*

He stepped out the door and watched from the porch as she grabbed the handlebars of her bike and started wheeling it toward his dad's buggy, which was parked near the barn.

The light rain that had begun falling during their trip home from Shipshewana had now turned to hail.

As Wayne started moving across the yard, the hail stopped as abruptly as it had started. A short period of calm followed. Then a loud roar that sounded like continuous thunder split through the air. The sky had darkened to a sickly green color, and a gust of wind whooshed through the yard so hard that Wayne could barely stay on his feet.

The whine of warning sirens blared in the distance—the kind that only went off in emergencies.

Wayne looked into the yard to see how Loraine was dealing with the harsh wind and gasped when she tripped and fell.

"Look up!" she shouted, pointing to the sky. "A funnel cloud's coming!"

Wayne's heart thumped wildly, and he rushed forward, almost falling himself.

Loraine struggled to get back on her feet, but the force of the wind dragged her across the yard and into the woodpile.

"Oh, no! Oh, no!" Wayne stumbled forward as quickly as he could. He reached Loraine just as the roof of the barn was ripped off and tossed into the air. They needed to find a safe place quickly, and the only one he could think of was the root cellar.

He bent down, grabbed Loraine under her arms, and lifted her up and into his arms.

"I'm too heavy. Put me down; I can walk," she panted.

Ignoring her pleas, Wayne started to run as fast as he could. A few feet from the root cellar, he stumbled and lost his grip on Loraine.

She screamed and fell to the ground.

With a sense of determination and a whispered prayer, Wayne grabbed Loraine's arms and dragged her over to the cellar. As he struggled to open the door, he heard a terrible crack. Glancing over his shoulder, he watched in horror as Pop's barn was torn asunder.

With his heart pounding so hard he feared it might burst right through his chest, Wayne grasped the cellar door handle and gave it a jerk.

It didn't budge.

He grabbed it again, pulling harder this time. *Snap!*—the handle broke off in his hand.

He looked up at the approaching funnel cloud and knew if they didn't find shelter immediately, they would surely perish.

CHAPTER 38

With a strength Loraine didn't know Wayne had, he reached into the seam of the door and pried it open. As they stumbled inside, Loraine sent up a silent prayer. *Oh Lord, please see us through this unexpected storm!*

Wayne turned and pulled the inside handle on the door, but the wind was so strong he couldn't get it to close. "Help me get this door shut!" he shouted. "We've got to get it closed now, or we'll be blown away!" A look of determination mixed with fear etched Wayne's face. He'd used all of his strength to get the door open so they could get into the root cellar; now she needed to help him get it closed.

Loraine scrambled to her feet and grabbed hold of the handle. Wayne did the same.

"Lord, give us strength," he prayed out loud.

Straining against the wind and blowing debris, Loraine gritted her teeth and pulled for all she was worth.

"Ugh!" She lost her grip and fell backwards, crashing into a box of potatoes. She tried to stand up, but the force of the wind whipping into the cellar held her down. Wayne, with another apparent burst of strength, braced his feet on either side of the doorjamb and pulled with all his might.

With one quick—*snap!*—the door slammed shut, and the room went dark.

Loraine's chest heaved up and down as she gasped for breath. "Th–this can't be happening! It's not tornado season, and there was no warning at all."

"Doesn't have to be. From what I've read about tornados, they can hit just about anytime," he panted.

A beam of light broke through the darkness as he shined a flashlight on her.

"Wh–where you'd get that?"

"Found it on the shelf behind me. We keep it in here for emergencies."

"Are we gonna be all right? Will the door stay shut?"

Wayne handed her the flashlight. "Hold this while I look for something I can use to secure the door." He scanned the room with a frantic expression and finally located a hammer.

Loraine held the flashlight so the beam of light shone on the door. She sucked in a deep breath and watched him struggle with the hammer, and she breathed a sigh of relief when he managed to wedge it in the handle of the door.

"We'd better pray that the handle holds, because if this door blows open, the wind could suck us right out." He pointed to the corner of the cellar. "We'd better get over there so we're not near the door!"

"O–okay."

Wayne grabbed an empty wooden box and turned it over and then lowered himself onto it and leaned against the wall. Loraine crouched on her knees in the corner beside him.

"Are you okay?" she asked with concern. "You didn't hurt your leg, I hope."

"I'm fine. Just tired and out of breath." He took the flashlight from her and snapped it off. "I don't know how old the batteries are, but we don't want to wear 'em down."

"I guess that makes sense." Loraine couldn't see Wayne's face anymore, but she was comforted by his voice. She didn't like being in the dark and wished she could throw herself into his arms and stay there until this nightmare was over.

"You're amazing, Wayne," she whispered.

"What do you mean?"

"You may only have one leg, but you're strong as an ox."

He snorted. "Don't think I've ever been compared to an ox before."

Loraine shifted, trying to find a comfortable position, and winced when a searing pain shot through her right leg. She reached down and touched the spot that hurt. Something wet and sticky oozed between her fingers. "I think my leg's bleeding. Can I see the flashlight a minute?"

Wayne snapped on the light and pointed it at her leg. "Ach, Loraine, you're cut!"

"I must have scraped it on something—maybe it happened when I fell into the woodpile."

"I can't tell for sure, but the cut doesn't look too deep. Might not even need any stitches." He reached into his pants pocket, withdrew a handkerchief, and handed it to her. "You can wrap this around your leg. It hasn't even been used," he added.

"Danki." Loraine wrapped it securely around her leg and tried to relax.

They sat in the darkness as the wind roared and shook the cellar door. "I'm scared, Wayne." Loraine's voice came out in a squeak, and fear churned like bile in her stomach. "I can't remember ever being in a tornado before, and I'm not ready to die."

"If your heart's not right with the Lord, then you need to pray and ask His forgiveness."

"I've done that already. I'm just not ready to leave this world yet. I want to get married and have children."

"Jake's children, you mean?"

Loraine's mouth went dry. Did she dare tell Wayne how she felt about Jake?

She drew in a quick breath and decided to plunge ahead. "I do care about Jake, but—"

"Figured as much."

"But not in the same way I used to."

"What do you mean?"

"When Jake and I were going out before he left for Montana, I used to think we'd get married some day."

The wooden box creaked beneath Wayne's weight. "Because you loved him, right?"

"Yes. No. Well, I thought I did." Loraine paused, searching for the right words. "I enjoy being with Jake; he makes me laugh and forget about my troubles." She reached over and touched Wayne's hand, sending a wave of warmth up her arm. "But it's not the same as when I'm with you."

"No, I don't suppose it would be. Jake's a whole man; I'm sure not."

"Jah, you are, Wayne. When we were out there in the midst of the storm, could you have carried me all that way if you weren't a whole man?"

"I stumbled and dropped you, remember?"

"But you dragged me to safety, and that took a lot of strength. Then when the door handle broke off, you pried it open and got us inside." She paused for a breath. "Then you closed and bolted the door all on your own. You were calm the whole time, and I have to think that you can do most anything you set your mind to do." She gulped on a sob and paused to gain control of her emotions. "Even if you couldn't do anything at all—even if you were confined to your bed—I would love you for the caring, gentle man you really are."

"You—you still love me?"

"Jah, and truth be told, I've never loved anyone the way I love you, and I never will."

"What about Jake? He's in love with you, Loraine. I can see it on his face when you're together. I can hear it in his voice when he talks about you."

"I don't know. I don't want to hurt Jake, but I know now that I can never make a permanent commitment to him because my heart will always belong to you."

∾ ≍

Wayne sat very still as he let Loraine's words sink into his head.

The breath he'd been unconsciously holding came out in a sigh of relief. *She loves me, not Jake. Even with Jake's good looks and playfulness, she'd rather be with me than him.* The revelation was almost too much to comprehend.

"You're awfully quiet. What are you thinking about?" Loraine's sweet voice cut into Wayne's thoughts.

"I'm thinking what a fool I've been for pushing you away. I'm thinking that I wish I could take back all the things I've said to you since the accident. I'm thinking that I made a big mistake even thinking I should move to Illinois."

"You were planning to move?"

"Jah. I thought if I moved away I could leave my past behind, and I wouldn't have to suffer the torment of seeing how happy you and Jake were together." He swallowed hard as his throat constricted. "All those things I've said about not loving you, they were lies. . .just a bunch of lies. I never stopped loving you, Loraine. I only suggested that you go out with Jake because I wanted you to be happy—to have a full life with a man who could give you all the things you deserve, a man who didn't have to rely on others for help."

"So you were giving me up so that I could be happy with Jake?"

"Jah."

"Oh, Wayne, don't you know I'd never truly be happy without you? If I chose Jake, I'd be choosing second best."

Wayne got quiet again, as he continued to mull things over. Could he and Loraine be together again? He'd proven today that he could be there for her in a time of need. In his own strength he could do little, but with God's help, he could do much. He thought of the words from Philippians 4:13: *"I can do all things through Christ which strengtheneth me."*

He reached through the darkness and took hold of her hand. "I love you, Loraine, and I want to spend the rest of my life with you. Will you marry me?"

He heard her sharp intake of breath, followed by a sob. "Jah, Wayne, I'd be honored to be your wife."

He squeezed her fingers as they sat quietly together, waiting for the storm to subside.

"What about Jake?" she whispered. "I don't want to hurt him, but I can't give my heart to him because it belongs to you."

"Want me to tell him?"

"No, I need to be the one."

"Maybe we can tell him together."

"Jah, okay."

Wayne stirred restlessly. "It seems quiet out there. I think I should open the cellar door and check on things."

"Are. . .are you sure?"

"Tornados happen fast and don't normally last too long. I think it's safe to go out." Wayne turned on the flashlight and made his way across the small room. He removed the hammer from the handle and pushed on the door.

It didn't budge.

Loraine jumped up. "I'll help you push."

They leaned their weight against the door and pushed with all their might, but it wouldn't open.

Wayne groaned. "Something must be blocking the door." He didn't say anything to Loraine, but he wondered how long it might take for someone to find them down here. He thought about an article he'd read in the newspaper awhile back about an Amish man who'd hit his head, passed out, and fallen on top of his wife, pinning her to the floor. It had taken several hours before someone came to help.

Bam! Bam! Bam! Loraine banged on the door. "We're stuck down here! Somebody help!"

Wayne pulled her to his side and held her tightly. "There's no point in banging on the door. There's no one out there to hear us. Pop took Mom to the hospital, and no one else is around." He gently stroked the side of her face. "All we can do is pray."

CHAPTER 39

As the wind whipped furiously against his body, Jake lay huddled in a ditch. He'd been heading to the Lambrights' to see if they needed help with their chores, when he'd heard a deafening roar that reminded him of a jet plane. Then he'd seen it—a huge funnel cloud heading his way. He'd pulled the buggy over, unhitched the horse, and then hurried to take cover in the ditch along the shoulder of the road.

With his arms over his head, Jake lay unmoving, praying for all he was worth.

When the storm finally subsided, he lifted his head and rose to his feet. The first thing he saw was pieces of his mangled buggy that had been scattered around like matchsticks.

Jake's horse was nowhere to be seen. Hopefully, he'd run somewhere safe and had escaped the wrath of the storm.

As Jake started walking along the edge of the road toward the Lambrights', his legs shook so badly he thought he could hear his knees knocking. He didn't know what might lie ahead, but he knew he had to keep going.

The tornado had whipped through with lightning speed, and what Jake saw along the road told him it had left a trail of destruction. Telephone poles had been knocked over; the roofs on several houses were missing; many barns had been knocked flat;

trees had been uprooted; and animals milled about in the fields, making pitiful noises.

Shivers rippled along Jake's spine as sirens wailed in the distance. With a sense of urgency, he picked up his speed.

By the time he reached the Lambrights' place, he was exhausted. The shock of what he saw there caused him to drop to his knees; everything seemed surreal. Crist and Ada's home had been leveled by the tornado, and so had their barn. A few sheep, including the ewe with three legs, milled about the place, apparently unharmed.

Jake looked around frantically. Nothing but rubble lay where the house had once been. Where were the Lambrights? Had they gotten out alive—maybe run to a neighbor's before the storm hit? Or were their dead bodies hidden under the pile of debris?

He cupped his hands around his mouth and hollered, "Is anyone here? Can anybody hear me?"

No response. Nothing but the moaning of the wind mingled with the animals' pathetic cries.

Jake's palms grew sweaty as he walked from one section of the farm to the other, searching for bodies. When he spotted a man's boot sticking out from under a pile of bricks, he halted. *Oh dear Lord, could it be Wayne or Crist?*

With his heart pounding and his mouth so dry he could barely swallow, Jake bent down and gave the boot a little tug. He heaved a sigh of relief when he discovered that it wasn't attached to anyone's foot.

He kicked at the ruins as he continued walking along, praying with each step he took that the Lambrights weren't here.

"Help!"

Jake tipped his head and listened. It sounded like someone calling for help. He looked all around but didn't see anyone or anything that looked like it might have trapped a victim.

"Help!"

There it was again.

Jake spotted a huge tree branch pushed up against the door of an old root cellar. Could one of the Lambrights be in there?

He moved toward the door and listened.

"Help! If anyone's out there, we're trapped down here!"

With his heart beating so hard it seemed to be echoing in his ears, Jake grabbed the end of the branch and pulled.

It didn't move an inch.

"Dear Lord in Heaven," he prayed out loud, "I need the strength of Samson right now!"

He gritted his teeth and yanked even harder. This time, he was able to pull the branch far enough away from the door that he could see that the handle was missing.

He stuck his fingers under the seam of the door and pried it open. A beam of light greeted him, and he saw two figures huddled together inside the cellar, one holding a flashlight, the other with eyes full of fear. Wayne and Loraine!

They scrambled out, clinging to each other as though they were each afraid to let go.

"Jake, what are you doing here? How'd you know we were in the cellar?" Wayne asked, clasping Jake's shoulder with one hand, while he held onto Loraine's hand with the other.

"I was on my way over here to see if you needed help with your chores, and the tornado struck," Jake said. "I jumped out of my buggy and took cover in a ditch. When the funnel cloud passed, and the wind had settled down, I came over here on foot." He drew in a quick gulp of air. "When I got here and saw the devastation, I was afraid you and your family might be dead. I searched through the rubble and found nothing. When I heard your cries for help, I discovered a tree branch had blocked the cellar door. I asked God to give me the strength of Samson so I could move it, and He did. Are you two all right?" Jake asked breathlessly.

"We are now," Wayne said.

"We didn't know how long we might be trapped down there, and I was getting more frightened by the minute," Loraine added tearfully.

Jake was relieved to have found Wayne and Loraine, but there were still two more people on this farm who were not accounted for. "Where are your folks? I looked everywhere for them, but found nothing," he said to Wayne.

"Mom fell down the basement steps trying to get some peaches, so Dad called 911, and the ambulance came and took her to the hospital to be checked over. Hopefully, they weren't in the path of the tornado." A look of shock and disbelief spread over Wayne's face as he gazed at the ruins of his folks' farm. "Ach! I'm so thankful they weren't in the house when this hit!"

Jake's mouth went dry. It didn't take a genius to see the look of love on Wayne's face as he gazed into Loraine's eyes. And it was more than obvious that Loraine felt the same way about Wayne. At that moment, Jake made a decision—one that would change the course of his life.

Loraine let go of Wayne's hand and moved toward Jake. "Wayne saved my life when he helped me get into the cellar, and now you've saved our lives by getting us out of the cellar." She blinked several times, and more tears gathered in her eyes. "There's something I need to tell you, Jake."

He held up his hand. "If you don't mind, I'd like to say something first."

She nodded. "Go ahead."

"I've. . .uh. . .changed my mind about staying in Indiana. I've come to realize that my place is back on the horse ranch in Montana." He looked over at Wayne and forced a smile, even though his heart was breaking. "It's obvious that you and Loraine love each other very much. I think the two of you are meant to be together."

Wayne's cheeks turned crimson. "You really mean that?"

Jake swallowed hard. "Jah, I really do." There was no way he could tell Loraine the truth—that he'd come over to the Lambrights' hoping she'd be here, that he'd planned to ask her out again, that he loved her and hoped someday they could be married.

"Danki, Jake," Loraine murmured. Tears flowed freely down

her face, and as much as it hurt, Jake knew he'd made the right decision.

"The tornado turned my buggy into matchsticks, and my horse took off, but I've gotta get home and find out how my folks fared the wrath of the tornado," Jake said, feeling an immediate need to go.

"I need to check on my family, too." Loraine looked up at Wayne. "There are so many in our community who might have been affected by this awful storm, but we have no way to get there except on foot."

"One of us could ride that." Wayne pointed to a bicycle lying in the middle of the yard.

Jake dashed over to the bike and picked it up. "It seems to be in pretty good shape," he called to Loraine and Wayne. He climbed on the bike and rode it back to where they stood. "How about if I ride this and you two wait here? I'll come back as soon as I know something."

"I guess we don't have much choice," Wayne said. He motioned to Loraine. "She's got a cut on her leg, and she probably wouldn't be able to walk very far. For that matter, neither could I."

"I'll be back as quick as I can." Jake started pedaling the bike down the driveway, but he'd only made it halfway when a van pulled in. It was Marge Nelson and her husband, Brian.

Marge rolled her window down and stuck out her head. "Is everyone all right here? Was anyone hurt?"

"Wayne and Loraine were the only ones here when the tornado struck. Loraine's got a cut on her leg, but I don't think it's serious." Jake turned and motioned to the farm. "As you can see, there's not much left of the Lambrights' place."

Brian nodded grimly, a pained expression on his face. "Our place is fine, but we saw destruction all up and down the road as we headed this way."

"I'm going home now to check on my folks and some of the others," Jake said, "but Wayne and Loraine are stuck here until I get back with some news."

"We'd be happy to give all of you a ride," Brian said. "You can put the bike in the back of my van if you like."

"It's not mine, so I'll just leave it here." Jake dropped the bike to the ground and climbed into the back of the Nelsons' van. Then Brian headed up the driveway to where Loraine and Wayne stood huddled together.

~e ɔ~

"I can't believe all this devastation!" Loraine exclaimed as they traveled down the road in the Nelsons' van. "So many people left without their homes. So many will have to rebuild."

Wayne squeezed her hand as they passed farms, homes, and places of business that had been affected in some way by the wrath of the tornado.

Brian steered the van around a large tree branch lying in the road and pulled into the driveway were Jake's family lived. "Looks like your house and barn are still standing," he said as he came to a stop.

Jake pointed out the window. "There's Mom, Dad, and the rest of my family. Thank God, none of them seem to be hurt." He looked over at Loraine, who sat between him and Wayne. "If you need me to come with you to your folks' place, I'll just check on my family and be right back."

Loraine shook her head. "You go ahead, Jake. I'm sure your family needs you right now."

"Okay. Let us know how everyone fared, and if you need anything, don't hesitate to ask." Jake whipped the door open and hopped out. "Thanks for the ride, Brian!" he called.

When they continued their drive toward Loraine's house, her heart began to pound as she thought about what they might find. The newfound joy she and Wayne had found when they'd expressed their love in the root cellar could be over if she found that anyone in her family was dead.

CHAPTER 40

Look, there's a buggy that's smashed up pretty bad!" Wayne shouted as they continued down the road. "I wonder if it belongs to someone we know."

"You'd better stop and see if there's anyone inside," Marge told her husband.

Brian pulled the van over behind the buggy and hopped out.

Wayne looked over at Loraine. "Sit tight while I check things out with Brian."

Loraine nodded as tears welled in her eyes. "I'm so afraid of what we're going to find at my place. What if—"

"Try to think positive." He gave her arm a gentle squeeze and stepped out of the van.

"There was no one inside the buggy," Brian said when he and Wayne returned a few minutes later. "I'm guessing whoever was in the buggy probably got out and ran for cover as soon as they saw that funnel cloud coming."

Wayne nodded. "That's what Jake did. He jumped into a ditch, covered his head, and waited out the storm." He looked out the window and scanned the area. There wasn't a soul in sight. "Whoever was in the buggy probably headed for home on foot as soon as they knew it was safe."

"I think you're probably right about that," Brian said as he pulled back onto the road.

They'd only gone a short ways when Loraine spotted three Amish people walking along the side of the road—an elderly woman, a younger woman, and a young man.

"Isn't that Sara Bontrager?" Loraine asked, looking at Wayne. He nodded. "And that's Fern and Freeman walking with her."

"We'd better stop and see if they need any help," Brian said over his shoulder.

Loraine knew they were doing the right thing by stopping, but she was anxious to get to her house and wished they could keep on going. What if something had happened to Mom and Dad? She'd had a disagreement with Mom this afternoon. She needed to make things right—needed to explain about her and Wayne getting back together.

When Brian pulled over, Marge rolled down her window again. "Do you folks need some help?" she asked.

Sara nodded but seemed unable to find her voice.

"We were heading home from Shipshewana when the tornado struck, and we had to take cover in a ditch by the side of the road," Freeman said. "Our buggy's wrecked, and our horse is missing, so we were on our way home on foot."

"We've got room for three more," Brian said. "So if you'd like to get in, we'll give you a lift."

"We'd be grateful for the ride." Fern motioned to her grandmother. "It's a long walk to Grandma's house, and she's already tired and pretty well shaken up by the unexpected storm."

Brian hopped out of the van and went around to open the back door. Fern and Freeman climbed into the seat at the very back of the van, and Sara sat on the seat beside Loraine and Wayne.

"How are things at your place?" Fern asked, tapping Wayne's shoulder.

"Not so good." He slowly shook his head. "The house and barn are gone."

"I'm sorry to hear that." Sara clutched Wayne's arm. "Where are your folks? Are they okay?"

"I hope so," Wayne replied. "Pop took Mom to the hospital in Goshen after she fell down the basement stairs, so unless the tornado hit there, they should be okay."

Sara looked over at Loraine. "How about your folks?"

"I...I don't know. We're on our way there now to see." Loraine's voice cracked on the last word.

Just then, they came across another buggy going in the opposite direction, a horse being led behind it.

"That's Ella and her daed!" Wayne shouted. "We'd better stop and check on them, too."

Loraine was tempted to argue, since Uncle Rueben's buggy looked perfectly fine; but he or Ella might have information to give them about Loraine's folks, so she didn't give a word of argument when Brian pulled alongside the buggy and signaled it to stop. "Are you folks okay?" he asked. "Did the tornado do much damage to your place?"

Uncle Rueben shook his head. "We're all fine. Nothing at our place was even touched." He and Ella stepped down from the buggy and came over to the van.

"We were heading to the Lambrights' to check on them and found this horse running along the side of the road," Uncle Rueben said. "Do any of you recognize it?"

"I think that's Jake's horse," Loraine said, looking out the window.

"I believe you're right." Wayne opened the door of the van and quickly told Ella and her father what had happened at their place and ended by saying, "We dropped Jake off at his house and were relieved to see that everything there looked all right."

"Have you heard anything about my folks?" Loraine called to Ella.

Ella shook her head. "We were going to go there after we stopped by the Lambrights' place."

"I'll tell you what," Uncle Rueben said, looking at Loraine, "Ella can ride with you over to Loraine's house, while I take Jake's horse over to him. Then when I'm done, I'll swing over to check on things at your place and pick Ella up."

Wayne opened the door, and Ella climbed in beside Loraine. "What a horrible day this has turned out to be," she said with a catch in her voice. "On the way here, we saw so many houses and barns that had been leveled. It will take a lot of rebuilding to get things back to the way they used to be."

"The community will work together," Wayne said.

"That's right," Freeman agreed from the backseat. "That's how it was for us in Ohio when several places were flooded out last year. Everyone pulled together."

"I'm sure a lot of the English men in our area will help with the rebuilding, too," Marge put in.

Brian nodded. "And I'll be one of them."

Ella nudged Loraine's arm. "How come you're holding Wayne's hand?" she whispered.

Loraine explained about being trapped in the cellar with Wayne, and said that even though they were scared, it had given them the time they needed to talk things through. "Wayne and I realize now that we've never stopped loving each other," she said.

"I'm so happy for you." Ella squeezed Loraine's hand. "I always did think you and Wayne belonged together."

"We both know that with God's help, we can work things out." Loraine's eyes misted. "I just hope that—"

"Hey, that's my daed's driver, Stan Burnet." Wayne leaned over the seat and tapped Brian's shoulder. "Would you stop and see if that's my folks he has with him?"

"Yeah, sure."

Loraine gripped the edge of her seat. She was anxious to see if Ada and Crist were okay, but every stop they made meant it was that much longer before she knew how her folks were doing. All she could do was to wait, hope for the best, and pray.

Brian honked his horn and motioned for Stan to pull over. Once both vehicles had stopped, Wayne climbed out and hurried to the other car.

Loraine watched as the backseat window rolled down and Crist stuck his head out.

"Looks like it is Wayne's folks," Marge said. "From what I can tell, they seem to be okay."

Loraine breathed a sigh of relief.

A few minutes later, Wayne climbed back into the van. "Dad said they were at the hospital when they heard about the tornado, but it didn't strike in Goshen at all."

"What about your mamm?" Loraine asked. "Is she doing okay?"

Wayne nodded and smiled. "I guess she suffered a mild concussion, and that cut on her head required a few stitches." He glanced down at Loraine's leg. "Looks like the bleeding has stopped on your leg. Does it hurt much?"

She shook her head. "I don't think it's anything to worry about." Her forehead wrinkled. "I am worried about Mom and Dad, though. Could we go there now?"

"Jah, sure." Wayne reached for her hand again. "I told my folks where we're headed and what to expect when they get to our place. Dad said he wants to see things for himself, and then they'll be over to your folks' right after that."

"We'd better get going then." Brian pulled onto the road again, and Loraine tried to relax.

When they finally pulled into her folks' driveway, her mouth went dry. Several big trees were down, the roof of the barn was gone, and the house was damaged extensively.

As soon as the van stopped, she jerked open the door and stepped out. She scanned the yard, and seeing no one, dashed across the grass, and was about to step onto what was left of the porch, when she heard Dad call, "Loraine! We're over here!"

She whirled around and was relieved to see Mom and Dad come around the side of the house. She rushed forward and grabbed them both in a hug.

"Are you all right?" they asked at the same time.

Loraine nodded. "How about you?"

"We're fine," Dad said. "When the tornado hit, we took cover in the basement."

Loraine quickly told them what had happened to her and Wayne, and how he'd saved her life by getting her into the root cellar.

"I'm so relieved." Mom's eyes filled with tears. "I've been feeling so bad about the disagreement we had earlier and have been praying that I'd get the chance to say how sorry I am for upsetting you like that."

Loraine clung to her mother, as tears splashed onto her cheeks. "I'm sorry for my part in all of it, too."

Wayne stepped up to them then, and Dad clasped Wayne's shoulder. "Danki for saving our daughter's life."

Wayne's face turned red. "No thanks is needed, Amos. I would have done anything to save the life of my future wife."

Loraine held her breath as she waited for her mother's response.

The minutes ticked by as Mom stood staring at Loraine in disbelief. Then she looked over at Wayne and said, "It does my heart good to see my daughter looking so happy, and I want you to know that I'd be real pleased to have someone as devoted as you for my son-in-law."

Wayne's smile stretched wide. "Danki. And I'll be real pleased to become part of your family."

As Loraine stood in the yard, holding Wayne's hand, she thought about Psalm 37:4, the verse that had been attached to the loaf of friendship bread Ella had given her several months ago—the same verse she'd read the other night. She realized now that God had truly given her the desire of her heart, and she determined that she would remember to pray for Jake in the days ahead.

Loraine inhaled deeply, feeling peace enter her like the fragrance of fresh roses. She wasn't sure exactly when she and Wayne would be married or where they would live, but she knew she'd be keeping the promise she'd made to Wayne last spring. For the moment, that was all she needed to know.

Loraine's Favorite Chicken

6 chicken breasts, skinned and boneless
1 (8 ounces) whipped carton cream cheese with onion and
    chives
1 tablespoon butter
Salt and pepper to taste

Preheat oven to 400 degrees. Flatten chicken to ½ inch thickness. Spread 3 tablespoons cream cheese over each. Dot each with butter and sprinkle with salt and pepper. Place in a greased 9 x 13 inch baking dish. Bake uncovered for 35–45 minutes or until juice runs clear.

AUTHOR'S NOTE:

NORTHERN INDIANA AMISH

In 1841, four Amish families moved from Pennsylvania to northern Indiana. In the succeeding years, that Amish community grew rapidly. Now, more than twenty thousand Amish live in Elkhart and LaGrange counties, making this area the third-largest Amish settlement in the United States. The population doubles about every twenty years.

While the majority of northern Indiana's Amish live on farms, few Amish men farm full-time anymore. In order to support their families, most Amish men either work in factories, a variety of stores, workshops, or in home-based businesses.

Elkhart and LaGrange counties have a large variety of Amish businesses, including quilt shops, buggy shops, furniture stores, bulk food stores, variety stores, window manufacturing, horseshoeing, bicycle shops, and numerous other stores. The Midwest's largest flea market is held in Shipshewana, where many Amish and English go to buy and sell their wares. A favorite place for tourists to stop when they travel to the area is Menno-Hof, a Mennonite-Amish interpretative center, also in Shipshewana. There, one can learn about the Amish and Mennonite way of life and discover how and when the Plain People came to America as they fled persecution.

The Old Order Amish living in northern Indiana use bicycles and horses and buggies for their transportation when traveling locally. The larger buggies are referred to as "queen buggies." For longer trips, they hire an English driver. While telephones and electricity are not permitted in their homes, the Amish make use of phone sheds and, in some cases, they use cell phones or have telephones in their places of business.

Amish young people in Elkhart and LaGrange counties often have Saturday get-togethers, where they play volleyball or table games. Some groups of young Amish women raise money for people in need by having candle parties or volleyball tournaments. Some meet to make things for Christian Aid Ministries.

Ice cream suppers are a tradition among the northern Indiana Amish. They fellowship with one another as they share a casserole dish or hot dog meal that is furnished by the hostess. Others who come to the supper bring things like chips, fruit, cookies, and cake. The evening is ended with servings of ice cream.

The Amish of northern Indiana strive to maintain their heritage. They believe it's important for Christians to be separate from the world, which is reflected in their dress, their language, their form of worship, and their minimal use of technology. They value hard work, simplicity, and a closeness to God, as well as to their families.

DISCUSSION QUESTIONS

1. A tragic accident can change the course of a person's life. Of the six people who survived the van accident in this story, whose lives do you think were the most affected?

2. A lot of blame was spread around after the accident. Was Loraine justified in blaming herself for suggesting that she and her friends take a trip to Hershey Park? Was her guilt self-inflicted, or did it come about because of the comments Wayne's mother made?

3. At times in people's lives, they become consumed with guilt over something they think they should or shouldn't have done. What are some ways we can work through such guilt? How can we help someone who is riddled with guilt and blames themselves unnecessarily for something that happened?

4. When Wayne learned that he'd lost a leg as a result of the accident, he fell into depression and called off his wedding, thinking he was less of a man and could no longer provide for a wife and a family. What, if anything, did Wayne's friends and family do to help him come to grips with his loss?

5. Some people might have a tendency to overprotect or smother someone who has gone through a tragedy such as Wayne did. What are some things that Wayne's mother could have done differently to help Wayne deal with his loss?

6. Even though Wayne seemed determined to push Loraine away, she was equally determined to keep her promise to marry him. Do you think this was a result of her guilt over the accident, or did she love Wayne unconditionally and want to be his wife despite his disability?

7. When Jake Beechy, Loraine's old boyfriend, returned to Indiana, she felt comforted, yet confused. She'd been in love with Jake once and wondered if she could love him again, yet she still had feelings for Wayne. The more Wayne pushed Loraine away, the closer she got to Jake and the guiltier she felt. Were Loraine's feelings for Jake deep enough that she should have been able to let go of the promise she'd made to Wayne? Or should Loraine have kept her promise to Wayne despite her past feelings for Jake?

8. If Loraine decided to choose Wayne because she felt sorry for him, how do you think her motivation might have affected their future?

9. Is there ever a time when it's all right to break a promise you've made? If so, what are some examples of when it might be all right?

10. Was Loraine's mother right in thinking that Wayne would be a burden to Loraine if she married him? How might Priscilla have been more supportive to her daughter during such a difficult time?

11. Loraine's cousin Ella was opposed to Loraine going out with Jake. What were her reasons and were they justified? How did Ella's attitude toward Jake affect her relationship with Loraine? How might Ella have been more supportive?

12. What life lessons did you learn from reading *A Cousin's Promise*, and which scripture verses from the story spoke to your heart the most?

About the Author

Wanda E. Brunstetter enjoys writing about the Amish because they live a peaceful, simple life. Wanda's interest in the Amish and other Plain communities began when she married her husband, Richard, who grew up in a Mennonite church in Pennsylvania. Learning about her Anabaptist great-great grandparents increased Wanda's interest in the Plain People. Wanda has made numerous trips to Lancaster County and has several friends and family members living near that area. She and her husband have also traveled to other parts of the country, meeting various Amish families and getting to know them personally. She hopes her readers will learn to love the wonderful Amish people as much as she does.

Wanda and her husband have been married over forty years. They have two grown children and six grandchildren. In her spare time, Wanda enjoys photography, ventriloquism, gardening, reading, stamping, and having fun with her family.

In addition to her novels, Wanda has written an Amish cookbook, an Amish devotional, several novellas, stories, articles, poems, and puppet scripts.

Visit Wanda's Web site at www.wandabrunstetter.com and feel free to e-mail her at wanda@wandabrunstetter.com.

OTHER BOOKS BY WANDA E. BRUNSTETTER:

DAUGHTERS OF LANCASTER COUNTY SERIES
The Storekeeper's Daughter
The Quilter's Daughter
The Bishop's Daughter

BRIDES OF LANCASTER COUNTY SERIES
A Merry Heart
Looking for a Miracle
Plain and Fancy
The Hope Chest

SISTERS OF HOLMES COUNTY SERIES
A Sister's Secret
A Sister's Test
A Sister's Hope

BRIDES OF WEBSTER COUNTY SERIES
Going Home
On Her Own
Dear to Me
Allison's Journey

White Christmas Pie

NONFICTION
The Simple Life
Wanda E. Brunstetter's Amish Friends Cookbook

CHILDREN'S BOOKS
Rachel Yoder. . .Always Trouble Somewhere Series:
School's Out! (Book 1)
Back to School (Book 2)
Out of Control (Book 3)
New Beginnings (Book 4)
A Happy Heart (Book 5)
Just Plain Foolishness (Book 6)

The Wisdom of Solomon